Her
Counterfeit Christmas

GRACE J. CROY

Copyright © 2024 by Grace J. Croy

This ebook is a work of fiction. The names, characters, places, and incidents are the products of the author's imagination or are used fictitiously. Any resemblance to actual events, business establishments, locales, or persons, living or dead, is entirely coincidental.

All rights reserved. Without limiting the rights under the copyright reserved above, no part of this publication may be reproduced, stored in, or introduced into a retrieval system, or transmitted in any form or by any means (electronic, mechanical, photocopying, recording, or otherwise) without prior written permission of the copyright owner. The only exception is brief quotations in printed reviews. The scanning, uploading, and distribution of this book via the internet or via any other means without the permission of the copyright owner is illegal and punishable by law.

Cover Design by Blue Water Books

To the Anderson sisters: Rheta, Lahla, and Helen.

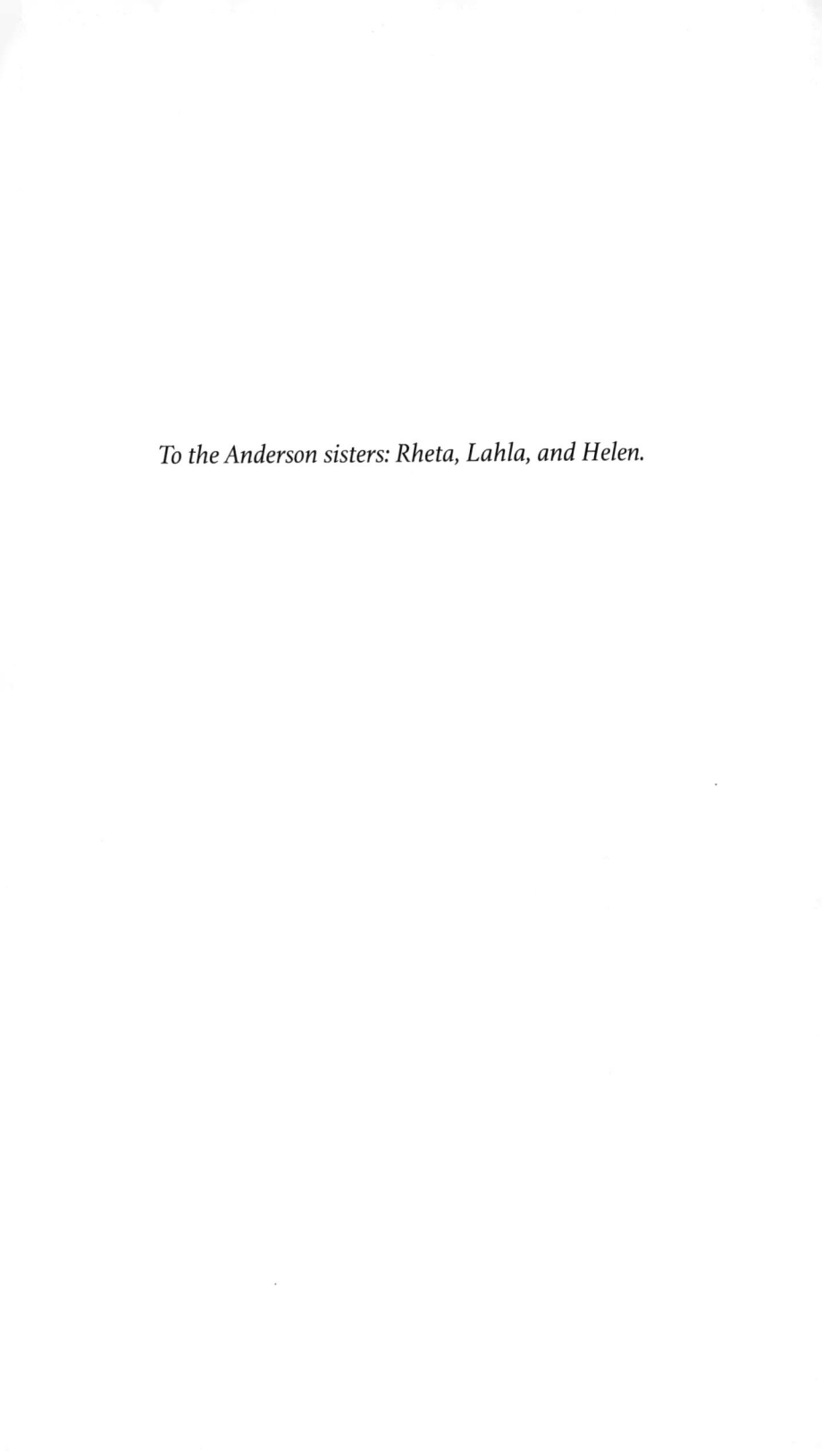

Chapter One

LAYLA

THE DEFINITION OF CHAOS READS: A STATE OF UTTER confusion or disorder; i.e., fifty middle school choir students during the last period on the last day of school before winter break.

My students probably think my whole life is teaching, but they're not the only ones counting down the minutes until the final bell rings. My plans for the next two weeks involve sweatpants 24/7 and celebrating the holidays with my roommates by consuming our weight in sugar cookies and homemade caramels. I can't wait for the holiday to officially begin.

Today is an early out day, but it still feels like school will never end. When at long last the bell rings, my room clears in under a minute. The last student calls out, "Merry Christmas, Ms. Adler," before the door shuts behind her.

Freedom. My body relaxes in the silence. I grab my

belongings from my desk and lock my door. Before leaving the school, I stop by the English classroom of my roommate and best friend and stick my head inside.

"Bye, Livy. I'm off to visit Nana."

She looks up from her desk. "Layla! We survived!" She pumps her arm above her head.

I give jazz hands, my excitement unable to remain contained. Some weeks, survival feels like a miracle.

"We've earned the next two weeks off," I say. "From this moment on, we're not allowed to mention anything that has to do with school."

"Agreed. I have some errands to run, but I'll see you at home later to celebrate the first night of winter break."

"Our Christmas movie marathon awaits."

Once outside, winter wind tugs at my hair and stings my cheeks. I huddle deeper into my coat. We're expecting a big snow storm tomorrow afternoon, just in time for Christmas. I love winter. I love seeing Salt Lake City covered in snow.

Traffic is horrible, especially just after school ends. It takes me twenty minutes instead of ten to get to Nana's assisted living center.

As I pull into the parking lot, my chest tightens and my head feels light. Most of the time I can live in denial about my financial situation, but every time I arrive at Brock Pine Home for the Elderly my anxiety makes an appearance.

I close my eyes and breathe through the panic.

When Nana moved to Brock Pine Home five years ago, she had a sharp memory and between Opa's life insurance, retirement savings, and the sale of her house, she had enough money to support herself for years to come.

That was before she was in bed for weeks after she had a

pacemaker put in and her memory began to fade; before a despicable human played on her generosity and compassion to scam her out of most of her money; before dementia sunk its claws into her mind. I've reached the point where I don't know how I'll pay for Nana's care beyond next month, and the future terrifies me.

When I'm able to force down my anxiety, I fold up my fears like a to-do list I have no intention of starting and leave it on the passenger seat. I can't allow Nana to sense any of my despair.

With a bag of yarn slung over one shoulder, a stack of sheet music in my arms, and a bundle of peppermint candy canes clasped in hand, I head inside.

The front desk attendant looks up from his computer. "Layla!"

I hand him a candy cane with a tight smile. "Merry Christmas."

"Thanks."

I'd like to ignore him completely after he let Nana slip out of the front doors last week and get herself lost for the afternoon. A lot worse could have happened than scraped knees and palms. Lucky for him, everyone gets a candy cane for Christmas, per my mom's tradition.

The custodian smiles as I approach. "Merry Christmas, Layla."

"You too! How's your wife?"

"Baby's due in two weeks."

I give him three candy canes. "I can't wait to see pictures. Two of these are for your wife so your baby in utero can have a taste."

He laughs and tucks them into his shirt pocket. I knitted

a blanket for his baby I haven't wrapped yet. I make a mental note to bring it tomorrow.

As I head to the recreation room to drop off the sheet music before visiting Nana, I wish a "Merry Christmas" to everyone I pass and hand out ribbon bedecked candy canes to all. I'm almost to my destination when I hear a dog bark. I freeze. Another bark.

Is Owen here today with his dog Greta? This isn't his week to visit. I lean against the wall and peek inside the room. My heart skips a beat at the sight of him standing twenty feet away talking to a resident. I don't know who because I can't look away from him. Especially not when he leans his head back and laughs.

His dark hair could use a trim and curls around the collar of his baby blue t-shirt. Over the past few months, he's grown a beard. It shadows his jaw and highlights his sharp cheekbones. I thought he was handsome before, but facial hair takes him to the next level of gorgeous.

As usual, he's wearing shorts in winter. The audacity of it makes me smile. As do his nicely shaped, athletic calves.

What's even more attractive is how patient he is with the residents. He's a big, broad-shouldered man. The type that probably excelled at college football. Instead of this frightening them, they flock to him. After his visits, they chat more about his kindness than they do about his therapy dog.

I have told no one about my massive crush on Owen, especially not my roommates. They would want to know everything and bring him up after each one of my visits to Nana. I'm not ready for that kind of long-term commitment to someone I've never spoken to. Instead, I secretly look forward to when he brings his therapy dog: a few hours in the afternoon every other week on Monday, Tuesday, and Friday. This is his week off. Why is he here?

Greta puts her front paws on the chair's armrest and licks the resident on the face. I'm pretty sure that isn't appropriate behavior for a therapy dog, but the resident giggles.

If I was close to Owen's broad chest in that snug, cotton t-shirt, I'd be giggling too. That wide grin of his is dangerous. Every time I catch sight of it my stomach swoops.

Owen scans the room, and I quickly pull back fully into the hallway so he doesn't see me peeking.

The first time I saw him was this past summer. June twenty-first, if I want to be specific. I stumbled into the recreation room in a rush because I was late for the scheduled singalong, when a dog bark startled me, and my sheet music slipped out of my arms and onto the floor. A golden retriever stood on the other side of the room, an unusual sight here at Brock Pine Home, but not any more unusual than the man holding her leash.

Everyone in the room must have heard my gasp. Or maybe not; most of them wear hearing aids. Owen heard at least, because he turned and looked at me. His eyes widened, and his smile had enough wattage to brighten the entire room. My fingers and toes tingled with electricity.

He took a step in my direction, his eyes intense and shining with interest. I fled as fast as my thrifted Louboutin sandals allowed. Shame pumped through me for finding him breathtaking when I was dating another man. My boyfriend at the time, Spencer, was handsome and suave, but he couldn't compete with Owen's tough and rugged looks.

From that moment on, I've avoided Owen, even after

Spencer and I broke up. I don't know why except that on the inside I'm a ridiculous fangirl. If Owen were in movies, like the Christmas Hallmark ones ('tis the season and all), every woman in America would be infatuated, just like I am.

I dare another peek inside the room. Owen looks directly at me, shooting me one of his toe-tingling smiles. I jerk back, my heart pounding. Caught.

That's my cue to speed-walk down the hall toward Nana's room. To do so, I have to pass in front of the open doors. Without turning my head, I look out of the corner of my eye. Yep, his attention is on me, a big old gorgeous grin on his face. Once I'm past the doors I can breathe again. I only look back twice to see if I've been followed by dog or man.

In this instance, everyone is *not* getting a candy cane.

I stuff the last of my candy canes in my coat pocket before I knock on Nana's door. I open it to find her sitting in her chair watching an old black and white movie while she knits, her hands moving so fast the needles blur.

Her eyes sparkle at seeing me. "Layla, you're here."

She remembers who I am today. My shoulders relax. Sometimes she thinks I'm a staff member. Other times she believes I'm my mom. Worse was the time she thought I was breaking into her room. I never know if her confusion will make her sad or mad; either response is difficult for me to witness. On her angry days, I feel like a wadded up, used tissue. She's always been the most even-keeled person I know, and witnessing her erratic behavior is devastating.

"I'm here." I kiss her cheek.

"Care to watch *Bringing Up Baby* with me?"

"Of course."

This is Nana's favorite Katherine Hepburn film. She

watches it regularly and still laughs at all the same parts even though she's seen it hundreds of times. I have every line memorized, and I haven't watched it nearly as much as she has.

Two laundry baskets sit along the wall. One for yarn, the other for knitting projects. Essentially, all she does is knit, watch movies, sleep, and eat.

I upend the bag of yarn I brought into the almost empty basket and pack up the projects she's completed over the past few days from the full one. There are two scarves, a pair of fingerless gloves, and a teal cable-knit sweater. The Merino wool is soft and I hug the sweater to my chest. It smells like the lavender soap I bring her. It's something I want to keep for myself, but it will end up on my website to sell because we need the money.

For as long as I can remember, Nana sold her knitted items at craft fairs. I can't count how many weekends I spent with her, listening to music on my headphones while people flocked to her table. That ended six years ago when she decided she was too old. That doesn't mean she stopped knitting. It was her surplus of knitted projects that gave us the idea of opening an online store. I sell things I make as well, mostly special-ordered items. The added income doesn't help as much as I wish it would, but every little bit is appreciated.

Nana's room is only big enough for her bed and Opa's old recliner. Since she's on the chair, I sit on the end of the bed and take my knitting from my purse. I'm working on a pair of rainbow striped knee socks since they sell well online. I've shipped all of our Christmas orders, and our shop is closed until the New Year so I can bulk up our inventory.

"You look beautiful this morning," Nana says. "Did you get your haircut?"

Not in the last few months, but I always agree with whatever Nana says. It's easier on both of us. "Yes. I'm glad you like it."

"How is school? Is your voice coach still picking on you?"

This clues me in to what year she thinks we're in—my sophomore year of college when I took private voice lessons. My hair was longer then. Nana's time-shifting is another thing that's been hard to get used to.

"She has been kind to me lately," I say. "She's becoming a good friend."

In reality, she was never kind and we were never friends, but I want to minimize any distress Nana might feel.

"Good, good."

From the hallway, the sound of a group singing "We Wish You a Merry Christmas" floats through the shut door. Nana's brow wrinkles in confusion. Christmas is her favorite holiday and not so long ago she would've jumped up and joined them. Now, she doesn't remember Christmas is a few days away. It's hard on me, but it's better for her to be ignorant of the upcoming holiday or she'll worry about not being prepared. When she forgets why she's worried the anxiety lingers, sometimes for days.

The song finishes, her brow smooths out, and her focus turns back to the movie. Our needles clack softly. For these short thirty minutes, I can almost believe everything is as it was two years ago, with mild memory issues and no financial problems.

The ending credits roll as my phone buzzes with the alarm I set earlier.

"Nana, I'm playing the piano in the recreation room. Do you want to come and listen?"

"Oh! How wonderful!" She claps. "I would love to come."

I've been playing here for years, but I'm never sure if she remembers or if she thinks this is the first time. I thought losing my mom to cancer when I was fourteen would be the hardest thing I'd have to get through in this life, but watching Nana slowly forget me and the big, full life she's lived is harder.

She fluffs her hair in the bathroom mirror and applies red lipstick, then we leave together. On the way, my phone buzzes with a text from my ex-boyfriend, Spencer.

SPENCER: *Can you meet me tonight for dinner? I have something important I need to talk to you about.*

I half-sigh, half-laugh. It's just like Spencer to text me last minute on a Friday night and expect me to change my plans to meet him for dinner. We broke up in October for the third time. We ended our relationship on friendly terms and have met up once since then, also last minute. It's been a few weeks since I sent him a text, and he didn't respond.

If I didn't already have plans to watch a movie with my roommates, I would go to dinner with him to catch up. But since I have plans, the answer is no.

I start a text, but don't have time to finish typing because we reach the recreation room, and I have twenty rabid rock-and-roll fans waiting for me. I'm relieved to see Owen and Greta have gone.

"Any requests?" I ask the group as I settle behind the piano.

They come fast; all songs I've played for them dozens of times. The Beatles, Elvis, and the Beach Boys. I have most of them memorized, but they throw out a few requests I don't know as well, and I dig out the music books.

This kind of music is the stuff I grew up listening to, and I love how Nana sings loudest of all. She remembers the words. The hour goes by quickly, but once it's over, it's time for dinner and no one sticks around.

I walk Nana to her regular dinner table and leave her to chat with her table mates. I'm on my way out of the building when I'm stopped by the facility manager.

"Layla, I'm glad I caught you. I have a Christmas miracle."

She waves a hand toward her office door.

"I love Christmas miracles," I say as I silently panic and follow her inside.

What other people view as good news doesn't always translate to me the same way. Every service added to Nana's care adds an additional fee. It's why I do her laundry and clean her room every weekend.

I sit, feeling like I've been called down to the principal's office to find out I've been accepted to an exclusive after-school club that I have no money to pay for.

She leans against the side of her large desk, smiling at me like I won the lottery. If only.

"We have an opening in our memory care unit. If we get Ellen's first month's payment and the paperwork filled out by Monday, we can have her moved in by the new year."

Memory care unit.

This is what I've been hoping for. Nana needs to live somewhere more secure, with specialized staff who know how to handle her outbursts, and locked doors so she can't wander away. Even so, my stomach drops. Memory care is more money. I may be able to scrape together the extra thousand dollars for January, but what about every month thereafter?

"That's great." I hope my smile looks genuine. It's hiding my fear. No one will give me another credit card, and when I tried to get a second bank loan last month, they turned me down. I'm sunk.

We chat about this exciting opportunity until I'm able to escape from her office. I absently hand her a candy cane from my coat pocket on my way out.

My vision blurs with tears as I leave the building and walk to my car. Once in the car, I wipe my cheeks and look at myself in the rearview mirror. Raccoon eyes stare back at me.

"Everything will be okay. I don't know how, but we've got this far. We can get a little further. You're fine."

If only I believed my pep talk.

I push the ignition, pull out of the parking space, and almost reach the exit when something wet wipes along my neck under my ear. I scream and slam on the brakes. My heart lodges in my throat. Did a kidnapper sneak into my car? And ... lick me? I've listened to a lot of true crime, but I've never heard any mention of a licking obsession.

Before I can get too worked up, a head pushes between the seats. A dog head. The head of Owen's golden retriever.

How did Greta get into my car?

I turn in the seat and scratch her ear. She licks my cheek, not looking any worse for wear, while I think I have permanent heart damage.

Only now do I notice the folded down back seat with a dog bed. My boxes of sheet music have disappeared.

I scan the rest of my car. A can of Dr. Pepper sits in the

cup holder; the tan seats have black covers; the crack in my windshield is gone; the check engine light is off. On the dash is the key fob with a Nordquest Ski Resort keyring attached.

That isn't my key. This isn't my car. If I had to guess, it belongs to the owner of Greta.

Owen.

I scan the parking lot and see my car. A blue Honda Civic hatchback, the replica of this one, is a few spaces down from where Owen parked. I reverse and quickly drive back to where I began, but today just wants to rain distress upon my head because Owen comes out of the building before I'm able to park. He stops in his tracks when he notices his car is gone, then looks around as if he misplaced it. He's wearing a hoodie over his t-shirt. In this weather, if he isn't wearing a coat, he should at least have a scarf.

I know the moment he sees me because his brow lifts and his eyes widen.

I park and slowly open the door to stand. I could boil water for cocoa with how hot my cheeks burn. Why did I have to steal *his* car right along with his dog? Anyone other than the man I'm currently crushing on from afar and have been avoiding for months. From my pocket, I pull out a half dozen candy canes and hold them out in apology.

"I am so sorry. This is why you shouldn't leave your key fob in the car. You're just asking for it to be stolen."

He laughs as he takes the candy cane bouquet from my hand. Between the sound of his laughter and the second our fingers touch, my heart races. This is the first time we've ever spoken, and it's because I took his car.

"It seems I was lucky and had a thief who returns what they steal."

I point to my blue Honda a few spaces away. "That is mine. I was distracted. Greta let me know I'd made a mistake, but you shouldn't leave your dog in the car alone."

He grins. "I was only inside for a few minutes."

"A few minutes was long enough for someone to mistake your vehicle for theirs."

More importantly, long enough for me to make a fool of myself.

I need to stop talking because all that's coming out of my mouth is reprimands. I reach inside the car for my purse, the bag of knitted items, and my sheet music from the passenger seat. Greta licks my neck again, which makes me feel marginally better. Some of the music is on the floor, probably from when I slammed on the brakes, and I lean in to grab it. I can't reach it until I'm practically laying across the seat with my bum in the air.

Nice. Real nice.

By the time I make it out of the car, any dignity that remained has fled. "Sorry. Bye."

I turn to flee, but Owen speaks before I can.

"Tough visit? You seem upset."

Right. Raccoon eyes. Blotchy cheeks. I can see how he'd come to that conclusion.

I'd much rather talk to his dog, but it's not like I haven't talked to a handsome man before. I'm actually quite the conversationalist, though he probably wouldn't believe it with the way I've avoided him for the past six months.

He's only an inch or two taller than me, so I don't even have to look up to meet his kind eyes. They're brown, but it's impossible to know the exact shade with the parking lot pole lights the only source of illumination.

"It was a good visit. Just ... hard."

"I'm sorry." He holds out his hand. "I'm Owen."

His hand is large and swallows mine. I'm glad I was too distraught to put my gloves on earlier. My whole body tingles and grows hot at the contact. Not a terrible thing, as it's cold and growing darker by the minute. I don't want to let go, but I find the inner strength to not embarrass myself further.

"Layla," I say.

"It's nice to officially meet you, Layla." My name coming from his lips sounds like the beginnings of a love song. "Can I help you with anything?"

Can you loan me tens of thousands of dollars, interest free?

Not that I would ever say anything remotely similar out loud. Nana taught me to never talk about our financial situation, and I never have. Not with friends, not with my roommates, and definitely not with handsome acquaintances.

"No. Thank you, though." I take a step away. "Well, good night. Merry Christmas. Happy New Year."

Be quiet now, Layla.

I turn and take a few steps toward my car, rushing but not running, when Owen calls out my name.

"Layla."

I take stock of all my possessions, worried I lost one and hoping I don't have to go back to retrieve it. Then Owen is standing next to me.

"I know we don't know each other, but I've seen you around. I've been wanting to get to know you better. Would you be interested in going to dinner with me after Christmas?"

He's asking me on a date?

It should be an easy yes. It's just a date. Except this is Owen, the man I have a massive crush on. It feels like there is potential for something more, and that scares me.

Faced with the possibility of a date, I realize the real reason I've been avoiding him: I don't want him to know about my messy life. I like how he looks at me as if I'm beautiful and desirable. If he knew about the hundred thousand dollars I have in debt, he wouldn't see me the same way.

At my hesitation, he says, "Maybe we could get something to eat right now if you're not busy?"

No is on my lips, but I want to go. It's just one date; my credit score won't come up in casual conversation, especially not if I keep it short. My roommates won't mind if I bail on our plans for a handsome man.

Except, after my conversation with the home manager, I'm exhausted and want to decompress at home with my roommates. My pajamas are calling, and I want to answer.

Maybe I can do both.

"I have plans tonight," I say. His smile dims until I continue. "But I have time for fries."

I point across the street to the fast food drive-in.

He nods, and his smile perks up. "Perfect. I'll drive."

Chapter Two

OWEN

Layla leaves to drop her things in her car while I wait. For a second she disappears from view, and I half expect her to speed away, leaving me alone in the parking lot with my disappointment. But then she pops up and walks in my direction.

I can't believe this moment is happening. I have maybe an hour to make a good impression so that she'll want to see me again. I've admired this woman from afar for months now. She's gorgeous: long legs, long blonde hair, full lips, bright blue eyes. It's what initially captured my interest, but she's so much more than beautiful.

She's kind and chats with everyone at Brock Pine, even staff. They all love her here. As Greta and I have visited with the residents, they've all talked about her and shown me items she's knitted for them. Envy is not something I usually feel, but I'm jealous that out of everyone associated with Brock Pine, I seem to be the only one she avoids.

I've had to resort to subterfuge by hiding out in the hallway to listen to her sing-along. Her voice is clear and rings out above all the other voices. Her musical talent is awe-inspiring.

Someone might construe my actions as creepy, but I appreciate the music too, not just the musician.

I've tried to talk to her, but every time I take a step forward to introduce myself, she turns in the opposite direction. It's been a hit to my self-esteem, but I've noticed how she watches me and I've bided my time, hoping my chance would come.

Now it finally has. She can take Greta for a joy ride anytime she wants, if this is the outcome.

Layla meets me at the passenger side of my car. The black make-up around her eyes is gone and her lips show the hint of a smile that was absent minutes before. There's a slight tremor in my hand as I open the passenger door for her.

Once Layla is seated, Greta sticks her head between the seats and licks her cheek.

I lean down and meet Greta's eyes. "Greta, no." She's always been a face licker, and I'm never not embarrassed when she does her thing.

Layla laughs. It's a laugh I've become familiar with over the last six months, and I can't get enough of it.

"It's okay," Layla says. "Greta and I became best friends on our quick trip around the parking lot. She's a sweetie. Aren't you a sweet girl? Yes, you are." She scratches Greta's ears.

Greta is a great wingman. I'll need to give her an extra treat tonight.

I shut the door and walk in front of the car. *Do not screw this up.* I slip into the driver's seat and drop the half dozen candy canes into the cup holder next to my empty Dr. Pepper.

Layla glances at me for barely a second before turning her attention back to Greta. "How did you get into therapy dog work?"

I back up the car and ponder her question. Therapy dog work? "Greta isn't a therapy dog. She belonged to my former neighbor, but when he moved to Brock Pine he couldn't keep her."

Layla tilts her head and studies me. An adorable wrinkle forms between her eyebrows. "You're not a professional therapy dog handler?"

I look away before I do something stupid, like take her hand. For months, I've wanted to ask her out, and now she's *right here.*

"No." I'm proud of myself for sounding unaffected by her proximity. "I started visiting Norman, my neighbor, with Greta after he moved in. Greta's so friendly, the activity coordinator asked if I would mind taking her to visit other residents. It's become our thing."

"Norman's never mentioned you before." There's a teasing tone to her accusation.

"Do you think I'm lying?" I say with a laugh.

"I've talked to Norman about Greta, though he didn't tell me she was once his." She purses her lips. "He talks about his nephew Clark like he wants to set me up on a date with him, but Norman has said nothing about *you.*"

I clap my chest like I'm Tarzan. "I'm Clark. It's my last name. Owen Clark."

She shakes her head. "Clark is Norman's nephew, not his neighbor."

Layla studies my profile as if she's memorizing my face so she'll know exactly what to tell the police sketch artist when I get arrested for lying about knowing Norman.

I find a break in the traffic and speed across four lanes to the parking lot of the drive-in. I find an empty stall and park. This place has been here forever, and it's rundown and old school. We have to wait for someone to come out and take our order. I hope they don't rush.

"He calls me his nephew because he only has nieces." I hold up my hand and twist two fingers around each other. "Norman and I are close, like family."

She smirks like I'm cute for making up this elaborate lie. I pull out my phone and call the man, putting it on speaker.

"Clark!" Norman says. His voice rumbles like he smokes five packs a day. It's only one. "I just saw you. What do you want?"

Classic Norman. "I'm here with Layla, and she thinks I'm lying about being your neighbor."

"You finally got up the courage to do something about your infatuation, eh?"

This was obviously a mistake. Layla's heard enough to know I'm not lying, and I use my thumb to take it off speaker. Or at least, I try to, but the phone slips from my hand and falls to my feet.

"Maybe now you'll stop talking about how beautiful she is when I'd much rather watch *Seinfeld*." His voice is muffled, but definitely still audible.

I reach for my phone, but it's by the pedals and my fingers brush against the corner, pushing it further. I can't get my shoulder far enough under the steering wheel to grab it.

"Layla, Clark has smelly feet. Don't let him take his shoes off. I might call him my nephew, but we are not related by blood. My feet smell like daisies."

Unlike Greta, Norman is a terrible wingman. Using my foot, I knock the phone closer to my hand and finally pick it up. When I sit upright, Layla's cheeks are a bright pink, but she's also laughing. She looks happy to hear what Norman is saying, so maybe I can still redeem this night.

"Thanks for that, Norman." I hope he catches my sarcasm. "Good night."

"Merry Christmas, Clark. See you in the new year."

"After this, I wouldn't count on it," I say, but he's already ended the call. I glance at Layla. "Do you believe me now?"

"I sure do." Her lingering laughter makes her words uneven. "Why do you only visit Brock Pine Home every other week?"

A change of topic is a great idea. Whether it's because she's embarrassed or she's kind enough to save me from my embarrassment, I appreciate it. I also notice that she's inadvertently admitted to knowing my schedule. All is not lost.

"I spend one week in Salt Lake City and the other in Elko, Nevada."

She scrunches her nose adorably. "Isn't that a long drive?"

"Four hours tops. I grew up in Nevada. My mom and brother live there."

Her eyes light up. "I've always wanted a sibling. I'm an only child."

"He's eighteen years younger than me, so I was out of the house by the time he was born."

She settles in the corner between the door and seat back so she faces me. "Were you upset when he ruined your single child status?"

"Not at all. I love being a big brother."

She studies me for a few seconds. "I bet he loves having you as a big brother. So, if you're not a therapist dog handler, what do you do that allows you to live in two different states and spend afternoons at Brock Pine Home?"

I tap my fingers on the steering wheel. That can be a tricky question to answer, but I'll keep it vague. "I started a manufacturing company a few years ago with a friend. Our headquarters were here and I grew to love Utah. I sold my half of the business not too long ago, and now I'm trying to figure out what I want to do with my life." Before she can ask me what kind of company I sold, I continue. "Until I figure that out, I own and manage a landscaping business."

"Mmm. This isn't your normal week to visit."

It sounds like an accusation, but I'm glad for the change in my regular schedule because I'm here with her now. I'm not so happy about why my schedule changed.

"No, it's not. I was up in Elko this week, but my mom, brother, and I drove here yesterday because we fly out of the Salt Lake airport tomorrow to visit family for the week."

"Is Greta going with you?" She turns in her seat and pets Greta's head. If she were a cat she'd be purring.

"No. She likes the car but hates flying. I'm dropping her off at a friend's house tonight. I'll miss her." I rub Greta's chin just the way she likes. Greta's in puppy heaven with both of us giving her attention. "I've only had her since May, but she's family now."

Greta goes for a lick attack and gets my lips before I pull back. I don't even mind because Layla laughs.

The server taps on the window, and I lower it.

"What would you like tonight?" he asks.

I glance at Layla. "Just fries? Or would you like something more?"

I want her to order an extra-large meal so we have more time to talk, but she shakes her head. I stifle my disappointment.

"Just a large fry with lots of ketchup. I can get it." She opens her purse, but I wave away her offer to pay.

"My treat." I turn to the server. "Two large fries, please." I hand him my card and he heads back inside. "What is it you do for work?"

"I'm a middle school choir teacher."

I love that she's a teacher. "My dad was a teacher. Math."

She grimaces. "Not a subject I'm proficient in."

"But you enjoy teaching?"

"I love teaching choir." Her eyes shine with happiness. "Especially the students who are there to learn and not just to fill in an arts requirement. My tryout choir, Vocal Jammers, is amazing this year. They sound like high school students." She sighs and sinks further into the seat. "Though I am thrilled to have a two-week break. Middle schoolers take a lot out of me."

Talking about work is kind of a downer anyway. "Do you have fun plans for Christmas?"

"My roommates and I don't have family nearby to spend Christmas with this year, so we're spending it together." She pauses. "I'm excited, but sad. It will be a different kind of Christmas. My grandpa was from Germany, and we have a bunch of traditions that won't happen. With my nana's memory issues, my celebration with her will be complicated."

"Do your traditions include hiding a pickle ornament? I had a college roommate who said it was a German thing."

She laughs as she leans her head against the headrest and looks past me, her eyes distant as if she's remembering the past. "The first Christmas my grandparents were married, my nana found a glass pickle ornament at some store that claimed it was a German tradition to hide the pickle on the tree on Christmas Eve. Whoever found it first had good luck the following year. She brought the pickle home but Opa had never heard of such a silly thing and swore it wasn't German. Nana didn't care. Every Christmas Eve, she hid the pickle, and every year while I searched the tree, he sat in the corner looking grumpy. Yet he's the one who always gave me an extra gift for finding it."

Her grandparents sound quite different from mine—approachable and warm.

"Are you going to hide the Christmas pickle this year with your roommates?"

She shrugs, a smile dancing across her lips. "I hadn't planned on it, but I should. It would be nice to have some serious competition. It's difficult to find a green pickle in a green tree, but when I'm the only one looking, there's no sense of urgency."

Our fries arrive with a dozen little tubs of ketchup on a tray. He took Layla seriously when she asked for lots of ketchup, but this is overkill.

I put the tray on the console between us. The second it's down, Greta tries to reach it, her nose quivering like she's tracking prey.

I raise my elbow to keep her back. "Sorry. I meant to give her a bone before the fries arrived and got distracted."

Easy to do when Layla's talking to me. I could listen to her for hours. It isn't just her singing voice that's lyrical. Except now I need to get into the glove compartment to grab Greta's bone. A little awkward to get that close to Layla's legs during our first conversation.

I point. "Will you grab the marrow bone from the glove compartment?"

"Oh, sure."

Greta forgets all about the fries when Layla gives her the bone. She takes it to the back of the car and hunches over it like she's afraid I'll steal it back.

Layla takes a fry and scoops the ketchup like it's salsa. Odd. To each their own, I guess.

"What else do you do for Christmas?" I ask. "I'm not familiar with German traditions."

"We celebrate Christmas on Christmas Eve, not Christmas day. On Christmas Eve, we decorated the tree with candles, bird ornaments, and glass balls Opa brought from Germany. I spent the rest of the day looking for the pickle Nana hid. Dinner was always blutwurst sausages, hard rolls, sauerkraut, and mashed potatoes with curry gravy over everything. Then we read the nativity from the Bible, sang Christmas songs, and opened our presents."

She dips her next fry and licks the ketchup off her fingers. It draws my attention to her lips. I make myself look away.

"You open gifts on Christmas Eve?" I clarify. "Isn't that a letdown for Christmas day?"

She laughs. "Never. It was weird to me as a kid when I found out my friends at school waited until Christmas morning for their gifts."

"Then what did you do on Christmas day?"

"Stay in our pajamas, watch movies, and make stollen, which is the best holiday cake." She sighs and slowly chews her ketchup with a side of fry. "I haven't had proper stollen since my nana moved to Brock Pine Home. I can never get the texture quite right." Then she turns to look at me. "Sorry, I love Christmas and could keep going for hours. How do you celebrate?"

"The normal stuff. Presents Christmas *morning*," I say pointedly. "When my brother was a kid, our dad dressed up like Santa on Christmas Eve and brought us one gift we could open that night."

"Didn't Santa visit when you were a kid?" she asks.

"Santa freaked me out until I was at least twelve. My parents knew to avoid him."

Her smile grows. I've always loved how happy Layla is when I've seen her at Brock Pine. She has an infectious joy about her.

"The tree goes up on Thanksgiving weekend," I continue. "We drive through neighborhoods to check out Christmas lights. My mom loves caroling to the neighbors. Me, not so much."

She puts a hand to her chest and pretends to be offended. "Caroling is one of the best parts of Christmas."

"Your objection is noted, but not sustained."

"I thought you were a businessman. You sound like a lawyer."

That sobers me for a second, but I brush it away. I may sound like a lawyer, but I'm not one.

I go on. "On Christmas Eve we make cookies for Santa and then watch movies until late. When my brother was eleven, he became obsessed with *The Lord of the Rings,* so for the last three years we've watched all three movies, the extended editions, all day. My brother and I start the first one at eight in the morning and our mom drops in for her favorite parts."

Talking about how Christmas *should* be this year makes me angry. It was only five days ago that Grandmother called and informed me and my mom we were having Christmas with her. We've been fine not visiting for Christmas for over thirty years. That shouldn't change now. Mom disagreed.

"A *Lord of the Rings* marathon sounds amazing. I wonder if I could persuade my roommates to do that this year." She thinks for a few seconds, then shakes her head. "No, Meg only watches Christmas movies during December, and Livy and I follow her lead. I doubt I can convince her the gifts from Galadriel to the fellowship are for Christmas."

Now it's my turn to laugh. Every additional minute I spend with Layla, the more I like her.

The only fries left are the little ones that hide out at the bottom of the bag and have all the soft insides fried out of them. I love the crunchy fries, but notice Layla doesn't eat them. She wipes her fingers and lays her napkin on top of her half-dozen empty ketchup cups.

I'm afraid she'll want me to take her back to her car. I must keep the conversation going so she'll stay.

"Only eleven more days of December. Do you have any wishes for the new year?"

Her eyebrows raise. "Wishes? What about resolutions?"

"I don't believe in starting anything on January first. Too much pressure. If something matters to me, I'll start a goal in the middle of a month. Wishes for the new year is something my mom does. It's like sending out an intention, but more fun. Our wishes are rarely serious."

"What's your wish?" she asks.

I take my time before answering. Until an hour ago, my new year wish would have been a chance to talk to Layla, but I've already been granted that one. Though the wish is meant to be inconsequential, I find myself telling Layla an important one.

"I want to figure out what to do with my life. I don't like not having a plan."

Her joyful expression dims. "Not having a plan is the worst."

"You?"

She gives a heavy sigh. "I wish Nana's dementia would stop progressing."

"That sounds like a serious wish," I say. I don't mind. Talking about her nana might be just what she needs right now.

"But it's not a wish that will come true." She focuses her attention on her hands in her lap. "Her memory will keep getting worse and each month I'll have a little less of her. She started a new medication that will hopefully slow it down, but it might not. It's expensive enough that it better do something." She looks up. "Sorry. I didn't mean to bring the mood down."

"You didn't. I'm sorry that you're going through this."

"Thank you." She takes in a breath and lets it out slowly. "For the next week, I will not worry about anything. I plan to celebrate the heck out of Christmas. I just wish I had family to celebrate with, you know? My mom and Opa have passed. I'm losing Nana bit by bit. My roommates are great, but it'll be more of a girls' party. Christmas has always meant family to me."

If I were staying here, I'd invite her over to spend Christmas Eve watching *The Lord of the Rings*. My mom would spoil her. Brady would love having someone new to lecture on how the books differ from Peter Jackson's scripts. I'd love to give Layla happy family Christmas memories this year.

Another reason to resent Grandmother's insistence that my family visit her for the coming week.

LAYLA

I've definitely killed the good vibes we were sharing. I can't really blame myself. Owen is easy to talk to. I'd probably share my entire life story with him if I stayed in his car long enough. Which is why I need to end this sort-of-date and get going.

I should have said my wish was something like obedient

students, a raise, or the check engine light in my car to disappear.

When Owen's hand cups my shoulder, I almost jump out of my skin. I catch a whiff of his spicy cologne. His touch is warm and gentle. It's the softest touch I've received in a long time and tears spring to my eyes for the second time tonight. *Get a grip, girl.* I blink them away.

"My dad died eight years ago," he says softly. "Some days I'm doing fine, then out of nowhere I'll think of something he said or did, and it's like I've lost him all over again. The holidays are the hardest."

I meet his eyes. He gets my grief. Having an empathetic ear is something I didn't know I needed until right now. It hits me again just how handsome he is. I love the beard. It makes him look older, wiser. Kissable. Okay, that is an inappropriate thought. I look back at my hands.

"Talking about moms and wishes," I say. "My mom and I had this thing we'd do every time we caught eleven-eleven on a clock. We called it the wishing minute, and we'd repeat our wish as many times as we could until eleven-twelve. I haven't thought about our wishing minute in a long time."

"My mom would love that."

My phone chimes in my purse. Normally, I'd ignore a text, but I need a distraction from Owen. His hand is so comforting. In another minute, I might lean over the center console and snuggle into his chest.

"Sorry," I say. "It might be my roommates. Just a second."

His hand drops from my shoulder, and I shiver.

It's not Meg or Livy. It's Spencer again. I forgot to text him back earlier to say I wouldn't meet him for dinner.

SPENCER: *Meet me at L'oie Bleue. Our table is reserved for 7 p.m. I like you in the blue dress with the open back.*

Spencer is great in some ways, but completely oblivious in others. I move to slip my phone back in my purse, when I'm hit by a profound thought: Spencer is wealthy.

I can ask him for a loan. Banks have turned me down. As have Visa and Mastercard. But Spencer's generous. He might say yes.

It's a crazy idea, but it's the only one I have.

I type out a quick text.

LAYLA: *See you there.*

I don't want to go. I'd much rather stay here than have a fancy dinner with Spencer. But Nana. She comes first.

"I'm sorry, Owen. I need to be somewhere. It's important."

His expression turns from disappointed to worried in a nanosecond. "Is everything okay?"

"It will be. Thank you so much for the fries."

Owen leaves the tray outside and turns on his ignition. Lucky me, there's a break in traffic as soon as he reaches the curb, and we're across the street and next to my car in less than thirty seconds.

He puts the car in park. "Could I get your number? I'll be back next Saturday, and I'd love to take you on an actual date."

I can't recall an hour that I've enjoyed as much as this one, but I'm still hesitant to let him into my life. Even if Spencer gives me a loan, it doesn't solve my money problems. My fear of Owen finding out what a mess I am hasn't disappeared. If anything, it's grown. He might not know what to do with his life, but he owns a business. His car isn't overdue for a visit at the mechanics. He's put together; I'm a disaster.

I glance at Greta, who is gnawing on her bone at the back of the car, then smile goodbye at Owen.

"I'll see you around. Merry Christmas."

I'm out of his car and into mine in record time. It's like tearing off a bandage: a quick goodbye is better than a lingering one. Besides, if I'm going to make it to *L'oie Bleue* by seven, I need to speed back to my apartment to get ready.

Chapter Three

LAYLA

I don't have much time to look my best, but I do what I can to revive my hair by re-curling the limp strands and dousing it in hairspray. I refuse to wear the blue Veronica Beard dress Spencer requested because I'm not an accessory, and this isn't a date. This is a business meeting between friends, even if he doesn't know that yet.

Instead, I wear the L'Agence black wrap dress. It's simple, but elegant. Before Nana lost all her money, I went consignment shopping every weekend and found some amazing designer pieces. I adore a gorgeous, well-made piece of clothing and a reason to dress up.

I pair the dress with my lucky red Gianvito Rossi boots. They belonged to my mom, a small splurge to keep her spirits up when she first became sick. They kept her alive for four years past her doctor's initial prognosis.

I need their luck tonight.

I'm on my way out the door when Meg comes through it. Her green scrubs are sweaty and dirty. By the way she collapses on the armchair, her nursing shift at the hospital must have been arduous.

"You're back early," I say.

When I arrived home and neither of my roommates were here, I hoped I could get out before they got home. It would be a lot easier to explain in a text than in person that I'm missing our movie night.

Meg blows out a long, exhausted breath. "It will probably never happen again." She notices what I'm wearing. "Those aren't pajamas. Where are you going?"

She and Livy hate Spencer, so I hedge.

"It's a last-minute thing. I'm meeting up with a friend. I'm sorry to miss our movie night."

There must be something in my voice or look because her eyes narrow.

"Does this friend happen to be an ex-boyfriend who you keep taking back?"

How does she read me so easily? "Why would you say that?"

"Because I can't imagine anyone else you would ditch your roommates for at the last minute. Unless it's an emergency?"

Getting money to take care of Nana is an emergency, but Meg and Livy don't know about my money woes. Finances have always been personal and something for me to deal with by myself.

"No emergency."

Meg sags. "So, it *is* Spencer."

Caught. "It's only dinner. We're friends."

"You're wearing your lucky boots. What kind of luck are you hoping for with your *friend*?"

I slide my left foot toward the door. The right follows. "It's not a big deal."

She waves her hand. "Just remember how unhappy you were the last time you dated, okay?"

"I remember."

"Good."

Dating Spencer wasn't all bad, nor was I always unhappy, but I did him a disservice by complaining to Livy and Meg every time he canceled a date or completely forgot we made plans because he was busy at work. Now that's all they remember. They refuse to listen when I tell them how kind and generous he can be when he remembers my existence.

We tried dating three times and broke up each time because his work always comes first. I'd like a boyfriend who makes me a priority. I'm almost thirty, and I haven't found one yet.

Meg stands and stretches. "Don't worry about missing movie night. My parents surprised me by coming into town for the week. They're taking me to dinner. I was going to invite you and Livy to come with us."

"That's great they're here! Sorry I can't go to dinner with you."

She doesn't visit her family in Idaho often, so it's special that they came down to visit her. No time to chat about it. I've got to go if I want to make it to the restaurant on time.

"Tell Livy for me?" I ask.

"Sure, but you owe me. I hate being the bearer of bad news."

"Thanks."

I open the door and find a breathless Livy on the other side struggling with a half-dozen over-full grocery bags in her hands.

Drat. Caught twice.

I go through the entire explanation about Spencer and our platonic dinner again and finally make my escape.

During the drive to downtown Salt Lake City, and while I try to find a parking space, I rehearse how I'll ask Spencer for help. I have never had to ask for money from a friend before, and the humiliation might kill me if the crazy holiday traffic doesn't first.

L'OIE BLEUE IS OVERWHELMINGLY GORGEOUS, AND THAT'S FROM the outside. All sleek, black lines and warm-lit windows. When I walk through the front door, heated air whooshes past me, a blessed relief from the bitter winter night. Once I'm out of the wind, I take in the candle-lit tables, a live string quartet, and the waitstaff in their black shirts and slacks with white aprons and white hand towels over their left arms.

It's all I can do not to turn around and leave. When Spencer and I dated, he took me to fancy restaurants all the time, but not to *L'oie Bleue*. It's a cut above the rest and impostor syndrome hits like a sledgehammer.

I should have worn the blue dress like Spencer suggested.

"Do you have a reservation?" The concierge's raised eyebrows tell me he expects a no.

If he knew I had fifty-three dollars and ten cents in my

bank account, he would kick me out in an instant. That wouldn't even cover an appetizer.

I hope he doesn't catch my nervousness as I speak. "Yes, it's under Spencer Eccleston?"

The concierge covers his tablet with a hand as he scans the screen for Spencer's name, then gives me a pointed look like he thinks I'm lying about knowing Spencer to get out of the cold. "Mr. Eccleston has yet to arrive. Shall we show you to your seat?"

"No," I say quickly. "I'd like to wait here."

Because if Spencer cancels due to a work obligation, I'd rather not feel compelled to order anything. This is the type of restaurant that doesn't print the prices of their entrees on the menu.

I turn away so it's not so awkward and stare at the ornate door.

Please show up. Please show up. Please show up.

I catch myself chewing on my thumbnail and hide my hands behind my back, clasping my fingers tight to keep them away from my mouth. The nervousness makes me want to keep my hands busy, but sadly, this isn't the place to pull the sock I'm knitting out of my purse.

As nervous as I am about what I plan to ask Spencer, my thoughts keep turning to Owen. This restaurant is gorgeous, and I'm sure the food is divine, but I'd rather be in his car with sappy Christmas tunes playing on the radio and eating subpar fries than here. I like him. A lot. I surmise the feeling is mutual. He did ask for my number so we could have a real date.

Thoughts about Owen lead back to my staggering debt that will only get worse as the years go on. Is there a point in going out with him on an actual date when anything serious between us would lead to pulling him into my depressing financial future?

No, which is why I didn't give him my phone number. The situation makes me sad.

I glance at my watch. Spencer's twenty minutes late. He hasn't contacted me with an explanation or cancellation. How long do I wait? When do I accept that he got tied up with work and isn't coming?

After twenty-six minutes, the concierge clears his throat, and I know he's about to escort me off the premises, but then the door opens and there's Spencer. He came. I'm so relieved, I feel limp.

A gust of winter wind sweeps in after him, and his long coat rustles around his knees. He's just as striking as ever, with light brown hair slicked back in a pompadour. Hazel eyes, high cheekbones, and thick eyebrows make him look classically handsome. Like always, I'm surprised he's here with me.

He's six inches taller than my five seven height, and he leans down to kiss my cheek. Then he takes my hand between his gloved ones and gives it a tight squeeze. It does not make my heart race.

"Thank you for meeting me at the last minute, Layla." He's earnest in his greeting, and it dispels my anxiety over his tardiness. "It's good to see you."

"It's good to see you too, Spencer."

It really is. We don't work as a romantic couple, but we're friends, and he's so busy I rarely see him.

"They should have taken you to our table," he scolds. "It's cold in the entry, and you shouldn't be made to wait here."

The concierge and I wear twin blushes.

"No," I say. "I wanted to wait for you before being seated."

He shakes his head like he doesn't understand why I wanted to wait by the door when I could enjoy my wine while sitting at a table.

"Mr. Eccleston," the concierge says. "May I take your coats?"

Once relieved of our winter wear, we're led to a table along the windows that look out on the city lights of Salt Lake City. Spencer pulls out my chair. I've always appreciated him for being a gentleman.

What I don't appreciate is how work is his first, second, and third priorities, as illustrated when his phone rings and he takes the call as he sits down. I look out of the window as the waiter fills our wine glasses and brings appetizers.

I should wait for Spencer to finish his call before digging into the crusty bread with olive tapenade and cheese spread, but after five minutes, I give up. The fries I shared with Owen are long gone, and I'm hungry. It's Spencer's fault if he misses out on the delectable appetizers.

Spencer's call ends, but he doesn't look up as he types on his phone. "I called ahead and ordered our meal. What do you think of the tapenade?"

"Delicious." I'm not sure he hears my answer. His brow furrows as he reads something on his phone.

So, this is not a rare night where I'll have his undivided attention. I hope whatever he has to tell me isn't about us getting back together, because right now is a perfect example of why we're better at being friends. While we dated, his distraction with his phone drove me mad.

I understand he worked hard to become the youngest

lawyer to make senior partner in the history of his grandfather's corporate law firm, but how that translates into real life is that the law firm *is* his life. While we dated, I shared most of our time together with his clients.

The appetizer plates disappear, and small bowls of French onion soup, with a slice of crusty bread and melted cheese on top, take their place. Only then does Spencer put his phone face down on the table.

"Sorry," he says with an apologetic grin. "I know you hate when I bring work to dinner."

I shrug. "We aren't dating anymore."

He chuckles like he thinks it's funny I'd say we're not dating. I pause with the spoon halfway to my mouth. That doesn't bode well for me. I don't want to tell him no, but I'll have to if he asks.

Through each course that follows, salad, beef stew, and cheese, he asks me about my job, my roommates, and Nana. I don't ask about his job because we've already spent too much time with it tonight. Instead, I ask about his plans for Christmas.

"I'll be in Maine with my aunts, uncles, and cousins on my dad's side."

So much family. A tinge of jealousy pings my heart, just as it did earlier when Owen spoke about his mom and brother. Nana is all the family I have left.

"When do you leave?"

He studies my face as he says, "Tomorrow morning."

Speaking of family, now is the time to discuss my situation. If I put it off much longer, I might not get a chance before he has to rush off.

"There's something I want to talk to you about." I push away the cheese plate and sit up straighter.

He nods and takes a sip of his wine. "I need to talk to you about something, too. Ladies first."

The waiter takes away our dishes, giving me a few moments to collect my thoughts. Dessert arrives. A little pot of crème brûlée for Spencer and chocolate cake for me. Spencer is observant and thoughtful to order me cake, my preferred dessert, and not crème brûlée, which reminds me of slime. He has a remarkable memory.

The cake smells amazing, but I don't let myself get distracted. I force myself to look at Spencer even though I'd rather study the tablecloth, and do something I promised myself I would never do: beg.

"Nana needs more care than she's getting. Her dementia is growing worse, and it's time to move her into the memory care unit." I swallow down the lump in my throat. "She needs somewhere that is more secure and where the staff understands dementia better."

Spencer leans across the small table and lays his hand on my arm. It's a warm weight that makes me feel less alone. Kind of like when Owen put his hand on my shoulder earlier tonight.

"I'm sorry, Layla. I understand how hard this must be for you."

I nod, acknowledging his sympathy. When he listens, he knows how to listen.

I take a breath to calm my racing heart. It doesn't seem to help. This next part is humiliating. I ignore the way my face heats and push forward.

"We've already gone through our savings. I don't have the

money I need to pay for Nana's care. Will you give me a loan?" I rush on, not giving him a chance to respond before I finish. "I promise to pay you back with interest, but it will take time. If you write up a contract, I'll sign it."

I can't even begin to pay him back until after Nana passes. The thought makes my throat tight.

He crosses his arms, his friendliness melting into business. "I can have a contract drawn up after Christmas. No interest. I'd like to help Ellen. I know how much you love her." He pauses. "Or I have a better offer." He studies me for a few drawn-out seconds where I think my heart will beat up my throat and choke me. "We help each other, and you never have to pay me back."

My stomach rolls. I'd never have to pay him back? It feels like a dream, but what does he expect me to do in exchange for a check with as many zeroes as I'll need? I lean back in my seat, leery. "What can I possibly give you in return?"

"Do you remember my grandfather died in April?"

"Yes."

"He left everything to Grandmother." He huffs out an angry breath. "She's never in her life managed money until now, and I don't know what financial advisor she's hired, but he's a crook. That's the only way I can explain her ridiculous behavior."

I'm unfamiliar with this side of Spencer. He's usually calm, almost to a fault. Now he runs his hand through his hair with a furious sweep.

"Spencer, I'm sorry for whatever she's done, but I don't understand how I can help you."

He closes his eyes and collects himself. "I found out a few days ago that Grandmother has decided to give the bulk of her fortune to charities. She's not waiting until she's dead. She's liquidating many of her assets now."

I still don't know how this relates to me, but I don't interrupt.

"Though she refuses to explain most of her updated will until after Christmas, she has mentioned how much each grandchild will receive as an inheritance. It's a joke how little she's leaving us. Grandfather inherited his fortune from his own father. It's generational wealth, which means it should pass from generation to generation."

I've always known Spencer is wealthy by the cut of his suits, the restaurants and entertainment he takes me to on our dates, and the Porsche he drives. I thought it was from his career as a lawyer with a thriving corporate law firm. I had no idea he was the product of generations of accumulated riches.

I cross my arms and sit with this information, surprised at how it intimidates me.

"There is one bright spot in all of this," Spencer continues in a calmer voice, oblivious to my own inner turmoil. "Grandmother has it in her head that her grandchildren are at the age where they should be married. She will double the inheritance for wives and children."

He looks directly into my eyes. He doesn't say it outright, but I make the connection. This is a marriage proposal. I laugh, ill at ease.

"You can't be serious." There's a slight tremor in my voice. "We have fun together, but that doesn't mean we'd make a good married couple."

"I disagree. I think we'll get along well." He clears his throat. "There is another reason I want to get married sooner rather than later. I have a client who doesn't take me seriously because I'm thirty-four but not in a serious relationship. I can understand how you might find this sudden, but I have no hesitation in saying you're the wife I want."

My head feels dizzy. This makes little sense.

"We have never once spoken about marriage," I say.

He studies me. "We are now."

From his inside coat pocket, he takes a small ring box and lays it on the table before opening the top and sliding it toward me. Inside is the largest diamond ring I have ever seen. Emerald cut with smaller diamonds along the platinum band. I don't want to guess how many thousands of dollars it cost him.

That is a serious ring. This proposal is serious.

I glance around, grateful no one notices our conversation. Attention would make this scene even more ridiculous.

"Put that thing away," I whisper. "It's going to blind someone."

He flips the lid closed but doesn't take it back. He studies me like I'm a problem he needs to figure out how to fix. "If we get married, my money is your money, and you don't need to repay anything. You'll have whatever you need to take care of Ellen."

Even if I am desperate for money, I'm not *that* desperate. I won't entertain the thought … except I do. No debt. No more stress about Nana's bills. No penny pinching for the rest of my life. No more stress knitting. I can knit because I love it and not because of desperation. For that one moment, the relief I feel makes my head spin.

Then reality catches up.

If I marry, I want it to be for love. I want my husband to love me more than his job. What Spencer and I have is not that kind of relationship.

"We can't even make a dating relationship last longer than three months at a time," I say. "A marriage between the two of us wouldn't survive."

"You broke up with me last time," he says with conviction. "Remember how I begged you not to?"

I wouldn't call him saying, "Please, Layla, give me another chance," after he missed our second date in a row as begging.

"I want a relationship with you to last longer than a few months at a time," he says. "If giving you a comfortable life and everything you need to take care of those you love is the motivation you need to commit, I'm going to leverage those things to my advantage. Layla, give me a chance to prove to you what kind of husband I can be."

I sigh. "Not a good one for me if work remains your only priority."

He doesn't argue the point. "I can't say my commitment to the firm will change going forward, but I can be better at listening to you. For example, I will stay off my phone during dinner."

My eyes widen at the audacity of such a statement from him. If that were a possibility, why hasn't he implemented it sooner?

He laughs at my expression. "I'm a work in progress, but if you're with me, it will be worth it." He points to my cake with his spoon. "Eat. Think."

He cracks the top of his crème brûlée as if he hasn't a care in the world. A stark contrast to five minutes ago.

The first bite of cake melts in my mouth. Spencer loves good food and only when I'm with him do I get to indulge. If we married, dinners like this would become a regular part of my life. I could eat here every week if I wanted—though more often than not I'd be eating alone. I don't mind being alone, or even eating at restaurants alone. What I would struggle with is knowing Spencer doesn't care if I'm alone because he would have more important places to be.

I swallow thickly. "Spencer, I plan on marrying for love."

"I refuse to marry for love," he says with conviction as he places his spoon on the table. "Love doesn't last. My dad has married three times because he *fell in love,* and within five years, all three marriages ended. In contrast, my grandparents were practically strangers when they married, pushed together by their parents, and they lasted over sixty years through mutual respect. That's the marriage I want." He takes my hand from where it lies on the table. "I respect you. We get along. We're honest with each other. That's what makes a successful relationship. Not love."

"And the money your grandma is offering." It's my turn to study him.

He smiles, but doesn't disagree. "Money makes everything in life easier."

I can't argue. I'm exhausted from being broke. Worn thin from stressing about money and worrying about how I'll give Nana everything she needs.

Would financial security be worth the loneliness I know I'll feel married to Spencer? Can I let go of the idea of marriage for love and be content with one of camaraderie? I grew up watching Nana and Opa together. I've dreamed of a marriage like theirs. A marriage between me and Spencer would be an imitation of love; a counterfeit of the real thing.

In a month, will I regret turning him down? In a year, will I regret saying yes?

My thoughts turn to Owen. Tonight was the first time we'd ever spoken, and yet, being with him I felt comfortable and accepted. If I say yes to Spencer, I have no chance with Owen. Not that I did before because I refuse to bring him into my financial troubles. Still, the loss feels deep, which is ridiculous because we officially met only hours ago.

Spencer's phone buzzes with a call and our glances clash across the table. It's a moment of truth. Will he resist the siren call of work? A war wages inside of him, and it's visible across his face. He pushes the button on the side, sending the call to voicemail.

I'm surprised. I didn't think he had it in him.

"Why do you want to marry *me*?" I ask. "There must be innumerable women who would jump at the chance to marry you." Somewhat hesitantly I add, "Someone who is in your social class."

He shakes his head before I've finished. "I don't want someone who wants me for my name or my money."

I laugh at that. "That's exactly what you're offering me."

He smiles sheepishly. "It's different between us. Wealth doesn't go to your head like it does other women I've dated. I love how sensible and frugal you are. Layla, believe me when I say I've given this a lot of thought. When Grandmother mentioned wanting to see her grandkids married, you were the first person who came to mind. Everyone else I've dated can't compete."

I'm not sure if I should be offended or flattered. "What about the model you dated in August?"

"She wouldn't eat with me watching." He leans close and talks as if he's telling me a dirty secret. "Unless we went to a restaurant with a private dining room, and I moved my chair so I wasn't facing her, we never went out to eat."

I try not to laugh. It's a surprise they lasted a full month considering how much Spencer appreciates good food.

His expression sobers. "Layla, I love you. Not the way you expect me to with this proposal, but I do. We're good friends. That's a solid foundation for a marriage."

I'm reminded of something Nana said to me once, about how there are layers of love. Romantic love. Family love. Friendly love. I love Spencer, too. I value his friendship and the time we spend together. But marriage?

"What are your expectations for this marriage?" I ask.

He grins like he's already convinced me. Maybe he has.

"We build a life together. Buy a home. Make a family. Grow old together."

A family. That's all I've ever wanted. Without this enormous debt I've accrued, I could actually have one.

"You'll love my family," he says, chipping away at my resolve to tell him no. "Fly with me to Maine tomorrow. Let me introduce everyone to my fiancée."

I laugh at the audacity. He expects me to drop everything and fly to Maine with only a few hours' notice. Classic Spencer.

"I can't leave with you tomorrow. It's four days before Christmas. I have plans."

"Spend eight days, starting tomorrow, in Maine with me,

and at the end, I'll give you fifty-thousand dollars outright. It'll be enough to cover Ellen's expenses until we marry."

My heart literally stops. Fifty-thousand dollars. Does he realize how tantalizing the money is to me? He must. It's a carrot to get me moving in the direction he wants. Annoying, but effective.

What is my other option? Nana being evicted from Brock Pine Home. She'd be taken into state care, and they'd get to choose where she lives and how she's cared for. I've looked into the care homes the state will pay for, and I can't let Nana live in any of them. I want her to get better care, not less.

In the end, it's not such a difficult decision.

I open the ring box and study the ring. It sparkles in the candlelight. I look up at Spencer. Engaged to a friend isn't the worst way to end the evening. In fact, I feel hope for the first time in this year. Spencer's proposal offers me help and support; both of which I desperately need.

"Yes," I say.

The grin that spreads across his face is almost a gloat, like he won a competition, and I'm the prize. Maybe I should've made him work harder for my acceptance. I'm positive his favorite aspect of being a lawyer is winning. I've never met anyone so competitive.

He removes the ring from the box. I hold out my left hand, and he slips it onto my finger. It's a little snug, but that's good. The diamond is enormous; if the band were loose, it might slip off.

It's only now that I consider how my roommates will respond to the news of my *engagement* to Spencer. Meg was worried I'd *date* him again. Marriage? She will freak.

I burst out in nervous laughter.

"What?" Spencer asks, looking up from my hand.

"Can you imagine what Meg and Livy will say when they find out?"

He shakes his head. "They'll try to talk you out of it, I'd guess. They hate me."

He speaks the truth. They have longer memories than I do.

Leaving tomorrow for a week will mean I don't have to deal with their suspicions about our sudden engagement, though I feel terrible about bailing on our plans. Then I remember Meg's family is visiting, so our plans would change anyway. They'll be fine without me.

One thing that will be challenging is not being here for Nana. I haven't gone more than two days without visiting her since she moved into assisted living. Either she'll be oblivious to my absence or worry when I don't visit, both terrible options. I tell myself this week away will be worth it because it will provide a way for me to take care of her going forward.

"Tell me about Maine," I say, consciously making myself not think about Nana being alone.

Spencer swallows his last bite of his crème brûlée. "My grandfather owns a cabin on the coast. Or, I guess it's Grandmother's now." He shakes his head as if trying to dislodge the oddness of the situation. "It's right by the ocean with a remarkable view of the sunrise over the water. My cousins and I grew up spending summers there every year. When I worked with my grandfather at the New York law office before moving to the Salt Lake City office, we spent weekends at the cabin. For such a small town, they have decent food."

It sounds idyllic. "Can you get me a plane ticket by tomorrow?"

"Already done."

I can't help but feel a bit manipulated. "You were that sure I would say yes?"

"No, but in case you did, I wanted to be prepared. I'll send a car to your apartment to pick you up at eight. Pack warm. Maine winters are cold. Colder than Salt Lake, even."

Another concern rises. "Are you going to leave me alone with your family while you work?"

He shakes his head. "My trial is scheduled for mid-January and it's solid. We'll be able to enjoy the holiday together."

I've always had to compete with Spencer's clients. It will be a new experience to have uninterrupted time with him.

He leans close. "I can't wait for you to meet my family. You will love them."

It's the perfect thing to say to me. "I'm excited to have a family Christmas."

He points to my dessert plate. "Are you finished with your *gateau*? Shall we go?"

"Yes."

As we walk the few blocks to where I parked, he holds my gloved hand. It's just the two of us, and it's lovely. Freezing, but lovely.

When we reach my car, Spencer leans in for a kiss, his gloved hand on my cold cheek. His lips are firm and sure. I feel no zing or tingles at his touch, but the kiss is familiar, just like him.

Only as I'm crossing in front of my car to the driver's side do I see the ticket attached to the windshield. The parking meter must have expired. My heart sinks at another expense I can't afford, but before I can open it, Spencer whisks it from my hand.

"I'll have my assistant take care of it," he says.

Just like that, the stress over my debt disappears. Until this moment, it didn't hit me how much I'd appreciate having Spencer as a fiancé.

He waits as I climb into my car then waves as I pull away from the curb.

The emotional fallout hits within seconds. My shoulders shake with sobs and my vision turns blurry. I pull over into a parking lot because I'm afraid I might crash into something. For so long, I've been alone with my worry over Nana, and now I'm no longer alone. The weight of a year-and-a-half of stress lifts from my mind. I'm not going to the modern equivalent of debtors' prison.

My future holds hope for the first time in ages. As long as I don't let myself think of what I'm giving up in exchange for Spencer's support. I focus on my gratitude for what he's doing for me and Nana. Everything will be okay and that is a miracle.

When my sobs wind down to hiccupy tears, the clock on my dash reads 11:11. I think of my mom, who believed in the magic of a wish.

"I wish to be happy in my marriage." I whisper it again and again.

I'm marrying Spencer Eccleston. There is no turning back. All I can do is wish for the best.

Chapter Four

OWEN

Since the beginning of the year when I sold my half of the company I co-founded, I've slept in until eight most mornings. So, I don't appreciate waking up to my brother jumping on me at five a.m.

"You're fourteen," I croak. "Way too old for this."

I groan and try to shift him off my lungs. He may be young, but he's already six feet tall. That's a lot of weight making it impossible for me to breathe.

He slides off my body and onto his knees. He pokes me in the side.

"Mom said you have to get up. We leave for the airport at six-thirty."

Our flight doesn't leave until nine, but it's no use arguing with Mom's logic. If she needs to be there two hours early to wait at our gate, then so be it.

Still, five a.m.?

"That's in an hour-and-a-half."

I'm thirty-two, which means I'm too old to be woken up by my mother, especially not in my own house. Sometimes she forgets that I have successfully lived on my own for fourteen years.

Brady grabs the cup of water on my bedside table and throws the remaining half-inch in my face.

I wipe it away with my hand. "Really?"

"Mom said I can't leave your room until you're up."

"I'm up."

I don't move to get out of bed, but my words must be enough because he finally leaves. I flip my pillow to the dry side, and I snuggle deeper in my blanket. I can sleep for at least another hour and still be ready by six-thirty.

Except Brady doesn't leave my room quietly. He flips on the light and plays Mariah Carey at full blast. I jump out of bed to grab his phone, but he isn't stupid, and runs down the hallway. When he disappears into the kitchen, I let him go and return to my room.

"Owen," Mom calls from the kitchen before I'm able to shut the door. "Your omelet is ready. If you go back to bed, it will be cold and chewy. Get it while it's hot."

I debate. Get more sleep? Or have a hot breakfast? May as well enjoy a non-chewy omelet.

Brady's cheesy omelet and a large glass of milk are half gone by the time I sit across from him, his attention on a thick fantasy book open on the table.

He takes after mom, with a lighter complexion and leaner build. He hasn't cut his light brown hair in years, and it hangs in waves past his shoulders. There's a bit of scruff on his upper lip and chin. It might be time to teach him how to shave.

I'm jealous of Brady's height. He'll probably grow a few more inches before graduating high school. I'm five nine, broader, and more compact like dad. Dad wanted me to play football like he did since I have the build for it, but once I hit middle school, I didn't have time for sports. Instead, I worked hard to earn an associate's degree before I graduated high school and got my bachelor's degree at twenty. All so I could be like Mom's dad: a lawyer. Decisions I regret now.

Mom places a plate in front of me and ruffles my hair. Again, not a kid. When she visits me in Salt Lake, she acts like this is her house and I'm sixteen. I rarely mind, but I'm not usually out of bed at five a.m. either.

"I'm hopping in the shower now," she says. "Who's next?"

"I don't need one," Brady says. He doesn't look up from his book.

We stayed up late last night so he could tell me about it. I tried to follow, but had a hard time because I kept thinking about Layla. I hope she's okay after the way she acted when she received that text. I wish she had given me her number so I could check and make sure.

Mom raises her eyebrows and stares at the top of Brady's greasy mop of hair. He must feel her attention because he glances up at her.

"You need a shower," she says. "You smell like a wadded-up swimming suit left in a towel, forgotten in the back of a closet for a month. You'll have to survive without your book for twenty minutes."

"It's the exciting part," he whines.

She puts her hands on her hips. "It's always the exciting part when I ask you to do something. Shower, got it?"

He nods reluctantly, then goes back to the book.

"Be ready by the time I get out of the bathroom," Mom warns before she moves down the hallway.

The moment the bathroom door shuts, Brady looks up and focuses on me. "Why are we going to Maine? Mom won't tell me anything except Grandmother invited us. It sucks because I'm missing my Dungeons and Dragons session."

As upsetting as that is for Brady, I'd bet he's more nervous about meeting his grandmother, aunts, uncles, and cousins he's barely heard about. Mom was ostracized by her family when she married Dad. I spent summers in Maine when I was a teenager but, besides our cousin Tori, I haven't spoken to the rest of the family in eight years.

Even if Mom doesn't want Brady to meet her family with any preconceived notions, he should understand what we're walking into this Christmas.

"What do you know about mom's parents?" I ask.

"Just that they didn't like Dad. Mom hasn't seen them since before I was born. After Grandfather died, Grandmother started talking to her occasionally. Mom goes into her room and cries after every call. It's weird."

Mom's family is weird, and I blame it all on Grandfather.

"Do you know why Mom's family didn't like Dad?" I ask.

"Because he didn't have money?"

"Yep, and he wasn't planning on making any either. Math teachers aren't exactly wealthy, and money means everything to the Ecclestons. When Dad proposed, Grandfather warned Mom she'd be disowned if she married him."

"She married him anyway." There's pride in Brady's tone.

"From that day until I turned ten, her parents, brother, and sister ignored her existence. Grandfather decided a male grandchild was worth breaking his silence for, and he reached out to Mom about having me live with them."

He tilts his head. "To live with them forever?"

"Yeah. They were raising our cousin who's a few years older than me, and Grandfather wanted us both to grow up to be like him. Mom said no way. Grandfather offered her money. She refused. He said he'd pay my college tuition when I was old enough to go to college. She compromised and said I could stay with them for two months over the summer, but only if I wanted to."

Brady leans back in his chair. "How did you get Mom to tell you all of this? She never talks to me about her family."

Mom's family is a taboo topic. I think it hurts too much for her to talk about them.

"It was Dad who told me."

His confusion over how I know so much clears. "They have a lot of money then?"

I laugh at how understated that sounds. "Yes, they have a lot of money. Grandfather thought that gave him the right to dictate everyone's lives."

"They would've liked Dad if they had known him."

Brady was six when Dad died. He never got the chance to know him like I did, but everyone loved Dad. At his funeral, former students, college friends, and people from all over the city packed the place. Our grandparents missed out by dismissing him because of his profession and lack of family connections.

"I think so too," I say.

He twirls his fork along the top of the table. "Grandfather called the summer I turned ten and asked if I wanted to visit. I didn't want to."

Mom never told me, but it makes sense. I'd already distanced myself from Grandfather. Maybe he thought I'd failed, but he still had a chance to mold my brother into his image.

I'm glad Brady didn't go; he would have been miserable. Grandfather wouldn't have let him read all summer, at least not fantasy. Nonfiction and law were more his style, and because he liked those types of books, everyone else should too.

"Why didn't you go visit?" I ask.

He shrugs. "I didn't want to spend a month with strangers. Besides, I knew you didn't like them, so why would I?"

"I didn't always feel the way I do now," I say. "We have cousins my age, and the three of us hung out every summer. Grandfather had expectations about how we had to behave and what things we needed to study, but it wasn't all work. He took us to museums, baseball games, and New York City. I never would have experienced those things if I had stayed home."

Brady, whose greatest passion is books and who finds fictional friends better company than real ones, isn't impressed.

"If you had so much fun with him," he asks, "Then why do you hate him?"

My answer to that question shows what an unappreciative jerk I was to our parents when I was Brady's age, and I hesitate.

The water in the shower shuts off, but we still have at least twenty minutes before Mom will be out of the bathroom. It's a family joke how long she takes to get ready in the mornings. It's why she can't understand how it only takes me thirty minutes from the moment I get out of bed to when I'm out the door.

"Are you going to tell me?" Brady prods.

"Our cousins are wealthy and sophisticated and lead completely different lives than I do, especially when we were kids. They'd been to Europe multiple times when I met them, and I'd been on a plane once because Grandfather bought my ticket. They had the newest phones, laptops, and expensive clothes. I was an average kid from a podunk town who wore jeans and t-shirts and didn't know any better. Instead of being angry at Grandfather for disowning his daughter, I was mad at Dad for having such a lame job."

Anger flashes in Brady's eyes. "He didn't have a lame job."

"I know that now, but I wasn't as smart as you are. I wanted to impress Grandfather and prove that I was like him and not our parents. From my very first summer, I decided I'd earn a law degree and work at his firm."

"But you changed your mind. You graduated with a business degree."

"My bachelor's degree was in business, but then I went to Harvard and earned a law degree."

He laughs. "You're kidding."

I give him a rueful smile. "Nope. You were only five, so you don't remember, but Mom and Dad threw me a huge party when I passed the bar. They supported me in everything."

Even when I didn't deserve it.

Brady's looking at me like I'm a stranger. "Then why aren't you a lawyer?"

"I worked at Grandfather's corporate law firm for a year, but then I quit."

"Did he treat you like an intern and make you get the coffee for the whole office and then, when you got his order wrong, did he make you remove staples from boxes of documents for hours and hours?"

I laugh. "That's oddly specific."

"I saw it on a TV show."

"The reality of law was much less dramatic and a lot more boring. I wanted to love it like Grandfather did, but I didn't. I don't know if you remember, but when dad first went into a coma, I was working in New York. After Mom called, I flew into a panic and booked a flight home. I rushed to pack while Grandfather was cool as a cucumber. He said, 'We're in the middle of a merger, and you've committed to see it through. Ecclestons never leave a job half-finished.'"

This was his response to my dad being hospitalized.

In an instant, a man I strived to emulate became the man I no longer respected.

To him, it was a mere inconvenience. Work responsibilities came first, no matter what happened in our personal lives. He had shared his work philosophy many times, but that day I learned what he meant.

"I left on my flight and never saw him again."

Brady studies me. "Are you still angry at him?"

"Looking back, I would've been surprised if he had acted any other way. What I most resent is how he warned Mom's family not to attend Dad's funeral. He held all the purse strings, and no one wanted to go against him. Mom could've used their support. It was Grandfather's last dig at the man he felt stole his daughter away from him. I wouldn't go this Christmas if Grandfather were still alive, no matter what Mom said."

"What about grandmother? Are you still angry at her?"

I shake my head. "Grandmother never stuck up for Mom or Dad, but she said nothing bad about them either." I shrug. "I'm okay seeing her, but I'd rather not go at all."

Brady gives me a long look. "I'm giving up Dungeons and Dragons to go, so it better be a good trip. Are you going to be miserable and ruin Christmas?"

"No."

He tilts his head to the side and crosses his arms. He doesn't believe me.

"I'll do my best to have fun," I amend. It won't be easy. I have a chip on my shoulder as large as a city block.

He keeps staring. It reminds me a lot of Dad.

I put my hand over my heart. "This will be the best Christmas we've ever had."

"If you fail, you'll regret it."

I don't doubt it.

The bathroom door opens. "Brady? Your turn."

Chapter Five

LAYLA

A SLEEK, BLACK CAR WAITS FOR ME OUTSIDE MY APARTMENT building at eight the next morning. As soon as I come out of the door, the driver walks forward and takes my two suitcases. He adjusts his grip as his shoulders shift forward. He raises his eyebrows as he packs them into the trunk.

I struggled to know what to pack, which meant I over packed and brought something for every occasion I could imagine.

When the driver opens my door, I slip inside, then startle when I see Spencer staring at the computer on his lap. I expected to meet him at the airport and had prepared myself for the stress of him arriving late.

He takes a second away from his laptop to kiss me on the cheek. "I'm glad to see your roommates didn't talk you out of coming with me."

"No."

It's not that my roommates didn't want to talk me out of it, just that I didn't give them much of a chance.

The driver pulls out of the parking lot, and I look back at my apartment building. The lights on our Christmas tree shine through our third-floor window in the gloomy, cloud-covered morning.

Last night when I got home, Meg was in the living room. I gave her the abbreviated version of the proposal, making it sound romantic, then escaped to my room. This morning I woke Livy, and while she was half asleep broke the news and fled. I even made up a wedding date so they'd take me seriously. The size of the ring did the rest. I wasn't able to convince them I love Spencer. They're too smart for that, considering they've been with me through all three times Spencer and I dated. I understand their confusion. They don't know about my financial woes or the extent of Spencer's wealth.

Spencer's fingers clack along the keys of his computer.

"I thought you weren't taking your case with you to Maine," I say.

Did I really expect anything different from a workaholic for the next week? Yes, I did. It's a reminder that I need to keep my expectations realistic for our relationship going forward. His work is his priority, not me. I'm marrying so I'll have the money to take care of Nana. If I don't expect anything more from him, I'll never be disappointed.

"Our key witness backed out of our case," he says. "It was the phone call I didn't take during dinner last night. This morning we were given additional evidence by the prosecution that doesn't look good for our client. We had an airtight case, but now it's falling apart, and we have less than a month to put it back together. The judge won't give us another continuance."

I close my eyes and center myself. "Will you be working on the case all week?"

At his silence, I open my eyes to find he's studying me. "You have to understand, I don't have a choice. This case is important. I won't fail my client."

"I understand, but that doesn't mean I'm not disappointed."

"I'm sorry. You don't know how sorry I am." He goes back to his computer, typing while also talking. I'm not sure how he's able to do both at the same time. "I was thinking last night that it might be better if I propose on Christmas Day instead of arriving as already engaged. Is that okay with you?"

I don't care either way, so I take off the ring and hold it out to him. My hand feels lighter. My heart feels heavier. Christmas in Maine isn't sounding so appealing anymore.

He takes the ring box from his suit jacket and slips the ring inside. The lid snaps closed.

He goes back to his computer. "Because I'll be up late and early working on this case, you'll have your own room. I don't want to disturb you."

That's the first welcome news since I entered the car. I'm not ready to share living space yet.

"What about gifts for your family?" My enthusiasm for Maine might have tanked, but it's still Christmas. "I brought a few shawls Nana knit years ago. We can give them to your grandma and aunts. I brought wool to knit everyone else something. What do you think? Mittens? A scarf? A tea cozy?"

He lays his hand on my wrist but is still reading from the computer screen. "Layla, my family doesn't appreciate homemade gifts. The presents I brought will be from the both of us."

"I want to give them something. You should see the shawls. They're like gossamer. The ones we sold online fetched hundreds of dollars."

"Layla." His voice is sharp and his brow creases. "It doesn't matter. They won't want anything knitted. Besides, you don't want to spend your holiday making stuff."

His words hurt. My knitting isn't *stuff*. I create usable items. He dismissed me and Nana in just a few sentences.

I have to take a deep breath and remind myself that this is a new life I've begun as Spencer's fiancée. Or, secret fiancée until Christmas. It's a change in perspective I need to make.

We're silent until we arrive at the airport. The driver opens our doors and pulls our luggage from the trunk. Spencer's smile deflates as the driver places my two wheeled suitcases next to his on the curb.

"Those are yours?" he asks.

"Of course." Who else would have bags in the back of the car? "What's the problem?"

He huffs out a breath. "Layla, I think you're perfect the way you are, but my family has exacting standards. We'll have to buy you new luggage when we arrive in Boston."

There's an insult hidden within the information drop, but I ignore it. "Boston, Massachusetts? I thought we were going to Maine."

"We have an hour's drive from the Boston airport to the cabin in York."

Now I'm really confused. "The cabin is in New York?"

"No, *York, Maine*, not New York," he says, enunciating each word. "York is about four hours from New York." He studies me from toes to nose. "I don't want my family to look down on you. We'll need to buy you new clothes in Boston, too."

Right now, I'm wearing sweatpants and a hoodie, but they're Alo Yoga. I may have bought them from my favorite consignment shop, but that doesn't mean they're from the dollar bin at Walmart. I'm not stupid. I came prepared to impress his family.

"I have a dress in my carry-on to change into before I meet your grandma."

He lays his hands on my shoulders and leans close. "You always look amazing, Layla, but I need you to trust me on this. You don't know my family yet, and I want them to have the best impression of you. I know you can't afford a new wardrobe, so it will be my Christmas gift to you."

Spencer is a pro at sandwiching his criticisms within compliments, but it doesn't sting any less.

I think of Nana yesterday in the recreation room, smiling as she sang along to "Blue Suede Shoes." This is for her. She needs to be in memory care, not evicted from Brock Pine Home altogether.

If it's so important to Spencer that his family doesn't look down on me because my clothes are a few years out of date, then so be it.

"Okay."

He kisses my cheek, his breath minty and warm. "Thank you for understanding."

Spencer takes my hand and leads me inside the airport.

An attendant has our luggage on a cart and follows behind. I'm discombobulated by how quickly we're whisked through security, given a ride on a golf cart, and are deposited at our gate.

Just as we arrive, they call first class and in minutes we're down the jet bridge. Once we're on the plane, instead of heading toward the right, we turn left into the first-class area. A flight attendant leads us directly to our seats. Or … cushy recliners that turn into beds? Pods? I'm not sure what to call them, but the moment I sit down I sigh at the comfort. I've only flown a few times, but never like this. When I stretch my legs out, and my toes don't touch the seat in front of me.

Next to my pod is a bag full of what I assume are complimentary items: snacks, ear plugs, eye masks, lotion, European chocolate, and gum. The rich definitely live differently than normal folk.

The moment Spencer sits down, he's on the phone talking to a colleague about the disaster of their upcoming case. As frustrated as he must feel at these last-minute complications, there's a thrill in his voice. He lives for impossible situations because he loves being the one to figure out how to come out on top. It sounds exhausting to me.

As the other ten first-class seats fill in, I wave away the offered wine and grab my earbuds and knitting needles. When I couldn't sleep last night, I finished my sock. Now I'm working on a baby blanket. As I cast on, I realize I don't need to run my shop like a desperate woman any longer. Spencer is giving me something precious: peace.

I don't want to knit another baby blanket. I stare at my

needles for a long time as I try to decide what I do want to knit.

A hot pad. The first thing Nana taught me how to make and I haven't made one since I was a kid. The sweet feeling the memory brings has me smiling. I have wool in my suitcase. When I'm finished knitting the hot pad, I'll felt it to make it thick and durable.

I put the blanket away as we prepare for take-off. By the time the pilot comes on and says we're at cruising altitude, I'm half asleep. While Spencer types away at his laptop, I slip on the eye mask. With the seat reclined, this is more comfortable than my bed.

I sleep for the full four-hour flight. Without the worry over money, it's the best sleep I've had in over a year.

It's dark by the time we leave Boston to drive the hour to York. The moment we enter the rental, Spencer hooks his phone into the Bluetooth and talks to his colleague back in Salt Lake.

I don't mind at all. We spent all afternoon shopping together, and it was surprisingly fun. He has an eye for fashion that I've never witnessed before. He took a few calls and answered some texts, but mostly, I had his attention as we went from store to store and picked out clothing for me to try on. Since I was a teenager, I've loved high fashion, but I've never been able to afford any designer clothing except pieces I find at consignment stores. Marrying into wealth has its perks.

In the trunk next to Spencer's luggage lie two new teal

suitcases. I allowed Spencer to donate my old ones, but we mailed my clothes home. Those items took me years to curate. They're quality, even if they aren't the highest fashion and are a few years out of date.

My phone buzzes with another text from Meg asking how things are going. It's the seventh one she's sent since this morning. Surprisingly, Livy hasn't joined in—I'm grateful for small favors. I need to put a stop to their worry, or they'll text me nonstop for the next week wanting details.

LAYLA: *We've arrived in Maine. I won't have a lot of time to keep you updated, but know that everything is wonderful. Please stop worrying. I'm very happy.*

It's the truth; I am happy. I smile at the memory of all the compliments Spencer showered on me when I came out of the dressing rooms in outfits with heart-stopping price tags. He really is a sweet man.

Meg responds almost immediately.

MEG: *If this is a hostage situation, send a frowny face emoji.*

I roll my eyes and send a smiley face instead.

LAYLA: *Don't worry about me. I'll see you next week.*

I silence our group chat. They'll just have to believe me because I can only tell them so many times.

Spencer's call ends, and the car is silent. He doesn't enjoy listening to the radio. I catch myself humming and stop. He hates my humming. Talking it is.

"Tell me about your family?" I ask. "I've only heard you mention your grandpa and dad." And his dad's girlfriend Ginger, but he isn't a fan, so I don't mention her. For all I know, his dad and Ginger have broken up since the last time Spencer and I dated.

"Besides Grandmother, Father, and *Ginger*," there's a

small lip curl at her name, "My aunt Ellory and her husband Gerald will be at the cabin. They work in the New York office. Ellory's daughter Tori recently got divorced, and she has her daughter, who I think is around four years old. I've never met my aunt Marianne, but she'll be there too. She married someone of little consequence and Grandfather disowned her. The husband died years ago, but their son came out every summer to Maine and spent a few months with me and Tori. He has a younger brother."

My mouth falls open. "You've never met your aunt? Doesn't that bother you?"

"No. My cousin fell out of favor with Grandfather when he quit the firm. I figure the whole family is the same. No big loss."

His attitude toward his Aunt Marianne and cousins is unbelievably callous.

"I can't imagine not knowing my aunt if I had one," I say with a lightness and humor I don't feel. "If I had any family outside of Nana, I'd hold on to them like a barnacle. They'd never be able to pry me off."

Spencer glances over for a second before turning his attention back to the road. "I think it would depend on whether your aunt was worth knowing."

"True, but you've never met her, so how do you know she's not worth knowing?"

He shrugs. "I trust Grandfather. If he were still alive, she wouldn't be spending Christmas with us, and that's enough for me."

His words sound final. Time to drop the subject.

Including me and Spencer, I count twelve people. That must be some cabin to fit us all.

"That's everyone who will be there at Christmas?"

"Grandfather keeps a caretaker on staff at all times, and there are locals who work in the kitchen and clean the house while we're visiting."

Ah, to live like the wealthy and never have to cook or clean up after yourself. It takes a second, but I realize that will be my life as soon as Spencer and I marry. Not such a bad thing.

His phone rings, and he takes another call.

For the rest of the drive, I watch the scenery the headlights illuminate. I catch a few glimpses between the trees of what must be the ocean, but it's too dark to tell. There's no snow, which is disappointing. It doesn't feel like Christmas without it.

In my head, I sing through Sarah McLachlan's *Wintersong* Christmas album. I'm careful not to let any sound pass my lips. It's difficult. The car is one of my favorite singing venues.

Spencer exits the freeway and navigates down dark streets lined with bare trees. His headlights create shadows that make me feel as if we've entered a haunted forest. I don't see any houses and very few cars pass us.

We eventually turn down a long drive lined with more trees. It opens up onto a large gravel driveway that ends in front of a mansion.

"Where are we?" I ask.

"The Maine cabin."

When he told me we were staying in a cabin, I expected a large, rustic structure. The "cabin" we're parked in front of looks like a gargantuan castle nestled in a forest. If this is his grandmother's cabin, what kind of place does she live when not on vacation?

Spencer opens my car door, but I don't move. I'm not sure my legs have the ability to keep me upright. His focus is on his phone, and he doesn't notice my lack of movement. When my initial surprise fades, I stand and he shuts the door behind me. I lean against the car and take everything in.

In the middle of the circle driveway is a fountain with a statue of a woman draped in a robe, one shoulder bare. With it being winter, there's no water, but I imagine it's even more beautiful when there is. Ten feet away is parked a fiery red Aston Martin. Two Ferraris. A black Lamborghini. The Cadillac Spencer rented at the airport looks like it belongs on a shady used car lot in comparison.

I'm out of my depth. I suspected I didn't know what I was getting into last night when Spencer mentioned generational wealth. Then again, this afternoon when he spent tens of thousands of dollars on my new wardrobe to impress his family. Now I know for certain.

Spencer's grandfather exiled his own daughter because he didn't like the man she married. What will this family do if they don't like me?

He was right to buy me clothes. The dress I originally picked to meet his grandma would not impress his family. Hopefully, the Loro Piana midi sweater dress and Mackage wool wrap coat he bought does.

I pull my new Boudron shoulder bag in front of me as if it will protect me from whatever waits inside. It's my favorite purchase from today. Made from soft leather, it's dyed a light blue with five small, round, silver buttons on the front, each with a gold B in the center. It's an unmistakable brand, and I've seen these bags all over the entertainment magazines and social media the last few years. It's surreal to own one.

Spencer slips his phone into his pocket and takes my hand. I stumble, and he catches me with a hand to my upper arm.

"Are you okay?"

He's calm. He's always calm, and it goes a long way to calming me. Everything will be fine. They're just people, and I enjoy meeting new people. Feeling well dressed gives a needed boost of confidence. I've got this.

"Too much sitting," I say as an explanation.

I follow him a few steps before I remember our bags in the trunk. "We forgot our suitcases."

I turn, but Spencer tugs my hand and keeps moving forward.

"Miles will grab them and put them in our rooms."

"Who is Miles?" I ask.

"The caretaker of the house."

Another sign of wealth—an employee to do simple things like carry luggage inside. I'd rather bring it in myself, but I quiet that voice and follow Spencer. I'm entering another world, and I need to follow the rules. Rules I don't know and will have to learn as I go. Nausea rises in my throat.

The right side of the huge double doors open as we climb the front stairs, and an older man, maybe in his early fifties, with thick salt-and-pepper hair comes out onto the porch, a wide smile on his face. He wears slacks, a white button-down shirt, and a black tie.

"Spencer! I'm glad you've made it. I thought you were going to arrive hours ago."

They shake hands.

"We stopped in Boston for the afternoon. Layla, this is Miles. Miles, this is my girlfriend Layla."

Miles doesn't shake my hand, but nods his head. "It is wonderful to have you here this week. Welcome." He turns back to Spencer. "The family is gathering in the sitting room before dinner."

Spencer hands Miles the car key while we pass into the house. Miles shuts the door behind us. Spencer helps me with my wrap, and I shiver. It's not cold, but without the thick wool, I feel vulnerable.

While he hangs our coats in the closet, I try not to be intimidated by the foyer and fail. The ceiling vaults to the second floor. A wide staircase splits half way and goes up opposite sides to the landing above.

A huge Persian rug with bright reds and blues covers the floor. It's at least twenty by fifteen feet. On the ceiling is a painting of people reaching toward heaven and angels. It's the sort of thing I expect to see in a medieval cathedral, not a cabin in coastal Maine.

Between the ceiling, the marble floor, the bright chandelier, and the artwork that hangs on the walls, I feel like I've entered a museum. Statues bracket each doorway off of the foyer. Lions sit at the base of the stairs. I'm afraid to get too close to anything in case an alarm blares.

In all the beauty, there are no Christmas decorations.

It's sad. This is the perfect place for a fifteen-foot tree. The banister is lonely without lighted garlands leading up to the second floor. It needs a large, colorful wreath on the door, Christmas figurines on the hall table, and decorations along the edge of the large mirror.

A pit of disappointment lodges in my throat. It's Christmas, and no one would know by looking at this house.

The double doors to the left open, and a woman around my age exits with a child in her arms, the girl's head on the woman's shoulder. She walks as if the foyer is a fashion runway, and her green, floor-length silk gown adds to the illusion. If I had to guess, it's Armani. She has the same height and lean limbs as Spencer. Her hair is a deep brown with lighter highlights, but what stands out the most about her appearance are her striking bright green eyes. I suspect they're colored contacts.

The little girl hiccups like she's just stopped crying.

The woman smiles at Spencer. "What are you doing hiding out in the hallway? Your dad has been waiting for you." She looks in my direction and studies me from head to foot. Her perfectly plucked eyebrows raise. "I'm Tori, Spencer's cousin. And you are?"

Before I can answer, Spencer does.

"This is my girlfriend Layla."

I wish I still had my coat to protect me from her judgment.

She hums thoughtfully. "Grandmother knows how to twist you around her finger, doesn't she? Anyway, everyone is waiting for you. I need to put Sadie to bed." She notices my bag. "Is that a Boudron?"

I nod, my voice not making an appearance.

"Nice. I have a red one, but Sadie put all her markers inside. It ruined the lining." She shrugs like it isn't a big deal her daughter ruined a four thousand dollar bag.

Considering Sadie's tears stain the shoulder of her silk dress and she doesn't seem to care, it probably isn't. "Well, good luck."

Her parting words leave a feeling of doom in my gut as she walks away. The little girl, her tear-stained cheeks framed by light brown hair, looks at me forlornly over Tori's shoulder. She has the same green eyes as her mother. Not contacts then.

Spencer puts his phone in his inside jacket pocket and takes my hand. "Let's introduce you to the family."

Chapter Six

LAYLA

S‍PENCER OPENS THE DOOR AND WAITS FOR ME TO ENTER. I hesitate. In this situation, the lady should not go first.

Layla, you got yourself here. Don't show weakness now.

Barely breathing, I step inside with my shoulders back and a small smile on my lips.

No one notices my entrance, which feels anticlimactic.

It's a large room, blinding in its whiteness. White walls. White couches. White rugs and lampshades. The wood floor and the mantle over the large gas fireplace are the only splashes of color.

Spencer enters and the four adults sitting on the couches in front of the fireplace notice him. They're all drinking amber liquid from short glasses.

Two men stand. One has thinning hair and frown lines around his mouth. There is a resemblance to Spencer in the eyes and nose, and they have a similar build with the same narrow shoulders. This must be his dad, Dorian.

The other man must be Spencer's uncle Gerald. It's obvious his full, black hair is a toupee. With his thick arms, barrel chest, and skinny legs, he looks like the cartoon character Popeye. Uncle Gerald needs a more balanced workout regime.

The two women stay where they are, but both of them study me just like Tori did in the entry. I make sure I stand confidently, my limbs loose, and smile back at them.

Gerald heads to the drink cart. Spencer's dad walks in our direction.

"Father," Spencer says.

Dorian and Spencer hug. It lasts for a second at most, but even then I'm surprised. When Spencer talks about his dad, it sounds like a business relationship more than a personal one. He spent much of his childhood being raised by his grandparents.

My smile dies when Spencer's dad looks me over with a wolfish grin. My skin crawls.

"This is the girl?" he asks in a low voice. Spencer's dad must know about our arrangement, or at least Spencer's reason for bringing me.

Spencer looks over at me with an apology in his eyes, if not on his lips. "This is my girlfriend Layla." He speaks loudly so those on the couch can hear.

"Call me Dorian," Spencer's dad says as he holds out his hand. His handshake is firm, but he holds me for too long. I tamp down my discomfort. This will soon be my father-in-law. Yikes.

Dorian motions to the women on the couch. "My partner

Ginger. My sister Ellory. Her husband Gerald. We're happy to have you here for Christmas."

Ginger studies me with a pinched smile. Her bright red hair looks unnatural, and she's older than I expected. From the few times Spencer has mentioned her, I thought she was much younger than his father, though it's hard to guess her age because her skin is unnaturally tight and smooth from plastic surgery. Maybe she's in her early fifties? Her dress is a gorgeous gray and white floral that goes down to the floor. She's paired it with gray peep-toe heels. Stunning.

I stand straighter at her perusal and meet her glance as her eyes travel back up to mine. She raises her eyebrows and turns away, dismissing me, but I know she's found nothing to criticize with my appearance. I loosen my fingers from around the strap of my Boudron. This is a highly uncomfortable situation, but I'm holding my own. For now.

Ellory approaches wearing a tailored tweed business suit paired with a black turtleneck and is no less stunning. As she pulls me into her arms for a quick hug, I catch the scent of honeysuckle. "We're so happy to have you. Dorian was just bragging about the wonderful woman his son has been dating."

Now that Gerald has a full drink, he shakes my hand. "Nice to meet you. Unfortunately, we've had a case fall apart in the last twenty-four hours. Did Spencer tell you? We'll be working on reviving it for much of the week."

"Gerald, I've got it under control." Spencer's cheeks turn red. From embarrassment or indignation, I can't guess. "There isn't any reason for you to get involved."

"Nonsense," Dorian says. "This trial is worth millions. We can't lose. We're all putting in the time. This isn't your fault, so don't get defensive, but if the case fails it reflects badly on the firm. We have to do what's best for our client, not your ego."

Brutal. I look at Spencer to see his response. He doesn't argue, just purses his lips and gives a sharp nod.

Ginger wraps her arm around Dorian's waist. "Yes, the client comes first, but not tonight. Let's enjoy a few hours without talking shop."

Ellory laughs and lifts her glass as if to clink it against an invisible one. "Agreed. I could use a break from work. I was hoping for a week, but I'll take twelve hours."

Tori walks into the room and heads to the drink cart. "Why does Sadie have to be so difficult at bedtime? I would love to sleep for nine hours straight. She doesn't appreciate sleep like she should."

Ellory shrugs like she's heard this from her daughter before. "If you had a nanny, you wouldn't have to deal with her tantrums."

Tori takes a long swig of whatever she poured into her glass. "I'm raising my daughter myself. If a nanny can handle tantrums, so can I."

"Once Sadie starts school and you come back to the firm," Ellory says patiently, "You'll have to hire someone to help you. Now that you're a single mother, you can't do everything."

"Watch me."

Ellory shakes her head and raises her hand like she gives up talking sense into her daughter.

Tori collapses on the couch and lays her arm over her eyes. Her body sags with exhaustion. "Grandmother better make this week worth it. Does anyone know why she made us come early? We're not going through her will until after Christmas. There's no reason to make us stay here a week when we can get it done in a day."

"Just as long as I get the Manhattan Penthouse, I'll stay for a month," Dorian says.

Ellory stands straighter. "I get the Manhattan Penthouse. Father promised it to me."

"Yes, well, he's dead, and now Mother holds all the strings." Dorian taps his chest. "I'm the oldest. I get the first pick of properties."

"I'm the favorite, and that holds more weight with Mother."

"Will you two stop arguing?" Ginger says. She lays a hand on Dorian's arm. "We have this one night where you two won't be working. Let's enjoy it."

Dorian and Ellory's glares soften, and they nod. This is not the family I expected to meet in Maine. Where is the joy in seeing each other? These people don't seem to like each other.

It's going to be a long week.

Spencer tugs me toward the couches.

"What would you like to drink?" he asks close to my ear as everyone continues to belly ache about having to spend Christmas at a mansion in Maine with their extended family.

I shake my head. "Nothing, thank you."

My knowledge of alcoholic beverages extends to the cooler section of the grocery store. I have no idea what to ask for, and it's better if I keep a level head. I sit on the edge of the cushion furthest from the fireplace. It's already too hot in here.

Everyone else makes their way back over to the couches to sit.

Ellory sits next to me.

"It is nice to meet you," she says and pats my knee. "You're so kind to make the trip out here at such short notice. Granted, we all only had five days to make arrangements, but you must be missing your family."

I am. Not only Nana, but also my roommates. The Christmas before me looks bleak and lonely with Ginger and maybe Tori the only other people not working.

Instead of telling her the truth, I make up a pretty lie and hope I sell it. "No, I saw my grandma yesterday and she's my only family. I'm happy to be here with Spencer and to meet all of you."

Tori rolls her eyes. I tone down my chipper attitude. I don't want it to seem like I'm trying *too* hard. As someone who participated in musical theater in high school, I feel like I've entered from stage right into a dramatic production where everyone has a script except for me. I was never great at improv.

"How long have you and Spencer been dating?" Gerald asks from the other couch, effectively making sure everyone is looking at me.

I rarely mind attention, but attention from these people makes me squirm. Especially when I'm not sure how to respond. Spencer and I have dated for five months out of the last twelve.

Lucky for me, Spencer answers. "Almost a year." He sits on the arm of the couch next to me.

Tori narrows her eyes as she looks between us. "You've been dating for a year? And you've never told me about her?"

Spencer lays his hand on my shoulder and looks down at me with adoration. A+ for his acting skills. D- for laying a foundation for an engagement.

"We met at a New Year's Eve party last year," he says. "We spent hours talking. She was my first kiss of the year, and I knew it was serious."

He leaves out two important points: I was hired to sing at that party and the kiss wasn't over two seconds to celebrate the holiday. Spencer makes it sound like we shared a memorable, life-changing moment. Maybe under the watchful glare of his cousin, that's for the best.

Tori taps her chin thoughtfully. "Weren't you dating some model a few months ago?"

Spencer told his cousin about the model who wouldn't let him watch her eat, but failed to mention me? Ouch.

"Layla and I broke up for a time," Spencer says smoothly. "But we found our way back to each other." He holds out his hand for mine. I take it and hold on tight. He's the only thing familiar in this weird world I've walked into. "I love Layla. I know what we have will last."

Maybe he needs to tone it down a little.

"Good luck in this family," Tori mutters. She's about to say more when the door flings open. She screams, which startles me, and I jump in my seat. She runs to the door.

When I turn to see who entered, she's hugging a man. From the profile view, her head hides his face from me. Next to them stands a lanky teenager with long hair tucked behind his ears and a woman with thick, brown hair weaved through with gray. Her natural look is in stark contrast to the other women in the room. Her brown eyes glisten with tears.

This must be the aunt Spencer's never met and her two

sons. Marianne and ... I realize Spencer never told me his other two cousins' names.

Tori laughs thickly as she continues to hug the older cousin. "You doofus. Why didn't you tell me you were coming?"

"I was hoping my mom would change her mind," comes the muffled reply.

Dorian and Ellory move toward their sister and hugs are exchanged and tears shed, at least by Marianne and Ellory. Dorian seems to be focused on keeping a stiff upper lip.

Spencer tugs me toward Tori and the two younger arrivals.

When Tori finally pulls back, I catch my first glimpse of the new arrival. It's funny, because this stranger reminds me a little of Owen. They share the same prominent cheekbones and dark hair and eyes, but the resemblance stops there. The new arrival has close cropped hair and a trimmed beard. He wears tailored gray slacks and a black button-up shirt. It's just my mind playing tricks on me. I need to get Owen out of my head because I'm secretly engaged to someone else.

But then the stranger smiles, and he looks *exactly* like my Owen.

It can't be ... until he laughs and I know it is.

Owen is *here*.

My breath catches.

Layla, we have a problem.

I step behind Spencer's shoulder. Yes, I'm hiding, but not well enough. Eventually, Owen will notice me. I'd rather hide behind the couch. Under the circumstances, no one would blame me.

This is the family Owen told me he was visiting for

Christmas. How? There is no resemblance. Not just in looks, but in personality. First, Owen is kind and friendly. Second, he wears t-shirts with car wash logos and well-worn shorts, not Luca Faloni. Though right now, I don't miss the snug t-shirts. His black button-up showcases his broad chest and biceps and is causing me heart palpitations.

Not the type of thoughts I should have at this moment.

A new realization hits: I'm stuck with him in the same house for a week.

He could ruin everything. I went out with him last night. He'll see right through my arrangement with Spencer. Or worse, he'll assume I'm a heartless cheater.

"Tori," Owen says to Tori. "This is my brother Brady."

His voice is as smooth and deep as I remember. It's like a siren call. I might need to Uber some earplugs.

Tori grins at Brady and lays her hand on his shoulder. "Aren't you a handsome creature? You'll have all the girls running after you with that hair."

Brady turns a deep red.

"Owen," Spencer says in greeting.

"Spencer."

They size each other up like they're about to step into a boxing ring.

I know the exact moment Owen notices me. His eyes widen and his jaw drops. He takes a step back like he's received a physical blow.

"Layla? What are you doing here?"

Spencer moves so he can see me. I'm no longer hiding.

"You know my cousin?" he asks.

Tori's grin widens, renewed interest in me clear in her eyes. "This just got interesting."

Chapter Seven

OWEN

"I, UM, YEAH," LAYLA SAYS, ANSWERING SPENCER'S QUESTION. She glances between him and me. "I know Owen. He's friends with a man who lives in the same assisted living home as my nana."

The bigger question is how Layla knows Spencer. How did they even meet? The year we worked at the firm together, he spent all of his time at the office, and when not there or sleeping, he ran to keep in shape.

"How do you two know each other?" I ask, pointing between Layla and Spencer.

Spencer lays his arm around Layla's shoulders, an insufferable smirk on his annoying face. "Layla is my girlfriend."

Girlfriend? The surprise feels like a slap. I spent most of the flight here wondering about her, and she's dating my cousin? Then why did she go with me to the drive-in last night? Why did she tell me she was spending Christmas with her roommates? Is she a pathological liar? Or maybe a master manipulator? But to what end? To get two dollar fries out of me?

Layla won't meet my gaze. She's the first woman I've felt a connection to in years, and she's dating *Spencer*. Spencer and I have diametrically opposed views on almost everything, especially work and money. We're not similar in any way, yet we're drawn to the same woman. Of course we are.

To break the hold Layla's presence has on me, I glance at Mom. She's crying as she talks to her siblings. This is the first time she's seen them in thirty-three years. The injustice of the situation infuriates me, and I can't understand why she's not angry like I am.

I pull Brady forward to use him as a distraction. I didn't want to come, and now that I'm here, I can see that it was a bigger mistake than I anticipated. "Brady, meet your cousin Spencer. This is Spencer's friend Layla."

"Girlfriend," Spencer clarifies.

Brady's more interested in me. He studies me, then glances at Layla, then back at me. He's too smart for his own good. Or at least, my good.

Brady raises his hand in a half-hearted wave. "Hi."

"Hello." Spencer barely spares Brady a glance. "Owen, I wasn't sure you'd show up. Last time we spoke, you said you'd see me at my funeral."

I was twenty-four, bitter, and a bit on the melodramatic side. "I'm here because my mom asked me to come. Not for any other reason."

Tori pouts. "You didn't come to see me? I'm your best friend."

A grin spreads across my face without permission. I promised Mom and Brady I would make this a great Christmas, but I didn't expect to find much joy here. I didn't take into consideration Tori.

When I cut Mom's family out of my life, Tori wouldn't let me go. She called me daily until I finally picked up the phone. She would have attended Dad's funeral, but it was the end of her first year of law school, and she couldn't get away.

These days, we video chat at least once a week, and I fly out to New York every few months to see her and Sadie. I haven't been out since October, and it's good to see her.

"You could always come visit me," I say. "My house may be small, but I still have a guest bedroom you and Sadie can stay in."

She wrinkles her nose. "Me in Idaho? Isn't there cow poop everywhere? I won't ruin my shoes, not even for my favorite cousin."

"Hey!" Spencer says. "I gave you that Cartier diamond necklace for your birthday."

I laugh, something I did not expect to do this week, but otherwise ignore Spencer. "I live in Utah, not Idaho. We're known for national parks and skiing." She acts like anything west of Florida is podunkville. "However, my mom lives in Nevada, and they're known for gold mines and casinos if you'd rather visit me there."

Her eyes widen with interest. "Tell me more."

My attention annoyingly goes back to Layla. She's half-hiding behind Spencer's shoulder again. They never answered my question about how they met.

"Layla, how do you know Spencer?"

"They met at a New Year's Eve party a year ago," Tori says in a sing-song voice. She widens her eyes like she knows this is a lie, but we're all going along with it because it would be bad manners to call the two of them out as frauds. "Spencer knew from their first kiss that he couldn't live without her."

I want to gag. And punch that smirk off of Spencer's face.

"You know she's a teacher, right?" I say.

Layla blanches. "What has that got to do with anything?"

Everything as far as this family is concerned, but the dig I intended for Spencer hit Layla, and I open my mouth to apologize. I don't get the chance.

"This is a lovely sight."

Everyone turns as one to the door where Grandmother stands. She's ... smaller than the last time I saw her eight years ago. Mom mentioned she'd been sick the last month, but I assumed that meant a cold. Grandmother looks like she's been battling death. Her dark red blazer fits poorly over her narrow shoulders. There are hollows in her cheeks, and her eyes appear sunken. I fear she might topple over at any second.

"Marianne." She takes a step in my mom's direction, and Mom throws herself into Grandmother's arms, but gently.

They both cry, and then Ellory joins their hug, and she pulls in Dorian. It's the most emotional I've ever seen any of them. Especially Grandmother.

With that one hug, it seems everything is forgiven. I clench my hands into fists. This is what Mom wants, to be back with her family, but I can't forget how everyone ignored her and Dad for decades. Yes, it was because of Grandfather, but everyone in this room followed along like baby ducklings so they weren't disinherited as well. If he hadn't died eight months ago, Mom wouldn't have been invited to celebrate Christmas with the family, and we all know it.

Grandmother pulls back and comes to me. She lays her hand against my cheek. Her touch is soft, but her fingers are cold. She has too much skin for her bones. No matter how weak she appears, this is the happiest I've ever seen her. Her smile no longer hides behind a placid expression. I'm familiar with her speaking quietly, so it seems her voice booms around the room as she speaks now.

"Owen, you are looking well. I'm so glad you came. And this must be Brady. Your mom has told me all about you. She says you love to read fantasy and even started writing your own book. We're going to have a novelist in the family in a few years. Is that right?"

Brady looks stricken. No one knows about his dream of being an author. Surprisingly, no one laughs. Tori doesn't even roll her eyes, and eye rolling is her reaction to ninety percent of what she's told.

"I look forward to reading your first book," Grandmother continues when Brady gives no response.

She makes her way around the room, hugging and greeting each person. This is more out of character behavior. The grandmother I remember nodded her head and welcomed the family from an emotional distance. From everyone's surprised expressions, this change in personality is new for them as well.

When she reaches Spencer and Layla, she takes each of

their hands. "Spencer, Miles told me you brought your girlfriend. It is lovely to meet you, Layla."

"You as well, Mrs. Eccleston. Thank you for allowing me to come for Christmas." Layla stands poised and confident, no longer hiding behind my cousin.

"We're happy to have you. Please, call me Rheta."

I don't think anyone has called Grandmother by her first name since the day she married Grandfather.

Spencer glances at me for one second before he says. "Grandmother, Layla is a teacher. She teaches middle school choir."

Everyone holds their breaths as we wait for Grandmother's response. Grandfather disowned my mom when she married a *teacher*.

"What a noble profession," Grandmother says. "Dinner is ready. Shall we go into the dining room?"

That's it?

The family follows her from the room, I stay where I am, too angry to move. I don't want to be here. The hypocrisy stinks. I should have booked us a hotel in Boston and stayed there for an extra day. Or two. I didn't get my fill of the city, even though I spend the day showing Mom and Brady all my favorite haunts from when I was a student at Harvard. I even got my hair cut at the barbershop near my old apartment because Mom's been commenting about the length.

Brady stays back with me as the room empties. "This is weird," he says.

Mom waits for us at the door, wiping tears from her eyes. "Maybe a little. It's been a long time since we've been a family."

"Doesn't it bother you that they speak to you now because their inheritances aren't at stake?" I ask.

She walks to me and pats down my collar. "It makes me happy that we've become more inclusive as a family."

I finish the thought in my mind—*now that Grandfather is gone.*

She stops messing with my shirt and lays a hand on each of our shoulders. "Come boys, let's eat."

We cross the foyer toward the dining room when Miles comes through from outside. He's the person I've missed the most since I stopped visiting, and I shake his hand while throwing my free arm around his shoulder.

"Owen," he says as he slaps my back. "It's good to see you again."

"You, too." I pull back. "This is my mom Marianne and my brother Brady."

His smile grows as he looks at my mom. "I know Marianne. How are you?"

How does he know my mom? It gets stranger when they embrace.

"I'm great," Mom says.

I look between them. "How do you two know each other?"

"You're not the only one who spent summers in Maine." Mom looks around at the grandiose foyer. "Though not here. When we visited, we had a cottage further down the shore. Father built this place while I've been gone. Miles' parents worked for us. His mom is an amazing chef."

"She still is," Miles says. "They both retired about ten years ago."

Mom lays a hand on his arm. "My mother mentioned that your wife passed last year. I was sorry to hear that."

"Thank you. She'd been suffering for a while, so there is comfort in knowing she's not in pain anymore. I'm sorry about your husband."

"Thank you."

Something passes between them as they gaze at each other. Are they bonding over the shared grief at the loss of a spouse? It makes me wonder what they were to each other when Mom visited Maine as a teenager.

I clear my throat. Miles tears his eyes away from Mom and waves us toward the dining room. "Everyone is waiting. If you give me your car keys, I can bring in your luggage and have it waiting in your rooms."

I hand over the keys. "You can't miss it. It's a red, fifteen-passenger van." And not a sleek, shiny one. It's a box on wheels.

His eyes widen. "A van?"

Mom laughs. "We were lucky enough to get the last rental in the whole airport."

She takes a moment to explain the mix-up with our car rental reservation, as though hesitant to say goodbye. I glance at Brady to share the bizarreness of this situation, but he's looking at the painted ceiling. It's a replica of a circular painting in the church of Saint-Roch in France. As a kid, I was fascinated by the people who look like they're climbing toward heaven through puffy clouds. Now it hits me as pretentious.

"I thought this was supposed to be a cabin," he says. "It looks like a palace."

"It's called a cabin because it's a rural location. You

should see the other vacation homes. The villa in Italy is amazing."

Honestly, I'm surprised Grandmother chose Maine for Christmas since she hates the cold. Maybe she assumed Mom couldn't afford the trip if she chose somewhere international.

Mom finally says goodbye to her pal Miles. When we enter the dining room, everyone is indeed waiting for us. Grandmother sits at her normal seat at the end of the table with Dorian, a redheaded woman, Tori, Spencer, and Layla on one side, and Ellory and Gerald along the other. The table is too large for the small group assembled.

The three remaining seats are on the side nearest the empty end chair where Grandfather always sat. It feels as if he's about to walk in and my body tenses. I remind myself he's gone.

Silently, we take our seats. I'm on the end, across from Layla. Not a great seating arrangement.

A moment later, two servers bring in a pureed soup. We wait until Grandmother has her first taste before we eat. It's delicious and creamy. Not as good as Miles' mom's soup when she worked here, but almost.

We eat our soup silently. The servers clear the dishes and serve us salad. In the past, Grandfather directed the conversation during meals. It seems without him, we're at a loss.

"Layla," Grandmother says into the silence. "Spencer. Tell me how you two met."

I watch them gaze at each other as they share their story. If I keep staring at them, I'll lose my appetite, so I force myself to focus on my plate.

They've been dating for a year. I saw Layla for the first time on June twenty-first. I have to wonder what this week would look like if I'd met her before she met Spencer. Except a year ago I spent all my time working to grow my manufacturing company, and we would never have crossed paths.

Even though they weave a believable account of their relationship, their story doesn't add up with what I've gleaned from watching Layla over the past half year. I might not have talked to her, but the residents talked about her. There was never any mention of a boyfriend.

During our main course of chicken Kiev, asparagus, and crispy roasted potatoes, Grandmother keeps up the conversation. She wants to know about Mom's job as a secretary, Layla's students, Tori's daughter, Ellory's pro bono cases, and Brady's schooling. She asks me what I've been up to, and I tell her I'm a landscaper. It's barely the truth since I own the business and do little of the actual physical labor. Spencer looks at me with pity.

One thing Grandmother does not bring up is the law, which I appreciate. Under Grandfather, every meal was about the law.

I don't think I'm the only one who notices Grandmother eats very little. By the time dessert is served, she doesn't pretend anymore and waves away a plate of strawberry cheesecake, my favorite.

"I am so happy that we are all here," she says. She motions to a server, and they pull out her chair. She stands, leaning heavily on the table. "It's been too long since we've been together as a family. This year we will have a traditional family Christmas. Schedules for the week are in your rooms. Sleep well. I will see you tomorrow morning at breakfast."

She leaves, the door closing softly behind her.

"Well," Ellory says with a sigh. "I think we all know now why we're here for the week."

"She wants to see her family," Mom says.

"Yes," Ellory agrees. "Because she's dying."

"And holding our inheritances over our heads, so we'll play along with her 'traditional family Christmas,'" Dorian adds.

Chapter Eight

LAYLA

It's past ten by the time I finish filling out the paperwork for Nana's upgrade to the memory ward and email it to Brock Pine. With a shaking hand, I submit January's payment in four partial transactions. Between the last of my bank loan, the money I put aside for my own rent, and my almost maxed out credit cards, I just manage to make the full payment. I can't let myself imagine what I would do in February if Spencer hadn't proposed.

I get ready for bed in the attached bathroom. It's colossal. The shower has so many knobs I can't imagine what they all do. There's a separate, jetted tub. A TV is mounted on the wall across from the toilet.

Once my teeth are clean, I turn off the light and climb into bed. The blanket is weighted, and I sink into the mattress. My body is in heaven, but my brain won't shut off.

I'm haunted by the way Owen looked in that black shirt

Her Counterfeit Christmas

and hate how I preferred it to the sweater vest and sports jacket Spencer wore. Or maybe I just preferred the man inside.

Ahh! Shut up, brain.

I just have to get through this week. It seems Spencer and Owen dislike each other, so I won't see Owen at family events. I'll take care to avoid Brock Pine when he's usually there, so I won't run into him. A prospect that should bring me peace but makes me more agitated. I enjoyed spying on him.

I toss and turn but can't find relief from my thoughts.

According to the schedule I found on the dresser, breakfast is at nine every morning. Tomorrow I'd like to go for a run before breakfast, which means I need to sleep now. But the shock and dismay on Owen's face when he first noticed me won't vacate my head.

I sit up and flick on the bedside lamp. Is there any cheesecake leftover from dinner? Maybe it has magical properties and a small slice will help me forget about the guy I can never think about again.

There's only one way to find out.

I grab the teal sweater Nana knit and I planned to sell. Now that I have Spencer, I can keep it for myself. I bring it up to my nose and make out the faint scent of Nana's lavender soap.

The hallway is empty and dark but for a light over the staircase. No light shines under any of the other bedroom doors. At the bottom of the stairs, I begin my search for the kitchen. Through the dining room seems like a logical place to start. I tiptoe across the room to the door opposite where the servers came through at dinner. On the other side of the door is a small room with counters. No cupboard or anything useful. I wonder if this is some sort of anteroom used as a staging area for service and a buffer from the kitchen noise. Once again, I'm amazed at the way the wealthy live.

There are three doors besides the one I walked through. I feel like I'm on a game show. Which one holds the prize I'm looking for? I pick the one closest to me. I must be lucky, because here is the kitchen.

I flip on the light over the oven, which gives the room a glow and makes me feel extra sneaky. I go to the industrial sized refrigerator and look inside. There are dozens of clear containers filled with food, many of them seem to be prepared for tomorrow's meals. It takes me a few minutes, but I finally locate the container that holds the cheesecake.

I have to open a dozen cupboards before I find plates. The silverware is easier to locate. Before I cut myself a slice, I hear voices from the anteroom I just came through.

It could be anyone, but that means it could be Owen.

Panic engulfs me. I don't want to get caught stealing food, especially not by him. How am I supposed to explain my behavior to him? I stuff everything back in the fridge, plate and spoon included, and run to the glass doors that lead outside onto a deck. When the door shuts behind me, I move out of sight just as the kitchen light turns on.

I'm not prepared for the cold. I'm wearing pajama pants, the cardigan over a tank top, and socks. Winter air attacks every millimeter of skin left uncovered. I wrap my arms around myself and bounce in place, hoping to conserve body heat. It's little help.

A peek through the door shows Marianne and Brady

interrupted my midnight scavenging, and not the person I feared. Now that I'm outside, I don't feel comfortable enough to go back in and admit my idiocy. I'll wait until they leave.

The sound of waves makes me move closer to the edge of the deck. The moon is almost full and gives me light to see. The ground slopes down, with the ocean maybe a third of a mile away. The tops of the trees are a little taller than the deck, and I can make out the rocky beach. I'm sure it's beautiful in the sunlight, but it's too cold to be in the wind, and I move back to the side of the house where it's mostly blocked.

I peek inside. Marianne and Brady are eating my cheesecake! It's hard to watch, not only because my stomach grumbles, but because it reminds me of nights I spent with my mom in the kitchen. I move out of their view and wait for them to finish. The longer I stand with my back against the house, the worse my body shivers.

Finally, the lights turn off. I immediately grab for the knob.

It's locked.

I rattle the door, but it doesn't magically open. My teeth chatter. My toes are in danger of frostbite. All the dignity I possessed fifteen minutes ago has fled. I knock, hoping Marianne might be close enough to hear me. I'd rather be humiliated than dead. They don't come back.

I waste precious seconds banging my fist against the door, then pull myself together. I need to find another way inside.

The deck disappears around the corner of the house. Maybe there's an unlocked window or another set of doors. I'd call Spencer, but I left my phone in my room.

Once around the corner, light spills out from a door cracked open further along the deck. I head toward the hope the light offers.

OWEN

I can't sleep. The images of Layla with Spencer at dinner won't leave me alone. They don't make sense together. Maybe it's because I'm jealous, but them as a couple is a burr in my brain. I can't let it go. I need to know how this happened and maybe then I'll be able to sleep.

I knock on Spencer's bedroom door. The fact that he's not sharing a room with Layla is another reason I question their relationship.

Spencer's always been a light sleeper, so if he were in his room, he would answer. He doesn't, which means he must be working. I head downstairs to Grandfather's old study on the main floor. It's at the back of the house, next to Grandfather's room. Grandmother's bedroom is further down the hall.

I push open the door. Spencer sits at Grandfather's desk, and for a moment it feels as if I've traveled back in time. He looks a lot like Grandfather, without the wrinkles and gray hair.

The room hasn't changed since the last time I was here. Bookshelves filled with legal books line the walls. An enormous desk sits in the center on the right of the room, opposite a couch and loveseat. Double doors open up onto the deck that runs along the back of the house and overlooks the ocean. This room has always felt stuffy, but the view is amazing.

Spencer has the deck doors opened a few inches, and the room is chilly from the night air, even with the gas fireplace blazing. As I step inside, I can understand why he's left the doors open. A musty smell mixed with Grandfather's cigars lingers.

Spencer doesn't glance away from his computer as I shut the door behind me.

"I need nothing else tonight, Miles."

"I'll let him know," I say.

His head jerks up, then his eyes narrow as he leans back in his chair and crosses his arms. "What are you doing here? I thought you were allergic to work and those who are productive members of society."

I want to laugh at what he perceives as a slight. "You don't think being a landscaper is work?"

"Not the kind of work Grandfather would esteem."

"Maybe that's why I do it."

He huffs out a breath and goes back to his computer. "Did you come for a reason other than to distract me from *my* work?"

I sit on the arm of the loveseat and prepare myself for the mocking that is about to come my way when he figures out I care about his girlfriend. "I don't get why Layla is here with you."

With a snort, he glances over for a few seconds before going back to his "work."

"She's my girlfriend. Why wouldn't I bring her home for Christmas?"

"You can't expect me to believe you've been dating her

for the past year. That lie might work on Grandmother, but I know Layla, and she never mentioned a boyfriend."

I wonder if she's shared with Spencer how little I know her, but he doesn't call me out for stretching the truth, so she hasn't said much.

"We've dated off-and-on, but now we're on for good." His fingers fly across the keyboard, and I'm impressed at his ability to type and talk at the same time. "I'm surprised you didn't bring a girlfriend. If anyone needs double the inheritance, it's you."

I bark a laugh. "If you thought Grandmother's ploy to get me married would work, you don't know me at all."

He shrugs indifferently. "It has been eight years. You're practically a stranger. There was a time when you dreamed of being rich and wanted to distance yourself from your parents' humble lifestyle."

Shame burns inside my chest. He's right, however much I wish he wasn't.

"I'm not that person anymore. You, however, haven't changed at all. You brought Layla here for the inheritance money, and for no other reason. Does she know?"

It's a stab in the dark in my quest to understand why they're together, and he doesn't deny it.

"Of course she knows. Unlike you, she understands the value of money and wants Grandmother's inheritance just as much as I do."

My stomach sinks. I don't want to believe she's the type of person who wants a millionaire husband. Maybe the reason she avoided me for six months was because she believed I was a humble therapy dog trainer? Except, if she wanted money, why is she a music teacher?

"I don't believe you." I sound like a petulant child, and immediately wish I could take the words back.

Spencer chuckles. "Then you don't know her as well as you think you do. I'll marry her no matter what, but with Grandmother's ridiculous will, it'll happen sooner rather than later. Twenty million as an inheritance? Doubled when we're married? Pathetic. Grandfather's estate is worth a few billion. Grandmother has to know that my father and Aunt Ellory plan to fight her on this."

The greed in this family is stifling. This is one reason I wanted out of the family firm, and why I won't accept any of Grandmother's money. I don't want to be involved in this lifestyle.

"Don't you care that Grandmother might be sick?" I ask.

I'm not sure if I agree with Ellory and Dorian's supposition that she's dying, but she's eighty-one years old. It is a possibility. One they don't seem too concerned about.

"Of course, I care." He pauses his typing and runs both hands through his hair before dropping them onto his lap.

It's hard for me to accept; I've thought of him as a heartless product of the family for so long. I hope Grandmother's mortality matters to him. Our grandparents practically raised him.

"We just lost Grandfather." He swallows thickly. For the first time in years, he appears human to me. "I'm not ready to lose Grandmother. However, as sad as this situation is, I can't do anything about it if it's true."

Maybe work tonight isn't just work, but a distraction from the possibility of her death?

"Why do you want to marry for more money?" I ask,

honestly curious. "You and your father are partners in the firm. You have plenty of money. When will it be enough?"

"There is no such thing as too much wealth." His shoulders straighten as his focus returns to his computer. He's transformed back into the man I know and dislike. "Unlike Grandmother, I'll give my children an inheritance they can take pride in."

I swallow bile at the idea of Spencer having children with Layla.

"I'd rather take pride in my accomplishments than my bank account."

"Spoken like a true povo," he mutters.

That makes me lean back. "Povo as in poor?"

He stops typing and looks at me. "Owen, I'm busy. It's obvious you have a crush on Layla, and I get it. She's gorgeous. Intelligent. Talented. Independent. But I have something that you can't give her because you're too prideful to accept your inheritance: the freedom and safety wealth offers. She'll make the perfect wife for a lawyer. She's not meant to be the wife of a day laborer."

"What about love?" I ask.

He shrugs. "What about it? We'll build a life together that anyone would aspire to. Even you."

"Layla deserves so much better than a loveless marriage."

He throws his head back and laughs. "You're delusional. Love causes people to do stupid things."

"Lack of love causes people to be miserable."

He speaks clearly, as if I won't understand otherwise. "Let me prove my theory that people do stupid things for love by using an example from your own life. You threw away your law career to go home to be with your dad when he was in a coma. He didn't even know you were there. If you'd been smart, you would've waited until the end of the merger. You leaving early destroyed your future, but made no difference to him."

"It made a difference to me," I say quietly. "And to my mom and Brady."

In a way Spencer is right. After his stroke, Dad was in a coma for eighteen days. Not finishing the merger got me home a week earlier, but he never knew I was there. He never woke up.

I'm ashamed to admit that the person I was eight years ago might have stayed through the negotiations if Grandfather had shown a modicum of compassion. Instead, he ridiculed my family and gloated over my dad's hospitalization. As if Dad deserved the stroke for stealing his daughter from him when he's the one who disinherited her and pushed her from the family for being disobedient to his demands.

Spencer sounds just like him.

Does Layla know what kind of man she's marrying?

The callousness of this family still infuriates me, and for a minute I can't speak. I've seen what love looks like with my own parents. I want the love that grows stronger in health and in sickness, in poorer and in richer. What Layla has with Spencer is not that.

He has no idea what he's missing out on in his pursuit to accumulate more money.

Grandmother is right—get rid of the money because wealth like the Ecclestons hoard distort reality and bring unhappiness in the long run.

LAYLA

"You're wrong," Owen says.

"About what in particular?" Spencer sounds annoyed and tired of this conversation.

Through the crack in the door, I see Spencer sitting at a large desk. He's focused on whatever is on his computer screen and doesn't seem to pay his cousin much attention by this point. I can't see Owen, but his voice keeps me outside in the frigid cold. I blow on my fingertips. They sting painfully.

"You're wrong about everything," Owen says. "Going to my dad was the right decision. Leaving the law firm was the right decision for me and my mom and brother. Life is about more than accumulating money."

I need Owen to stop talking and go away. The more I hear of this conversation, the more I sympathize with him and not Spencer. My secret fiancé is wrong in so many ways, especially about Owen's dad. He was in a coma and Spencer believes Owen should have stayed to finish a business deal? No. Owen's priorities are sound; Spencer's are honestly embarrassing.

It's a harsh reminder that any children Spencer and I have will come in second place to the law. Not an appealing insight, but what am I supposed to do? Not even an hour ago I paid Brock Pine Home every penny I could access. The only thing that's keeping me moving forward is knowing in a week I'll have fifty-thousand dollars in hand. It's so much, but to Spencer, it's so little.

The words *twenty million as an inheritance? Doubled when*

we're married? Pathetic, cycle through my mind. I'm worth twenty million dollars to Spencer. How can he believe that amount is paltry?

"The most important aspect of life is our relationships with others," Owen says.

Spencer laughs. "Owen, you're naïve. We'll never agree. You've made your choice. Just know that if you don't accept Grandmother's inheritance, you'll have nothing that Layla wants. As for me, I'm locking in my inheritance now because with Grandmother's spending spree, there might be nothing left by the time my father takes what's left of the estate."

Too many thoughts bounce around my head. My teeth chatter. I can't feel my ears and nose. Not only do I not want to hear any more of this conversation, but I need to get inside. I'd rather not enter while they're talking about me and my love of money. Humiliating myself in front of Spencer isn't so bad, but I can't give Owen anymore ammunition to think I'm a garbage human. I'd like to keep some dignity intact at the end of this day.

"If Layla's only love is money, then she isn't the person I thought she was."

There's so much disgust in Owen's voice, his words hit my heart. Tears prick my eyes, but I quickly wipe them away before they can freeze my eyelids closed.

"Life isn't worth living if you don't have any money at all," Spencer says. "I'd think you'd learned that by now."

What a stupid thing to say, and that comes from someone who has no money. Owen must feel the same because his laugh is edged with disbelief.

"Good luck on your case," Owen says. "I'm glad it's you and not me."

A door opens and then closes. I push inside and shut the door behind me. Spencer startles.

"What were you doing outside? It's cold."

"Y-yeah it i-is," I stutter. I immediately go to the gas fire and hold out my hands.

"Are you okay?"

"I go-got locked ou-outside. Long st-story."

He comes over immediately and rubs my arms. The friction is delightful, but I'm reminded that I'm not wearing a bra and wrap the cardigan over my chest before crossing my arms

My face and hands tingle as I defrost. My teeth stop chattering.

"Are you okay?" Spencer asks.

I don't answer his question. Now that I'm inside, there are more important topics to discuss. "Twenty million dollars is the tiny inheritance you're outraged about?"

He pulls back and looks down at me. "You heard my conversation with Owen?"

"Yes. Did you have to make me sound like a gold digger?"

Maybe it's an accurate definition, and it rubs me wrong because it's so right.

Spencer rubs my back. "My goal was to get him to leave you alone. He has a puppy-dog crush on you that will prove annoying this week if we don't stop it now."

It's best if Spencer doesn't find out I reciprocate Owen's puppy-dog crush. Though after the last ten minutes, I doubt Owen still feels the same. He'll avoid me from now on, and I hate how much that hurts my heart.

I'm secretly engaged to Spencer! I remind myself. *Who cares about Owen?*

Spencer gives comforting hugs, even if I can feel him check his watch behind my back. I hold on tighter so he won't let go.

"I want to go running tomorrow morning," I say into his collar. "Will you come with me?"

"No, I'll use the treadmill in the gym to save time."

I'm assuming that's an in-home gym. His response is unsurprising, but it was worth a try.

"Do you know a good place to run? All I saw coming in tonight was the main road and I'd rather not get hit by a car."

"There's a neighborhood where Owen and I used to jog. I'll text you the directions."

"Thanks. That would be great."

The door from the hallway opens, and we pull apart to look.

Owen.

He takes a step back and glances between us in confusion. "Layla, were you outside?"

I step away from Spencer and pull my cardigan tighter around me. I'm chilled through, still shivering. But more significant in this moment is that Owen's seeing me in my pajamas with my hair falling out of my ponytail. Then I hate myself for caring. Owen is a distraction I can't afford. Literally.

Spencer looks between us before shaking his head and sitting back down at his desk. "What did you want now, Owen?"

"I, uh, can't find my phone."

He comes closer to where I stand and looks at the loveseat. His phone lays on a cushion.

"Must've fallen out of my pocket." He meets my eyes, and my stomach swoops.

Time to get out of here.

"Good night," I say to both men as I walk past them and out into the hallway. I hurry toward the staircase, but not fast enough.

"Layla, wait," Owen calls out quietly from behind me.

Against my best judgment, I stop and turn. I expect him to question my motives and why I'm here, like he did with Spencer. This is his first opportunity since we arrived, and I feel I owe him something after last night.

"Look, Owen, I'm sorry about last night. I shouldn't have gone with you to the drive-in. I'm sorry I ran off so suddenly, but I…" My words dry up, unsure how to explain the last thirty hours. He guessed Spencer was marrying me for his inheritance and Spencer told him I'm marrying for money. That's the truth. What more is there to say?

Owen looks away, a small, sad smile on his lips. "It's better that you ran. I might have kissed you, and I'm not the cheating type."

My mouth flaps open and closed. I would've enjoyed a kiss, and it's mean of him to tell me what I missed out on. It can never happen now.

"You have beautiful blue eyes," he says quietly. "They look almost teal next to your sweater."

I close my eyes to hide. Why am I torn between two men? *These* two men in particular? I have chosen Spencer, but I still want Owen.

I'm a horrible person.

OWEN

Layla is absolutely gorgeous. Her hair is a halo around her face. Her disheveled appearance reminds me of the first time I saw her as she rushed into the Brock Pine recreation room six months ago. She's even more beautiful now. Her arms wrap around her stomach like she can't get warm, and her shoulders shake as she continues to shiver.

The things I learned about her from Spencer tonight don't jibe with the woman who so selflessly gives of her time to play songs for senior citizens. She visits her grandma almost every day. She's kind to everyone, residents and staff alike. They've told me how they're invisible to most people, but not Layla. I've dated women who are more interested in my money than in me, and that isn't her.

Sadly, I will never discover the truth. From what Spencer said, they plan on marrying. To me, she can only ever be the wife of my obnoxious cousin.

I've saved up a lot of questions to ask her, but now that I have a chance, it's better if I don't start. She's made her choice, and I will respect it by not digging into what's really going on between her and Spencer. If it's money she wants, it's better she gets it from him. That isn't the kind of relationship I'm looking for.

I shouldn't have complimented her eyes. In the future, I need to keep similar thoughts to myself.

"You don't owe me an explanation," I say. "I wanted to wish you a good night. Are you okay? You look cold."

"I'm fine."

Nothing I can do here. I move around her to go up the stairs.

"Wait," she says. "Can you tell me where you run? I'd like to go tomorrow morning, but I don't know where to go."

"Spencer knows this place better than me. You can ask him."

She glances over her shoulder in the direction of the office door. "I did, but I don't think he'll remember to text directions."

I scratch at my bearded cheek, not sure if I should say what I'm about to say. I'm supposed to avoid her, not be alone with her. Oh, what the heck. I'm a trustworthy guy. I won't make a move.

"I was planning on running tomorrow morning at seven," I say. "Do you want to go with me? There's a two-mile loop through a nearby neighborhood."

"There's a neighborhood?" she says with a lopsided smile, though it seems more for show since I get the impression she's uncomfortable talking to me. "All I saw coming in was a barren forest."

I laugh softly to dispel her discomfort. "I can give you a tour of the area at the same time."

She chews on her bottom lip, but then nods. "At least I won't get lost. I'll see you at the front door at seven."

This time when she leaves, I let her go ahead and follow at a much slower pace.

When I get to my room, I text Miles. I'm not sure he'll answer this late, but Layla was shivering. Even if she doesn't want my help, I have to do something.

OWEN: *Is there a heating pad somewhere? Layla could use it.*

MILES: *Sure. I'll grab it and bring it to her room.*

OWEN: *I don't mind bringing it to her if you tell me where to find it.*

MILES: *I got it. Get some sleep.*

It'll be better if it comes from Miles instead of me, anyway. Then she'll assume Spencer sent it up. You know, the man she's dating.

OWEN: *Thanks.*

A minute later, I send another text.

OWEN: *Maybe bring her a cup of cocoa while you're at it. With a candy cane if you have any.*

Chapter Nine

LAYLA

From the moment my alarm sounds at six-twenty I begin an internal debate: Should I show up for the run with Owen? No. But will I? Probably. I'm jittery with energy I need to burn off.

Even though it was Miles who delivered an electric heating pad and a mug of hot cocoa last night, I know it was Owen who sent him. I wish it was Spencer, but I'm not that naïve. Happiness is a mug of hot cocoa, and it was just what I needed to warm up. The cold outside had sunk into my core and a pile of blankets would not do the job.

Why does Owen have to be a nice guy? It would be so much easier to ignore my attraction to him if he wasn't kind. He should be a jerk and then I would easily forget about him.

No matter my reservations about running with him this

morning, I'm ready and waiting at the front door five minutes before our meeting time. When Owen comes down the stairs, he's whistling. My Opa was a whistler, and it makes me smile. I force a frown. Owen can't think I enjoy spending time with him, or he might invite me out again, and I can't trust myself to say no.

"Good morning," he says with a sunny smile. Someone got up on the right side of the bed.

"Morning," I grumble.

Outside is cold and dark, though the sky is lightening to a robin egg blue to the east. Running in winter is not for those with weak resolutions, and I'm glad Spencer bought me cold weather running gear. Unlike my roommate Livy, I love winter. At least I do when I'm properly prepared for it. A crisp wind from the ocean caresses my cheeks with icy fingers.

After stretching, we start out at a steady twelve-minute mile down the lane and speed up as we get further. Our breath puffs out in a white cloud as our feet hit the pavement in a steady rhythm. This is the first run I've had in over a week, and I feel the stress and tension shed behind me.

Poor Spencer. This is a thousand times better than running on the treadmill.

I normally run with earbuds in, but that's because I run alone. It's rude when I'm with someone, even if we're not talking. That doesn't mean music isn't running through my head. Today's soundtrack is the Beatles' *A Hard Day's Night* album.

From the main road, Owen takes us to an offshoot lane

that does indeed lead to a neighborhood. The houses are colorful, with dormer windows and wide front porches. They're large, though not mansions like Rheta's home, and spaced far apart with stretches of barren trees and lawns between each one.

The light from the rising sun casts everything in a sunny glow. It's a gorgeous morning, and I don't realize I'm smiling until I catch Owen looking at me from the corner of his eye. I can't find the will to put the frown back on my face.

We finish the loop of the neighborhood, and Owen asks, "Are you ready to go back?"

My body has warmed enough that I unzip my jacket partway, but I'm not ready to end this yet. "Another loop through the neighborhood?"

"Sure."

We run in silence a little longer before he asks, "How did you get into running?"

My chest warms with the memory. "My mom. She was a cross-country runner in high school. One of my earliest memories is when she took me out with her in a running stroller. When I got old enough, I rode my bike as she ran."

"And you joined her running when you got older?"

"For a little while. She was diagnosed with cancer when I was ten and couldn't run anymore, at least not the way she wanted. It devastated her. I did cross-country in high school just like she did and even earned a scholarship that paid for a chunk of college. The sweetest part of running is how I feel my mom is with me."

I've said too much. My connection with Mom through running isn't something I talk to others about. "How about you?"

"Spencer, actually," he admits. His smile turns into a frown. "He's older than me by two years, but we started Harvard the same year. He picked up running for easy exercise he could squish in between classes. I followed his example. We trained for the Boston Marathon for a few years, but we never qualified."

I would never guess seeing them together now that they were once close and attended the same university. Owen attended Harvard? It surprises me almost as much as overhearing last night that he was a lawyer in the family firm before he quit.

I've always pictured Owen homegrown like me. Harvard is for the wealthy with connections. For the first time since arriving in Maine, I see him as an Eccleston. Or, at least as part Eccleston. His running jacket is old and frayed at the hem, not like my flashy new one. He's also the best running companion I've ever had, and I can't say the same for Spencer. He's all about getting the run done, and doesn't enjoy the journey.

"I have never paid for a race," I say. "The thing I love about running is it doesn't cost me anything."

That makes me sound poor, and I wish I could take it back.

"I love races," Owen says. "It gives me something to work toward."

"Since graduating from college, I love how running isn't competing against anyone but myself."

He huffs out a laugh and shakes his head. "My family could learn from you. All we know is how to push each other down so we come out on top."

"Rheta isn't like that," I say.

He shrugs but says nothing to support or refute my defense of her.

I think about dinner last night and Dorian's conjecture about Rheta. "Do you think she's dying?"

We exit the neighborhood and slow to a walk as we head back to the cabin.

"I don't know," Owen eventually says. "I haven't seen her for eight years and she's frail, but she's getting over the flu and also eighty-one. For my mom's sake, I hope it's not something terminal. They're finally getting the chance to have a relationship after so many years." He looks toward the horizon. "I think my uncle and Spencer will sue Grandmother for control of her estate. If she is dying, it's unfortunate her last months will be spent in legal proceedings with her family."

"I agree."

I like Rheta, and she planned this week to have time to spend with her family. It doesn't seem she'll get that if Spencer, Dorian, Gerald, and Ellory spend it working. So much sadder if they're secretly plotting behind her back.

We reach the stairs to the front door but both stop at the bottom. Is he as hesitant to end our morning as I am? I loved running with him. I loved our conversation. I love how easy we are together, like we've known each other for months and not days.

All terrible things. I jog up the stairs. "Thanks for the run, Owen."

"Layla, wait."

I turn. "Yeah?"

He fidgets with the zipper of his running jacket. "I know

being here together this week might be awkward, but I hope we can still be friends."

My heart grows two sizes at the pleasure his words give me. Friends hang out together. They don't feel the need to avoid each other. Sending cocoa to a shivering friend is acceptable behavior. As is complimenting their eyes. They can go on morning runs and not feel guilty for enjoying the time spent together. By sticking Owen in the same box as Livy and Meg, I erase all my conflicting emotions about spending the week with the two cousins in the same house. Owen equals friend. Spencer equals boyfriend-slash-secret fiancé. Part of me thinks they should swap places, but that part of me is stupid.

Friendship with Owen equals perfection.

"I'd like that too. If you're up for it, we should go running again tomorrow."

He smiles. "I'll plan on it."

I push through the front door before he can see my mouth mirror his. I hum Shania Twain's "Best Friend" all the way to my room.

I HAVE TEXTS WAITING FOR ME FROM MEG AND LIVY IN OUR group chat, but I don't read them. As much as I want to know how much fun they're having with Meg's family, it's easier if I keep my focus here in Maine. They're probably worried about my silence, but they would be so much more worried if they knew the truth.

If I were home, I'd stay in my pajamas all day, or at least yoga pants and a t-shirt. Instead, I curl my hair and apply makeup to smooth out my pinkish complexion and bring out my eyes. I wear the softest gray wool pants I've ever touched and a green silk blouse that feels like a cloud against my skin. Not my usual wardrobe for a Sunday morning.

I glance at the schedule. Today we're visiting the town of York and the Nubble Lighthouse. I grab the Valentino flats Spencer bought me since it seems we might walk a lot.

I'm excited about tomorrow's visit to a tree farm. This house needs some sort of decoration for Christmas, and a tree is perfect. On Christmas Eve, Rheta has planned Nordic skiing at Mount Agamenticus. I don't imagine she'll be joining us on such a rigorous activity. The day after Christmas will be Boxing Day at the community center, whatever that means. Friday is a family discussion with her lawyer about her last will and testament. I'll be officially engaged by then. Does that mean I'll be invited to the family meeting? Something that's not worth worrying about right now.

I knock on Spencer's bedroom door, but there's no answer. A glance at my watch shows its nine. He must have already gone down for breakfast. Except when I enter the breakfast room, I'm the first to arrive. I expected everyone to be prompt after Rheta's edict last night, but even she's not here yet.

The breakfast room is smaller than the dining room, with a table large enough to seat twelve instead of thirty. The east wall is completely glass, with a sliding door and windows that open onto the back deck. Beyond is the ocean where sunlight reflects off the water. It's breathtaking. This may be my favorite room in the house.

A server, a young woman who looks to be around age twenty, stands next to the sideboard and smiles at my entrance. The smile only lasts a few seconds until she looks down. I wonder if she isn't allowed to engage with the guests in the house. It bothers me if my guess is correct. Enough that I go to the sideboard, but instead of picking up a plate, I speak to her.

"Have you worked here long?"

She clears her throat. "Not long."

I lean close and say in a whisper, "This place is crazy, right? I counted ten bedrooms upstairs, all with their own bathroom. I hope you don't have to clean them all."

Now she looks up, her eyes dancing. "No, I'm kitchen help."

"Do you enjoy it?"

"I don't know yet. This is my second day, and it's only a seasonal position." Her face brightens. "But if Ms. Rheta likes my work, I could get a permanent spot on her staff."

"Doesn't the family only come for vacations?"

"The family, yes, but Ms. Rheta moved here permanently this past summer."

"I didn't realize." I wonder if Spencer knows. If so, he didn't mention it. "I'm Layla."

Her smile brightens. "Hannah."

A clatter comes from the anteroom and she straightens her back and looks down again.

"Miles said I'm to be invisible and silent."

I can understand how Dorian and Ellory might be offended if the staff started talking to them, but I'm not like that. Just a few days ago I would've been in Hannah's position, trying to make money during the holiday break. I relate to her more than Spencer and his cousins.

"Well, I am the one who spoke to you," I say. "It would be rude if you didn't respond. It's nice to meet you, Hannah."

"You too, Layla."

My stomach grumbles. Everything smells so delicious. The food spread out on the sideboard is enough to feed three times as many people as are staying here. There are biscuits, muffins, croissants, bacon, sausage, scrambled eggs, cut fruit, yogurt, and three fresh juices along with coffee and hot cocoa.

"Hannah, do you know if I should wait for everyone else to arrive before filling a plate?"

"I was told breakfast lasts until ten o'clock and that the family will come and go during that time."

"Thank you. That's very helpful."

My stomach grumbles again, and I reach for a plate. The door opens and I look over my shoulder as Owen, Marianne, and Brady enter.

Brady has a thick book under his arm, and Marianne reminds him there is to be no book reading during meals. "We're here to spend time with extended family, not fictional characters."

My eyes meet Owen's, and I'm hard pressed not to show through my smile how good it is to see him, even though we only separated an hour ago. It's not a big deal. Friends are happy to see each other.

Marianne comes up beside me. "Good morning, Layla. How did you sleep?"

"Very well, thank you. How about you?"

"Well enough eventually. Brady and I rummaged in the

kitchen for a midnight snack. I find traveling always wakes up my appetite."

I turn away so she doesn't see my cheeks pink from the memory of what happened to me when I tried to do the same thing.

Now that I have my breakfast, I have the dilemma of figuring out where to sit. The same end spot where I sat last night seems like a safe bet. A few moments later, the Clark family does the same and sit in their seats across the table. Which means my friend Owen is directly across from me. I meet his glance and we share a smile.

By the time Spencer, Dorian, Ginger, Ellory, and Gerald enter, we're half done with our breakfast.

Spencer's hair is wet, and he wears a fresh shirt and slacks, but there are bags under his eyes and he yawns. I wonder if he got any sleep last night. The other three look well rested. This case might be important, but they could take the night off. It's unfortunate Spencer didn't do the same.

His eyes find mine, and I smile and stand as he walks over and kisses the top of my head.

"You look lovely," Spencer says.

"Thank you. I wish I could say the same. Did you get any sleep last night?"

"A few hours."

When Spencer goes to the sideboard, I go with him. I want to grab another biscuit. They're heavenly. The last one melted in my mouth like it was fifty percent butter.

Tori enters, her daughter skipping beside her wearing a blue Cinderella dress. The moment Sadie sees Ellory, she runs over and wraps her arms around her grandma's leg.

"I pooped in the potty!"

Everyone chuckles while Tori covers her eyes with a hand. "Sadie, remember I told you we don't talk about such things during breakfast? Or in public ever."

Spencer frowns at Sadie, as if such a display of pride in her accomplishment is unacceptable. I think it's cute, and turn his attention back on me so the little girl doesn't notice his censure.

"How is the trial prep coming?" I ask.

"Not great. I wanted to get caught up on all the latest developments and do what I could before everyone gets involved. It was a solid case two days ago, and now it's falling apart. We'll all be working overtime on this one."

Knowing Spencer, I expect nothing less, but it makes me wonder. "Do you need to go back to Salt Lake?"

I can feel Owen looking at my back. I would miss my new friend if we had to leave. And my roommates would have easy access to me. It's better for me if we stay here.

Spencer shakes his head. "No, we have to stay. Grandmother wants us here, and if we leave, she might change her will again. Right now, the best course of action is to do what we can to make her happy. It will annoy her that half of us will work during the week, but at least we'll be present for meals."

He fills his plate with meat, and I grab my biscuit before we sit down. I glance up to see Owen studying me. I widen my eyes, asking silently what he's staring at. He grins and shrugs.

When Rheta enters, everyone stops eating and talking. The room is silent as she sits at the head of the table. Hannah disappears for a few seconds before returning with a bowl of what looks like runny oatmeal and lays it on the table in front of her.

"It is lovely to have my family with me this morning," Rheta says. "I hope everyone is looking forward to our visit to York today. As stated in our schedule, we shall leave at ten-thirty."

Dorian is the one to break the bad news to her. "Mother, we have an issue with a case that arose yesterday and unfortunately, Ellory, Gerald, Spencer, and I need to work on it today."

Rheta's smile instantly disappears. "Yes, well, I can't say that's unexpected."

"You demanded we visit only a few days ago," Ellory says. She's in another tailored business suit, this one a deep burgundy. "You can't expect us to spend all week without working."

Rheta nods. "I understand."

"I'm sorry, Grandmother," Tori says, "but Sadie doesn't sleep well in new places and kept me up most of the night. Miles found me a sitter for a few hours so I can take a nap."

"I'm off to Boston for a spa day." Ginger dabs at her lips with the cloth napkin. "I scheduled it weeks ago."

Rheta looks around the table at her family while they share glances with each other. Dorian tugs at his shirt collar. Ellory bites her bottom lip. Spencer hides a yawn. They must wonder how their refusal to participate in the holiday she has planned will affect their standing. Rheta doesn't come across as vindictive, but this family is different from anything I've known, and I couldn't predict what any of them will do.

"There is nothing mandatory about spending Christmas

with our family." Rheta takes a fortifying breath. "This week in Maine was an invitation. It has been years since we've been together, and I wanted to mend broken relationships, but it is a choice. Does anyone else have any pressing responsibilities that will make them unable to come to town with me today?"

I would rather go to York than spend the day alone at the house, but it isn't lost on me that I will spend it with Rheta, Owen, Brady, and Marianne. Essentially, the Clark family and grandma.

"No, Mother," Marianne says.

"Wonderful." Rheta beams. "We will have a lovely day. I hope the rest of you will get your obligations in order to join us tomorrow for picking out a Christmas tree and ornaments. This year I intend to be involved with every stage of decorating the house. We shall do it together."

"Mother," Ellory says. Her tone is one she might use with a child. "We've never picked our own tree or decorated the house before. I'm sure there are staff that can do that for us."

Rheta hits her palm against the table. "Not this year. Why pay someone to have our fun when we can experience it for ourselves?"

That's a weighted question that no one answers, but I wholeheartedly agree.

Rheta eats her oatmeal. We eat our breakfast. No one says a word.

When Rheta's bowl is empty, Hannah pulls out her chair.

"We leave in forty-five minutes," she says to Marianne before turning to me. "I'm so glad you can come with us, Layla. Everyone else have a lovely day. I'll see you at dinner."

The door shuts behind her with a soft tap.

"Yep," Dorian says. "She's definitely dying."

"She's not dying," Marianne says. "She's old, and she's had the flu. Is the case really so important that you can't give Mother what she wants for Christmas? Time with her family?"

"Yes, it really is that important." Ellory's voice is calm but her eyes blaze. "You've been away from the family and the firm for too long. We have a reputation to uphold, and we won't lose this case because of Christmas."

"I didn't choose to leave this family," Marianne says softly, but her voice carries. "I was pushed out of it."

Ellory sniffs. "You went against Father. What did you expect?"

I want to sink into my chair and disappear. I'm an interloper in this family drama. Owen meets my eyes across the table, again. His jaw ticks.

Dorian waves his hand in the air, as if he's dismissing this petty argument. "What's done is done. We can all agree that Father was a controlling—" He breaks off when Tori glares and waves her hand over Sadie's head. "Man," he finishes lamely. "I for one am glad to have Marianne back in the family."

Marianne's expression softens. "Thank you. That means a lot."

Ellory lays her cloth napkin on the table. "I am too, Marianne."

Dorian nods, giving the impression that a few words have healed everything. "This is a time to unite and convince Mother not to throw the estate away in pieces. Marianne, since you're the only one able to go today, we're relying on you. Now it's time the rest of us get to work."

He stands. The lawyers in the room follow his lead. Spencer kisses my temple before his departure. From the way he glances at Owen, I'm positive he only did it to annoy his cousin. He doesn't realize that Owen and I are only friends.

I lean back against my chair, exhausted from the Eccleston family drama, and I haven't even been here twenty-four hours. Six more days to go.

Chapter Ten

LAYLA

At ten-thirty a black SUV waits for us with Miles behind the wheel and Rheta in the passenger seat. It looks like an FBI vehicle or a security detail for the President. It's surreal climbing inside. The radio plays classical music, and it grounds me in reality.

I sit in the very back with Brady, leaving Owen and Marianne the middle seats. As we pull out onto the main road, Rheta, Marianne, and Miles laugh about something, but I can't hear their conversation over Tchaikovsky's *Waltz of the Flowers*.

Owen shifts and looks over his shoulder at me. His beautiful brown eyes now remind me of the color of hot cocoa after me sent a mug to my room last night. I expect him to say something, but he just smiles. I can see myself spending the entire drive to town smiling back, but staring at each other is a strange thing for two platonic friends to do.

I turn to face Brady. "What are you reading?"

He doesn't look up from his book. "The last book in the best fantasy series of all time."

It's obvious he wants me to stop talking so he can actually read the book, but I'm good at ignoring what teenagers want, though usually it's for their good and not mine.

"Tell me about it?" I ask. "It's been a while since I've read a book that sucked me in so deep, I didn't want to leave."

Brady studies me for a few seconds, decides I'm serious, and launches into an enthusiastic and detailed description of the first book in the series. I give him my full attention.

The center of town is about fifteen minutes away, and even after Miles parks in a lot behind Main Street, Brady is still telling me about the main character's emotional journey.

As I climb out of the car, Owen holds out a hand to help me down. Without thinking, I place my hand in his. My skin tingles with the contact and once on solid ground I tug my hand away and fist it in my coat pocket.

Brady follows me out of the car still talking about his book, and I nod like I'm still listening. Owen's touch has short-circuited my brain, and it's impossible to focus on anything but him.

Owen gives me a look like he knows exactly why I started up this conversation with his brother and finds it funny I'm now stuck. He doesn't look affected by our contact at all, which is irritating—I mean, good. We're friends. Friends don't have this kind of physical response to a quick hand hold. I'm being ridiculous.

Miles grabs a wheelchair from the back of the SUV and

wheels it past us on his way to the passenger side door. Brady falls silent. Marianne covers her mouth with a hand. Expressions range from anxious to worried at what seems to be an unexpected wheelchair appearance. We watch as Miles helps Rheta from the vehicle.

"Don't worry about me," Rheta says with a wave of her hand. "In another month I'll be as healthy as a woman my age can expect. Unfortunately this week, I'm still weak after my bout of the flu. Shall we head to town hall to pick up a map for the Christmas Tree Challenge?"

Marianne shakes off her surprise at the wheelchair with effort. "How fun!"

Am I the only one who doesn't know what that is? No, because Owen asks his mom the same question.

"All the inns, hotels, and bed and breakfasts in the area decorate a tree in their lobby and visitors vote on their favorite. I haven't done the challenge since I was Brady's age. I didn't know York still did it."

"I thought you only spent summers here," Owen says.

"We came for Christmas a few times. Your grandfather hated cold so we went somewhere warmer most years."

We follow Rheta and Miles. People fill the sidewalk, bundled up against the cold. There are decorations on lamp posts, garlands along walls, and every business has a holiday display in their window. My favorite is the sweet shop where they've created a four-foot Christmas tree entirely out of candy. It finally feels like Christmas has arrived in Maine.

Not only are the decorations amazing, but the town itself is picturesque and quaint, with a small-town feel only historic downtown areas have. It also has a coastal vibe, with ocean paraphernalia and brightly painted buildings.

I love everything about this place. I can't stop smiling. There's a skip to my step.

We pass a street performer playing the opening chords of "Feliz Navidad" on his guitar. When he sings in a clear tenor voice, it's impossible to resist joining in. I stand off to the side singing softly, but he must hear my harmonization, because he waves me forward. I comply and sing loud so that everyone gathered around can hear. He grins at me. I grin back. His fingers run along the fretboard with more enthusiasm as he adds his own little flair to Jose Feliciano's song.

The surrounding crowd grows. I haven't performed in a long time, and I'm reminded how much I love it. My whole being feels buoyant and bubbly. My body warms and I open my coat to cool down.

He plays the last chord then, without a pause, continues with "Baby It's Cold Outside." I lose track of where I am as we finish, and he starts in on another. When the third song draws to a close, the crowd claps enthusiastically. A flood of people comes forward and drop bills and change into his open guitar case.

The musician holds out his fist, and I bump it with mine.

"Nice," he says. "Up for more?"

I glimpse Spencer's family in the crowd and am reminded why I'm here. Music has a way of making me forget time.

"I wish, but I have to go," I tell him regretfully. I drop all the change I have in my wallet into his case. "Thank you. You play beautifully."

He places his hand over his heart. "Your voice is angelic.

I'll be here the rest of the week if you're up for another round."

That makes me laugh as I step over to the family.

Owen's smiling. "That was amazing."

"Layla, you have a gorgeous voice," Rheta says. "Do you play the piano as well as you sing?"

I nod.

"Will you accompany us tonight as we sing Christmas carols?"

"I'd be honored."

Everyone is complimentary, even Brady, and I'm surprised he noticed anything outside of his book, but as we continue on our way, I can't shake the discomfort I feel about the situation. No one cares I stopped and sang on a public street, but I recall a date Spencer and I went on over the summer when I started singing a song as we strolled down a busy sidewalk. I don't remember why. Probably something he said reminded me of the lyrics. Spencer looked around to see if anyone noticed and then *shushed* me.

If Spencer were here, he wouldn't be complimentary like the rest of his family; he'd be embarrassed that I joined in with a busker.

"Hey, are you okay?" Owen asks.

"Yeah, of course," is my rote response.

But I'm not okay. I've prepared myself to keep my expectations low as Spencer's fiancée and future wife, but this is the first time I've considered what I would have to give up of myself in order to fit into his world. To him, teaching music is my profession, but to me, music is my lifeblood. I love performing and feel no shame singing in public.

I'm not sure what to do with this realization, or even if

there is anything to do. I follow behind the group and pretend not to notice Owen shooting me concerned glances.

At the town hall, we pick up our voting sheets and the map. York must be a popular vacation spot because the main part of town isn't big, but there are thirteen locations participating in the challenge within eleven small blocks.

Rheta plans out a route so that we walk in a big, wobbly loop. Rheta, Miles, and Marianne lead. Brady reads as he walks. Owen keeps looking my way.

I focus on the happy, festive people we pass and the trees we visit. My mood lifts enough for me to convince myself that Spencer and I will both adapt as we merge two very different lives. We'll come to appreciate what the other offers to our marriage. I don't believe it yet, but if I repeat it enough times, I'm sure it will become a reality.

Most of the trees we visit have themes, Like *'Twas the Night Before Christmas, The Polar Express*, and *Toy Story*. One tree has flocked white branches and only purple decorations. Another is decorated with colored ornaments in a rainbow pattern. They're amazing, and I take pictures of them all, but not as many as I do of my favorite tree titled "Candy Cane Land." It's decorated with red bows, small white ornaments, and hundreds of candy canes.

As we walk back to city hall to drop off our ballots, Owen comes up beside me and asks, "Why do you love candy canes so much? I noticed how you gave them out to everyone at Brock Pine and now that tree. You must have taken a hundred pictures."

I'm grateful for a distraction from my thoughts about Spencer.

"My mom loved candy canes. Anything peppermint,

really, but specifically candy canes. She would say, 'It's a sucker with an edible stick.' Every December she bought hundreds, decorated them with a green bow, and gave them to everyone she met through the whole month. I do the same because it reminds me of her."

I brought a small box of them with me to Maine, but I haven't given out a single one. When I ask myself why, the answer comes easily: Spencer would think it's odd. Not something I want to ponder on, especially not after my last realization.

I ask Owen, "Is there something that you do that makes you feel like you're celebrating with your dad?"

Owen doesn't have to think about his answer. "He really loved *The Muppet Christmas Carol*. My parents saw the movie on their first date, and we watch it every December with a box of See's chocolates. He made us sing along to all the songs. Mom, Brady, and I still do it every year."

That is the kind of Christmas tradition I want to incorporate into my own family someday. I can't see Spencer joining in. I don't allow myself to dwell on how that will disappointment future me.

"*The Muppet Christmas Carol* is one of my favorite Christmas movies," I tell him. "I make my students sing along to it the week leading up to Christmas break."

"Do they like it as much as you do?" He grins like he knows the answer is no.

I laugh. "Not at all, but that doesn't deter me."

With our challenge obligations complete, Rheta takes us to a burger place just down the street. Not what I was expecting, considering she is a billionaire.

The place is packed, but they have a table reserved for

us. A few waiting customers grumble, but the staff ignore them. Everyone who works here greets "Ms. Rheta" by name. Only Miles is unsurprised that they know who she is.

Once we're seated, our waitress brings us water. "It's a pleasure to have Ms. Rheta and her family with us today. Do you want any drinks?"

When she leaves with our drink order, Marianne asks, "Mother, how do they all know you?"

Rheta doesn't look up from the menu. "Oh, I've come here a few times for dinner."

Miles leans forward and whispers, "She set up a grant for local businesses. Biggs' Burgers was a recipient a few months ago. They're expanding into the next town over."

Rheta tuts. "Miles, if you give away all my secrets, I'll have to leave you at home for our next outing."

He puts a hand to his chest in mock offense. "Who will cut down your tree if I'm not there?"

She lowers her menu and looks at her grandson's arms. "I think Owen can handle the task."

I can't help but scan my own eyes over Owen's shoulders and arms, then down to his large hands and long fingers. Yes, I'm sure he can handle an ax quite well. It's only when the waitress returns with our drinks that I'm able to tear my eyes away.

We all order the cheeseburger and fries, while Rheta asks for her usual. Why she even glanced at the menu is a mystery.

"Miles, tell us more about what my mother's done around town," Marianne says.

Miles obliges. A new roof for the community center; three pickleball courts at the park; a bigger sign at the city limits; repaving some of the outlying roads. Each time he mentions something else, Rheta swats at his hand, though it's more like a pat.

Marianne thinks it's wonderful, but I can't help wondering how horrified Rheta's other two children would be if they knew how much she donated to York. They would definitely be annoyed Marianne isn't trying to talk her mother out of spending their inheritances. Maybe it's a good thing they didn't come today. I can't imagine they would like the conversation or this place. Spencer wouldn't.

When our waitress brings our food, I'm not surprised to see Rheta's usual order is four chicken nuggets and a small fry with a side of mustard. After watching her eat soup and salad last night and oatmeal this morning, a simple meal fits her.

Owen and I both reach for the ketchup at the same time. Our fingers brush and I jerk back.

"You first," I say.

"No. You. Let me be a gentleman."

"No, it's fine."

I'm not sure why I'm making a big deal about this, but my hand still tingles from our contact hours ago when he helped me from the car. I ball up my fist under the table and will myself to be indifferent to Owen.

I wait for him to grab the glass ketchup bottle. He waits for me. I'm afraid if I reach out he will reach at the same time. Then we'll have accidental contact again. It's when my skin touches his that I doubt my ability to remain just his friend.

It's Brady who lifts the bottle and plonks it down next to his brother's plate. "A gentleman listens to a lady."

"Something you picked up from your fantasy novels?" Owen asks with a lopsided grin, but he takes the bottle and shakes it over his plate.

When nothing comes out, he shakes more, then more violently. A large glob lands on top of his fries and drowns them.

"Want some fries with your ketchup?" Brady says with a smirk.

Everyone laughs at Owen's disgusted face. I remember how he barely dipped the fries in ketchup at the drive-in. Was that only two nights ago? It feels like weeks.

Owen hands me the bottle without a word. A few shakes and I get a small blob, probably because that's all that's left. I take his plate and push mine in front of him. We ordered the same meal, so the only thing he's missing is the ketchup lake.

"You don't have to do that," he says, reaching to take his plate back.

"I actually like ketchup," I say.

He stops trying to swap plates and falls against the seat back. "Thank you."

"No problem." I use my fork to free a fry. It's delicious. I love the sweet of the ketchup with the saltiness of the fry.

Rheta isn't the only one who wrinkles her nose. "We can get you fresh fries. There's no reason to eat ketchup soup."

"That is honestly the way she eats them," Owen says.

"How would you know?" Brady asks. He looks between me and his brother with more interest.

Owen says in a rush, "This burger is really tasty. How did you find this gem of a place, Grandmother?"

Am I the only one who notices he hasn't tasted his burger yet?

The food is decent, but the company is lovely. Marianne is kind and has a ready laugh. Miles can't seem to take his eyes off of her. Seeing Owen interact with his mom and brother is fun. He teases and takes teasing easily. Rheta enjoys watching them as much as I do. I wonder if she regrets the years she missed in their lives. How can she not?

When the waitress comes back to fill our water glasses, Rheta asks, "How are the plans coming for Boxing Day?"

Boxing Day at the community center is on the family schedule for the day after Christmas. I'm curious about the answer myself.

Our waitress deflates. "They're not. The flood at the community center on Wednesday did more damage than they originally thought. They can't get it fixed by Thursday, especially with Christmas in three days. There's supposed to be a snowstorm on Boxing Day, so we can't do it at the park either. We had to cancel."

Rheta is affronted. "Why didn't anyone tell me?"

"I suppose we thought the mayor did. Or Miles."

Rheta gives Miles a stern look. "They did not. Well, there's only one thing to do. We'll have it at my home. I have plenty of space to host the town."

The waitress's eyes light up. "Ms. Rheta, you would do that for real?"

"Of course. I'll talk to the mayor tomorrow and get it all squared away, but you spread the word, alright?"

She bounces up and down. It's a good thing the pitcher of water is now empty. "Thank you so much! I'm sure everyone will be thrilled."

Only after she's left does Owen ask, "What's Boxing Day?"

"I've actually never been," Rheta says. "I was looking forward to experiencing it this year. Miles, why don't you explain?"

Miles swallows his bite of burger. He doesn't look away from Marianne as he fills us in on the town tradition.

"It started fifteen years ago with a family who moved into town from New Zealand. Boxing Day is an actual holiday that started in England centuries ago as a time to give to the poor. This family invited others to join them the day after Christmas to exchange unwanted Christmas gifts and eat leftover food. Through the years, it has spread, and now it's a big town party where we eat turkey sandwiches until we want to pass out."

Brady wrinkles his nose. "Isn't it rude to give away presents?"

Miles shrugs and nods at the same time. "There are a few people we have to be considerate of when bringing things to the swap, but most of us think it's fun. The gift swap has become more than only Christmas presents, and now we all bring things we don't need any more to give it a new life. It's amazing what you find. And the leftover food is great too."

"I love a good turkey sandwich." Rheta pauses with a fry halfway to her mouth, then drops her hand. "There is one problem with hosting this year. We haven't put up any Christmas decorations yet. This week was a last-minute idea, and the flu kept me from getting the decorations purchased before everyone arrived. Tomorrow's trip to the tree farm is even more important. Miles, we need to find decorations for the house and enough ornaments for six trees."

"Six trees?" Marianne asks.

"We'll need one for every room on the main floor, with the tallest we can find for the foyer."

"There will be decorations to purchase at the lighthouse this afternoon and at the tree farm tomorrow," Miles says.

"Perfect. We also need people willing to decorate. I can't rely on my family to do it all." She nods her head decisively. "I'll pay them, of course."

Miles shakes his head. "Ms. Rheta, you won't have to pay people to help you."

"Nonsense. It's Christmas. They should be compensated for time away from their families." She looks around the table. "Is it okay if we cancel our plans for Nordic skiing on Christmas Eve and spend the day decorating the house instead?"

Everyone nods in agreement. I'm now impatient for Christmas Eve. I love decorating.

We leave Biggs' Burgers and walk back to the van. I ate too much and wish it wasn't parked three blocks away. Brady has the right idea. He jumps onto Owen's back and they stagger down the street, trying not to bump into anyone on the crowded sidewalk.

Today has turned out to be a better day than I expected, even with the internal crisis thinking about my future with Spencer. This is the kind of family I hoped to marry into one day. Though … Spencer isn't close to Owen's family. Once we fly home, I'm not sure how often I'll see any of them. I better soak in as much of their joy as I can this week because it will have to last me a long time.

Chapter Eleven

OWEN

DURING THE DRIVE TO SOHIER PARK AND THE NUBBLE Lighthouse at Cape Neddick, Layla and Brady talk in the back about *The Lord of the Rings* movies. I didn't realize she was such an aficionado on the topic. She even has strong opinions on Tom Bombadil, who was only in the book.

Brady is a Layla fan. We should create a club. We'd have to fight over who got to be club president, but I think I could win.

Earlier I thought she only talked with my brother to avoid talking to me, but now I rethink my earlier assumption. I may have a bit of an ego when it comes to Layla. She's such a huge part of my thoughts, I assume I'm in hers. Apparently not. She is dating my cousin, and we did agree to being friends, so the realization shouldn't sting as much as it does.

When we arrive, the small peninsula is packed. The

first time I came here, I expected Sohier park to actually be a park. It's more of a rocky outcropping with a grassy spot to one side. During low tide, a small stretch of rock reaches across five hundred feet to the rocky island where the Nubble Lighthouse sits. It's high tide now, and the ocean beats against the rock on both land and island. It's a dull rumble compared to the roar of voices from the hundreds of visitors who had the same idea as Grandmother.

On the left of the grassy area, Santa sits on a large red throne. A line of children and their parents winds back to the parking lot. Nearby are real reindeer grazing on hay. Bells twined through their antlers jingle as they move.

To the left are a line of pop-up shops, nothing more than tables, canopies, and homemade products ready to sell. From jewelry to jam, baked goods to loomed rugs. If anyone has procrastinated their Christmas shopping until three days before Christmas, at least they have a wide selection of gifts to choose from.

Layla twirls in a circle, her eyes bright as she takes in all the goods for sale and tells Brady, "My nana sold at markets like this almost every weekend until a few years ago."

"What did she sell?" Brady asks.

"Knitted items like socks, mittens, hats, and sweaters. I spent so much time with her. This is almost like coming home."

"Cool."

"Brady," Mom calls from a booth. "I want to show you this."

That leaves me and Layla at the back of the group. She stops at a handmade jewelry table and runs her finger along a necklace with an angel pendant carved from bone. The tag attached says fifty dollars. With a sigh, Layla moves on.

"You're not going to get it?" I ask.

Fifty dollars is nothing, especially when dating Spencer Eccleston.

"No. I don't need any more jewelry."

In my family, need is rarely taken into consideration when purchasing items. Her restraint is an admirable quality.

Or ... maybe it isn't restraint? The way she walks away so reluctantly has me wondering if it's because she doesn't *have* the money to purchase something frivolous. Not even fifty dollars. I count the clues: she's a school teacher. Her grandmother lives in an assisted living center. Layla has no family to help her financially. How did I not realize this earlier?

My entire perspective on Layla's relationship with Spencer shifts. Could it be that she isn't overly interested in money like he claimed, but instead she needs money to survive? Spencer said she wanted to marry for the safety wealth offered. I disregarded it at the time, but maybe that's the key to understanding the Layla puzzle.

Layla's phone rings. After looking at the screen, she quickly answers.

"Hello?" She glances at me for a moment, then weaves her way through the crowds to the perimeter of the shops.

I catch glimpses of her between groups of people passing. Next to me is a table selling popcorn. I buy a bag of caramel and munch on it while I wait. The longer Layla's on the phone, the more her free arm waves through the air as she speaks. When she finally hangs up, she's blinking back tears. I weave my way through crowds until I reach her.

"What's wrong?"

She wipes under her eyes. "Nothing."

"Maybe I can help."

She laughs bitterly. "You can help as much as I can since we're both in York and not Salt Lake." With a shake of her head, like she's dislodging something from her thoughts, she explains. "It's the daytime front desk attendant at Brock Pine."

"Bennie?"

"Yeah. Bennie." She says his name like a curse. She wraps her arms around herself as if for comfort. "My nana slipped past him and out the door. She was lost for most of the day until they found her in Target. Last time he allowed her to leave, she fell. This time she could have been hit by a car or, I don't know … kidnapped."

No one is going to kidnap an old woman, but Layla's scared and not thinking logically. I try to lighten her mood since her nana is safe now.

"Granny-napped more like."

Layla shakes her head like I'm ridiculous, but gives a small smile. I'd love to reach out and pull her into my arms, but that isn't my place as her *friend*. It's Spencer's, and the idiot isn't here.

"She's okay, I know," Layla says. "But I worry about her, and I feel so powerless, especially when she's so far away. Bennie better not let her get out again because I have a roommate who is devious when it comes to payback."

It isn't Bennie's job to keep the residents in. They can leave at any time, though they are supposed to check out before they go. But Layla's grandma has memory issues. That would be scary.

She walks back into the crowds. I go with her.

"Could you move her somewhere else?" I ask.

"It's too expensive." She glances up at me as if she's said something she shouldn't have. It reinforces my theory that she's struggling to pay for her nana's care. "I mean, it would be too confusing for her. Next week she'll be moved into the memory care unit, and that'll be hard enough. Taking her to a whole new place is too much." She gives me a sardonic grin. "For both of us."

Her first response was most likely the more honest reason, and it bothers me. She's dating Spencer. He plans to marry her. Why isn't he helping her with the expense? He dressed her in designer brands and bought her a Boudron bag, but he can't foot the bill for her grandma?

I want to stop listening to the voice that's telling me her relationship with my cousin is insincere, but I'm finding that impossible with this new hypothesis.

"Tell me again how you met Spencer?" I offer her popcorn, and she takes a kernel without looking at me.

"At a party last New Year's Eve."

"Spencer doesn't party. Unless it was a firm event, or a client invited him, he wouldn't be at a party."

She takes more popcorn and eats each kernel one at a time. People jostle around us, but we stick together, shoulder to shoulder.

"Did you lie?" I ask.

She stops at a booth of hand sewn aprons and flips through the child-sized rack without seeing them.

"We didn't lie," Layla says meekly. "I met him at a party. But, you're right, it was at the house of one of his clients."

"How do you know his client?" Spencer's clients are business people who make a million dollars a year, minimum. Layla doesn't hit me as the kind of person who hangs out with millionaires. That's one of the things I like about her.

She huffs. "Why do you care who I know?"

"I don't," I say with a shrug. "I want to understand how you and Spencer met. You're not his type."

"Because I'm a *school teacher*?"

She walks away, and I follow until I'm beside her again.

"I offended you with that comment last night, and that wasn't my intention. How well do you know the Eccleston family? My mother was disowned because she married my dad, a *school teacher*. It's a sore subject for me."

She slows her pace. "I'm sorry; I didn't make the connection. Spencer doesn't care about that sort of thing. He's never cared about my career, and as far as I can see, neither does anyone else in the family."

Probably because Grandfather isn't here anymore. If he were alive, there is no way Spencer would have brought Layla to Christmas. It's harsh, but it's true. I'm shocked Spencer started dating her before Grandfather passed. My cousin never rebels.

"He may not care about your profession," I say. I should not say another word, but she doesn't see how mismatched with is with Spencer, and that bothers me. "But he cares about your appearance because he picks out your clothes. How much did the Boudron cost you? Three thousand at least. And the coat? Another two thousand. I'd be surprised if those slacks were less than nine hundred."

She stops in the middle of the path and glares at me. I've hurt her and I hate it, but I don't regret what I said. She shouldn't settle for a guy who treats her like a Barbie doll.

"How do you know I didn't buy this coat myself?" Her voice quivers, but she glares with all the confidence in the world.

"Because I've seen you multiple times over the last six months, and you've never worn it until yesterday. Tori has a coat just like that in green, and it was new this fall. She wouldn't shut up about it when I talked to her last month."

Her stance softens. "I can't understand why you care."

"Because I care about you, Layla. Call me a fool, but I do. Are you in need of money? Is Spencer manipulating you?" I lean close and lower my voice. "Do you know he stands to inherit *twenty million* dollars when he marries?"

Her expression doesn't change as I mention the insane amount of money, which tells me she knows. Maybe I've gotten this wrong, and she's manipulating *him*. I instantly disregard that thought. Layla isn't the type to harm anyone, not even for her benefit.

She turns and stalks away. This time I don't keep up, but follow slowly behind. She catches up to Brady, who's trying on a green *Lord of the Rings* cape at a booth that sells fantasy costumes.

As I approach, Brady turns to me. "Owen, this is what I want for Christmas."

"I already got you a Christmas gift."

"I won't like it as much as this."

"You better like it because it's exactly what you asked for."

Brady's shoulders slump. "Come on. It's only a hundred and fifty. You can afford it."

This is what I don't like about money. The entitlement. I want Brady to learn the value of a dollar, not that he can get whatever he wants with no effort on his part. Once he inherits twenty million from Grandmother, it'll be too late.

When I say nothing, he deflates further.

"Brady," Layla says, "I could knit you a cape just like this."

His eyes light up. "Really?"

Layla nods. "I can have it done by the new year. I have the perfect wool at home that will work for this sort of project."

"Thanks!" Brady is thrilled.

I am not. It's nice of Layla to offer, but it's still time and money someone is investing without Brady doing anything to earn it. I'm caught between offending Layla again and disappointing Brady now that he has a promise.

It's better I accept Layla's generosity. I'm about to tell her to send me the bill for the supplies and her time when Grandmother calls out to her from the next booth over.

"Layla, what do you think of these?" She points to ball ornaments made from patch worked pieces of material. "I want to decorate the trees with items made by local artisans."

Layla goes to look and Brady follows, the glow of hero worship in his eyes, like she's the Pied Piper. It's enough to make me pause because I want to follow, too. Does that make me a rat?

I stay where I am and reevaluate why I'm asking her questions about her relationship with Spencer. She's a grown woman who can make her own decisions. I may not agree with them, but it isn't my place to make value judgments on what she does.

Instead of tagging along and forcing her to answer questions she doesn't want to, I head back to the aprons and buy the lady-bug print for Sadie. I'm not sure how often she's in the kitchen, if at all. Tori's cook probably doesn't appreciate Sadie's help, but she will look cute wearing it.

I browse the other booths on my own and buy a few items until I get a text from Mom telling me they're stopping for hot cocoa and cookies and to come meet them.

With only a few picnic tables available, it's easy to spot Rheta's wheelchair at the end of one. I don't know how they snagged it with so many people milling about, but I'd guess whoever was here before was thrilled to give up their table to "Ms. Rheta."

The town's hero worship of Grandmother is a paradigm shift for me. She was always Grandfather's shadow. He was the one everyone looked up to. It seems since his passing, she's finally found herself. It only took her eighty years, and that makes me sad for her.

The only place at the table for me is on the end, next to Layla. I stuff my shopping bag at my feet and offer a quiet apology.

"I'm sorry," I say under my breath, so that she's the only one who can hear. She stills, but doesn't turn to look at me. "What you do is none of my business. I respect your job as a teacher. You look amazing in blue and that coat is nice. I'm sorry that what I said came across as a judgment against you."

It was against Spencer.

She nods, still looking ahead. "Thank you," she whispers.

"I hope I can still call myself a friend. And as a friend, if you need anything, including money, I will help. No strings attached."

Her cheeks pink, but if I expected her to take me up on my offer and ditch Spencer, then I'm a fool because she says nothing.

Miles brings me a tree-shaped frosted sugar cookie and a cup of hot cocoa topped with whipped cream. Sticking out of the top is the hook of a candy cane. Even if I don't look at Layla, my thoughts are there. From now on, candy canes will always remind me of her tradition and the candy cane bouquet she gave me after she stole my car.

I slurp up the whipped cream, and dip my frosted sugar cookie in my cocoa.

"Don't do that," Layla says, exasperated, as if our previous conversation had never happened. "You're ruining a perfectly good cookie by making it disgusting."

LAYLA

Owen doesn't look at me, but he smiles down at his cocoa. "It's actually quite delicious. You should try it."

He bites off the cocoa soaked bit of cookie.

I grimace. "No. I don't like soggy desserts."

"Bread pudding?"

"Gross."

"Banana pudding?"

"Mushy Nilla Wafers? Yuck. I don't actually like the texture of pudding in general."

"Apple crumble smothered in ice cream?"

"I don't know if that would count as soggy. However, ice cream on cake? Blah."

He dips his cookie again, almost as a taunt. I look away, not because it's gross, which it is, but because he's charming while being gross.

Rheta and Marianne are reminiscing about a Christmas spent in Paris forty years ago, and no one is looking at this end of the table.

I should let our earlier conversation drop, but Owen has this effect on me where I want to tell him everything. It shouldn't matter under the circumstances, but I don't want him to dislike me or believe I'm a gold digger or a liar. I want him to understand me, because that's what friends do: they understand each other.

"I'm friends with members of a band," I say. "They were playing at a private party last New Year's Eve, but their singer came down with food poisoning. I filled in for her the night I met Spencer."

The soggy part of Owen's cookie falls into his cocoa. He doesn't seem to notice.

"The band was taking a break between sets when he came over and started talking to me."

I think back on that night. Spencer was sexy and suave with his slicked back pompadour and double-breasted suit. After our first conversation, I didn't lose track of him all night. I'd never met someone like him, and it felt amazing to have his attention when there were so many beautiful women there who were actual guests. Whenever I wasn't on stage, he sought me out. To say I found it flattering does my feelings a huge disservice.

"I thought he was slumming it with me," I say. "I was literally the hired help and everyone treated him like a celebrity. But he called me the following week and asked me out. He got my number through the host who contacted the band. Who puts in that much effort for a date with a jazz singer? He has only ever shown me respect." I smile sardonically. "Unless it has to do with putting his phone away during meals or arriving on time. Then he's a lost cause."

Owen smiles but quickly sobers. "You've been together ever since?"

He has to be thinking about our fry night. Is telling him the truth about how I came to be here better or worse? I can't decide, but I know I don't want to lie. He must suspect I need money for Nana because of his offer to give money after my call with Brock Pine Home. He knows part of my story already.

"No, we haven't. We broke up a few times over the year, but we always get back together. Spencer and I weren't dating when I went with you for fries. I'm sorry I left so abruptly. I got a text from him saying he needed to talk to me as soon as possible. When we met up, he asked me to come with him to Maine, and I said yes."

The intensity of Owen's attention makes my heart flutter. He nods. "Thank you for explaining."

"I know Spencer and I aren't a conventional match, but

we work as a couple. I'm not blind to his faults, but he's what I need in my life. Besides, I'm not perfect either."

I come with a lot of financial baggage.

Owen eats the last bite of his gross, soggy cookie and says under his breath, so softly I barely hear the words, "I disagree. You're nearly perfect to me."

He wouldn't think that if he knew the truth.

OWEN

As the sun sets, everyone at Sohier Park heads closer to the rocky shore and looks out at the lighthouse. Wispy clouds in the sky reflect the light from the sun as it sinks behind what looks like the edge of the world, coloring the sky pink and shadowed purple.

"I've never seen a sunset like this before," Layla breathes out with reverence. "It's beautiful."

I glance over. Her face is aglow with the last minutes of the sun's rays and I am in awe of the view. I couldn't agree with her more: beautiful. If she were mine, I'd hold her hand. She'd lay her head on my shoulder. I'd kiss her forehead. She'd snuggle into the crook of my neck.

A foolish dream that will only cause me pain because it will never come true. I'd step away from her, but we're packed in tight.

As the sky turns to a murky blue, the crowd starts a countdown from ten. Layla puts her hands to her chest and laughs. She meets my eyes and we both join in.

"Five ... Four ... Three ... Two ... One!"

Christmas lights outlining all five structures on the island, including the Nubble Lighthouse and the keeper's cottage, turn on at once. The crowd collectively gasps. Even Brady seems impressed as his eyes widen at the sight.

A cheer goes up, but I'd guess no one claps louder than Layla.

JUST AS GRANDMOTHER DEMANDED, BACK AT THE CABIN, everyone shows up at dinner. Once again, I'm seated across from Layla and Spencer during the meal. Whenever my eyes wander in their direction, Spencer touches Layla. A hand on her wrist. An arm along the back of her chair. If he leaned any closer to her, he'd tumble into her lap.

From the way Layla glances at him with a wrinkled brow and a slight frown, I'm left believing his behavior is all for my benefit. I want to tell him to grow up, but I don't want to give him the satisfaction of knowing how irritating I find the constant touching.

I stew about what Layla told me today: they hadn't been dating recently until they met up Friday night and he invited her to Maine.

I stew about what Layla didn't tell me: her love for Spencer.

If not love, then it must be all about the money. Her motivation is honorable if it's to take care of her grandma. It makes me sad. She deserves to be adored and spoiled with love by someone who will sacrifice and put her needs first. What a sorry situation that she's not marrying the kind of man who will do that for her.

Mom nudges me with her elbow. When I look over, she mouths, "Grumpy face, what's wrong?"

I sit up straight with a shrug and smile, banishing my grumpy thoughts.

Dorian shares a story about a client who got drunk, stuck his head through the bars of a handrail, and was then robbed by some marauding teens on their way to school the next morning. He's a talented storyteller, and everyone but me laughs throughout the telling.

I have never been with my extended family in a lighthearted situation like this. During the summers I spent here, meals were serious affairs. This is what it should have always been like. I understand why Grandmother brought us all together for the week: to make memories like this.

Since Dad's funeral, I've carried around a knotted ball of anger in my chest. Right now, as I watch everyone laugh and joke together, a few of those knots unravel. They've been the villains in my story for so long, it feels odd to see their humanity. I quite like my grandmother after today. Ellory and Dorian may be selfish, but they aren't evil.

Grandmother stands. "Shall we have our carol singing in the music room? Layla has graciously offered to play the piano for us."

I've always been confused by the house having a music room when no one plays music, but it comes in handy tonight. We file down to the basement and into the music room, which comprises a piano and a few dozen folding chairs.

Grandfather had the cabin built on a slope, so the basement opens into the backyard. Much like upstairs, the back of the house is mostly windows. No ocean views here, just trees.

As we pull out the chairs and set them up in a semi-circle around the piano, I overhear Layla speaking to Spencer.

"The case will not make itself," he says.

"Stay for thirty minutes. Everyone else is here." She points to Dorian and Ellory. Even Tori is here after putting Sadie to bed.

Spencer's erect posture softens when he notices me watching them. "You're right. I can stay. It's been too long since I heard you play."

I'm surprised he's heard her play at all, but I suppose they have dated some of the year, if not recently. Layla kisses his cheek before she sits at the piano. It's the first time I've seen her show him physical affection, and it turns my stomach sour.

Miles hands out music books. We start with "O Little Town of Bethlehem." I'm not sure Uncle Dorian has ever sung a note in his life, but under Grandmother's watchful eye, he joins in. We're not great, but we're not terrible either.

Grandmother claps and laughs. "I planned for us to sing to a recording, but this is so much better."

I can't help but think of Grandfather missing out on this Christmas. The first happy family Christmas we've ever shared. It must make him miserable to know he's not here to ruin it.

With each song, we get worse, and Grandmother's laughter gets louder. She finally ends the misery after our fifth song.

"Good night!" she says with a wide wave of her arm, like

she's Santa Claus. "Thank you for making this old woman's evening so memorable."

She's cackling as she leaves the room.

Layla plays a song with an unfamiliar melody. Spencer goes to the piano and talks to her for a few minutes, but her fingers never stop dancing across the keys. I can't look away. The music makes her happy, and she literally glows.

Everyone in the family leaves but for me and still Layla plays. I'm drawn to her and step closer until I'm only a few feet away. The last chord reverberates around the room. I feel it in my chest.

She looks up and says, "I thought everyone had left."

"You're an amazing musician."

Her cheeks turn pink. "Thank you."

"What song was that you just played? It's beautiful. I didn't recognize it."

Her blush deepens. "It's something I made up. It changes every time I play it."

I'm in even more awe of her. I curse Spencer for finding Layla first and relegating me to friendship. I don't want to say good night. Tomorrow is too long to wait to see her again.

"My mom, Brady, and I are having our sing along to *The Muppet Christmas Carol* in my room tonight. Do you want to come?"

She chews on her lip as she thinks. I have to look away because my fingers itch to touch her cheeks. My thumb wants to run along her full, bottom lip. She drives me insane.

Finally, she says, "Um, okay."

Chapter Twelve

LAYLA

Thirty minutes later, I knock on Owen's bedroom door, excitement thrumming as I anticipate singing along to a *Muppet Christmas Carol* with my friend and his family. People who actually want to sing and not my students.

Owen opens the door wearing a Harvard t-shirt and pajama pants with dancing candy canes. *Candy canes! Dancing!* They have eyes, a huge smile, legs, and two hands that hold a wooden cane. How did I not know such a thing existed? I'm finding them online tonight and buying them ASAP. Which means they'll sit in a digital shopping cart until I get paid next month. It will be worth the wait.

It's impossible not to compare Owen and Spencer, though I wish my brain would stop it. Spencer wouldn't get caught dead wearing something so ridiculous. Owen is adorable in his dorkiness. With the way my heart knocks around in my chest, I should turn around and go back to my room, but I'm incapable of moving. The view is too charming.

"Welcome," Owen says.

He opens the door wider, and two things hit me at once. Marianne and Brady are wearing the same dancing candy cane pajama bottoms. This family's adorableness is almost more than I can stand.

The second is the room is purple. Very purple. Everything has been purpled. From the walls, rug, bedspread, and pillow covers, to the dresser and upholstered couch. Even the lampshades on the bedside tables are purple.

"What?" is all I'm able to get out.

Owen understands what I'm not able to vocalize. He ducks his head and runs a hand through his thick hair.

"Yeah, I got to decorate the room my first summer here, and I went a little overboard. I blame it on my mom. She loves everything in taupe and grays. Color was a new experience for me."

I meet Brady's gaze, and we both laugh.

"I wanted to paint one wall in my bedroom blue," Brady says. "She about died."

Marianne shakes her head. "I'm not that bad."

"Yes, you are," Brady and Owen say at the same time, as if they scripted it.

"It was midnight blue! Who wants dark colors on their walls?" She gets no sympathy from her sons, and I'm trying not to laugh. She waves me over to the couch. "Don't listen to them. They have no sense of interior design." She points to the walls as proof.

There's room enough for one more person on the couch

next to me, and I hate myself for hoping Owen takes the spot.

I'm dating someone else, brain, so shut up! Owen is my FRIEND.

"It wasn't so bad last time I was here," Owen says, waving around the room. "Just the walls, floor, couch, and dresser were purple."

"Right. Not so bad," Brady deadpans.

Owen shakes his head. "Miles brought in everything else as a joke."

"No," Brady says. "He brought it in because he knows about your secret purple obsession and wanted you to feel at home."

Owen looks at me for support.

I shrug. "I have to agree with Brady on this one. Would you even know where you are if everything wasn't purple?"

He seems to accept that he's lost this argument and picks up the TV remote. A smile teases his lips. "Let's watch this movie."

"Yeah," Brady says. He points to Owen. "It's late, and we don't want the old man to fall asleep before the end."

Owen puts his arms around Brady's neck and pulls Brady's head into his shoulder. Brady is a few inches taller and is forced to lean down at an odd angle.

"Let's see who falls asleep first," Owen says.

Then they say together, "Mom."

"Hey!" Marianne says. "I'll stay awake. It's not even nine o'clock."

They snicker before plopping on the end of the bed. The camaraderie between the Clarks opens up the yearning in my soul for family. This kind of family, not the workaholics down in the office below.

Brain, I'm serious. One more thought like this and I'm making you go to bed immediately.

Family is family, and I'm about to be officially engaged to Spencer. No use thinking about what-might-have-been.

"What's in the bag?" Brady asks me.

I don't realize he's talking to me until all three of them wait for my answer. I forgot I was carrying it. "Oh. I'm knitting hot pads that I'll felt and sell in my online shop."

Brady's stare is blank. "Okay. Why?"

"Ignore him. Tell me about your store." Marianne pats my arm and leans closer. "I'm a quilter, and I've thought about selling things online, but it feels overwhelming."

I tell her a little about the platform while Owen cues up the movie. Unfortunately, he sits on the bed with Brady. I hope I hide my disappointment.

If I thought they were a fun bunch before, they get even more wild once the movie starts. Maybe it's caused by the Sees chocolate box being passed around, but the two brothers are hyper.

They try to out-sing each other, but neither of them are in the correct key and they don't care. I'm laughing too hard to do much singing myself. During Bob Cratchit and Tiny Tim's duet, they each take a part. When they're not trying to out yell each other, they aren't terrible, but it would help if they started on the right pitch.

Owen points to his mom. "Let it be noted that she is asleep, just as we predicted."

Marianne is slumped against the couch arm, her head at an uncomfortable angle that will definitely leave a crick.

Owen brings a pillow that he places under her neck. My heart melts at his thoughtfulness.

"She lasted longer than I expected," Owen says.

"Should we wake her up so she can go to her own bed?" I ask.

"No. She'll wake up during the credits and swear she never fell asleep."

"She was just resting her eyes," Brady explains.

Forty minutes later, when the credits roll, their predictions are once again correct.

"I was awake the whole time," Marianne insists as she stretches her arms above her head. "My eyes were a little tired. I need to put some eyedrops in. That's all."

I can't stop laughing as they tease each other. It's hard for me to leave because I want to bask in the family togetherness for hours longer, but I should get to bed. As I stand, I realize I didn't open my knitting bag. It's been years since I've been so engrossed in the company I'm with that I haven't worked on a knitting project while watching a movie.

Owen follows me into the hallway. "Let me walk you home."

I stifle my laugh so I don't wake anyone. "It's ten steps away," I whisper.

He shrugs. "You never know what might happen. It's dangerous out there."

We walk the ten steps, then stop in front of my door. I fixate on his chest. It's such a nice chest, especially in this snug t-shirt and not the loose button-up from earlier today. It's also better than looking into his cocoa-colored eyes.

"Still interested in a run tomorrow?" he asks softly. "I thought we could go to Long Sands Beach."

With the way I wish I could kiss Owen right now, I need to stay away from him. But sunrise on the beach. Running. The sound of the surf. I promised myself that I would have the best holiday break. Going on a run with Owen would definitely help me reach that goal.

Besides, after this week, I won't see him often, if at all, and I want to soak up as much of his friendship as I can.

"What time?" I ask.

"Six-thirty? It's about a fifteen-minute drive."

"Okay. Good night, Owen."

"Good night, Layla."

Neither of us move. I chance a glance up, and find his focus on my lips. He seems closer than he was before. Is he leaning forward? I want to do the same and burrow into his warmth.

It takes more strength than it should to open my door and walk through.

"Layla, can I get your phone number?" he whispers. "For logistical purposes. It's easier than pounding morse code on our shared wall."

"Sure." I recite my number, and he types it into his phone.

Only then do I force myself to shut the door on that beautiful chest. I go through my bedtime routine in a daze. My brain won't stop comparing Owen and Spencer; the one I want to date and the one I need to marry. Why can't it be the same person?

I ignore the flutter of guilt I feel about what I wanted to happen outside my door. Nothing did happen. Nothing will happen.

It makes me wonder if I should invite Spencer on our

run tomorrow morning. I don't bother. He'll say no. At least I hope so, which is why I don't ask.

For the second night in a row, I can't sleep. It's Owen's fault. He's planting doubts in my resolve to marry Spencer.

I know from past experience that when my brain is buzzing, lying in bed doesn't help me fall asleep. A change of scenery for a half hour does. A trip outside to the deck to enjoy the sound of ocean waves might do the trick. This time, I dress appropriately for the weather before venturing downstairs. I go through the breakfast room doors and make sure they're unlocked before I shut myself outside. See, I'm teachable.

I walk to the railing. The light from the moon offers a view of the ocean. It's quiet but for the sound of rolling waves. I snuggle deeper into my new wool coat and tug my knitted hat further down so it covers my ears.

"Are you having trouble sleeping?"

I jump at the voice behind me. My heart beats erratically in my chest as I turn and see Rheta on one of the patio chairs, her feet propped up on a second one.

"Sorry to startle you," she says, but there is a laugh hidden in her voice. "It's a beautiful night."

Concern for her health is my first thought. "Should you be out here when you're still recovering from the flu?"

"The cold air is good for me," she says. "My husband hated the cold, but I thrive in weather like this. I come out here most nights. It helps me sleep. Would you like to sit with me for a few minutes before I turn in?"

I'm afraid I might get an inquisition about my relationship with Spencer, but feel like I can't turn her down without appearing rude. I sit on the edge of the deck chair beside her.

I wait for the questioning to start, but it doesn't happen. We listen to the waves. A plane flies overhead. The cold nips at my nose and cheeks. We might stay out here silently for hours, if only because neither of us will find the words to say goodnight. My body relaxes in the silence.

"I love York," Rheta says eventually. "Charles and I were married in Augusta, about ninety minutes from here. My parents gave us a house down the coast a few miles as a wedding gift, and I naively believed we'd live there permanently. Charles thought of York as a vacation town and never cared for the house, so he built this."

"It's beautiful."

"It's where I felt most at home during our marriage. I hate New York and the noise and busyness of the city. Charles was kind enough to give me a few Christmases here when our children were young, and of course summers, but I always wanted to stay."

With all the doubts Owen's churned up inside of me, I have to know how she and her husband got along for sixty years. From what little Spencer told me the night he proposed, their relationship is a lot like ours: one based on circumstance, not love.

"Spencer told me you hardly knew your husband before you married. Was it an arranged marriage?"

"In a sense. We only met a few times before our vows, but I was smitten the moment I met Charles. If I hadn't wanted to marry him, my father wouldn't have forced me, though it was the match he wanted."

"Were you happy?" *Will I be happy married to Spencer?* It's a question she can't answer, but if anyone could give me a glimpse into my future, it would be Rheta.

She sighs. "Yes, and no. I had everything I could want in a material sense, but Charles was a force. I was young when we married, only twenty. My father was much the same, and I'd learned never to question either of them. I didn't speak up for myself or my family like I should have. It made for a lonely life."

It's not much different from what I expected her to say, but not what I want to hear.

"I miss Charles, but now that he's gone, I'm left with regrets over all the things I should have done differently. I tell myself the past is behind me and I can't change what's been. I'm trying to do better going forward. Not an easy feat for a woman my age."

"It seems to me you're succeeding. Everyone in York knows and loves you."

A joyful smile spreads across her wrinkly cheeks. "It's lovely to feel like I have a community. Dorian wants me to move to Utah so he can monitor me, but this is where I belong."

"You have a wonderful family." I feel I have to say so, but I don't disagree with it. Just because half of them are workaholics doesn't mean they aren't wonderful.

She pats my hand. "Yes, I do. Though I worry they spend too much time at work, just like their father. The most important thing in life is family."

"Agreed."

Its obvious family is Owen's priority. He reminds me of Opa. Opa was one hundred percent involved with any zany idea Nana came up with, even the made-up German pickle tradition. His complaining about the pickle was half the fun every year. If he were alive, he would've been in Owen's room singing his heart out to *The Muppet Christmas Carol* in his German accent I miss so much.

"That is why I'm glad Spencer has you," Rheta continues. "You're an excellent influence on him. I'm thrilled you're here, and I hope you'll stay much longer than one week as part of the family."

Right.

Spencer.

NOT Owen.

I wish I could have both men smooshed into one. What a terrible thing to think, even just in my head. I fall against the chair back, accepting that I'm a horrible person and not sure what to do about it.

"Tell me about your family," Rheta says. "Are they having a big Christmas celebration?"

Rheta has been honest and open with me. I want to give her the same in return.

"No. I only have my grandma still living. She has dementia and doesn't remember me half the time. She doesn't even know it's Christmas."

Being with Rheta makes me miss Nana even more than I already do.

Her expression sobers. "I'm sorry you're going through that. Neither of your parents are still with you?"

"I never knew my dad. He left my mom when she was pregnant with me. When I was ten, my mom was diagnosed with colon cancer. She hung on for a few years, but died when I was in middle school. Grandpa died six years ago. Heart attack. I'm the only one left."

Those last few words hollow me out. I haven't thought of my situation in that way before now: *the only one left*. What's even more depressing is that once married to Spencer, I'll still be the one that's left. He'll be off doing his work, and I'll be at the house alone. Wealthy. Able to pay for Nana's care. But still alone. How did Rheta say it? *A lonely life.*

"A heart attack is how my Charles left us," Rheta said. "It's difficult to lose those we love, isn't it?"

"Yes, it is."

Rheta has a way of listening that loosens my tongue. She reminds me of Owen. The more I get to know her, the more I respect and admire her. This might be the only chance to warn her of Dorian's plans.

"Your children aren't happy with the changes you've made to your will. Ellory and Dorian want to take control of your estate."

She brushes her hand in the air. "Oh, I know. They are talented lawyers, but I was married to an exceptional lawyer for sixty years. I've picked up a few things in my time, and my lawyer is just as smart as they are." She leans her head back and looks at the moon. "I hope they don't waste their time coming after me. I invited them here for Christmas so we could be a family. I realize it isn't working out the way I hoped, but I don't want to fight over money and land. Charles' focus in life was accumulating as much as possible. Now he's gone, and it does him no good."

She sighs, long and deep. When she speaks again, her voice is soft, as if she's inviting me into a secret. "This past month when I was sick with the flu, there were days I wanted to die because I felt so horrible. It put my life in perspective. I asked myself if I had missed out on living because I tried so hard to do what was expected of me. I didn't like the answer I came to. I don't want my children or grandchildren or even great-grandchildren to wonder the same thing the last hours of their lives. I hope to teach them to find joy in living in the now. Joy isn't found in accumulating wealth."

A noble goal, but she is the one offering twenty million dollars to any grandchild who marries. I'm not sure her plan will have much of an influence on their views on money.

"They won't get on board easily," I say.

"No, you're right, but I can hope this week will change their hearts. If not, they will be sorely disappointed when I die." She puts her feet on the deck and stands. "Thank you for staying with me. Good night, Layla."

"Good night, Rheta."

She moves slowly to the end of the deck and to what I assume is the door to her bedroom. I stay a little longer before heading back inside. My conversation with Rheta has given me a few things to think about.

First, I won't be a silent bystander in my marriage to Spencer. I will compromise, but he can't expect me to follow silently while he decides what's best for both of us and our children when they come along. I don't want to regret my life either.

Second, I will build a community wherever we end up. On those nights he stays at the office to work, I won't stay home alone. I have friends and hobbies. I can lead a full life, with or without him.

Last, I love Rheta's views on money. I don't want to hoard

it. Spencer said the night he proposed that what was his will be mine when we marry. I want to help people with what we have. I will be generous and bring Spencer along with me. I'll teach him there's more to life than accumulating wealth.

My marriage might not be the one I hoped for, but I can make it a good one.

Just before I turn out the light, I catch 11:11 on the digital clock on the bedside table. The wishing minute.

I wish to make a life filled with love and joy, like Rheta has, and I don't want to wait until I'm eighty to do it.

When I finally fall asleep, it's with a smile on my face.

Chapter Thirteen

OWEN

When Layla sees my rental van, she laughs. "This is yours? I thought it was Miles'. Did you bring a band and all their equipment, then secret them in the basement or something?"

Such a ridiculous question needs no response.

I open the passenger door, and she climbs in. Climb is the appropriate word to describe what she has to do to get into the van. It's high off the ground.

She looks to the back. "You could fit all twenty-four of my Vocal Jammers into this beast."

"There are only fifteen seatbelts."

"They're middle schoolers. We'd manage."

I shut the door and walk around the front. When I get behind the wheel, there's a twinkle in Layla's eyes.

She unbuckles her seatbelt and moves between the two front bucket seats to climb into the back. "If there are any hills or speed bumps, don't slow down. I'll be judging you on how high I bounce."

In the rearview mirror, I watch her progress to the last row. "You're seriously going to leave me up here alone?"

"Of course. You're my chauffeur, so don't make me dock your pay."

"I'm getting paid?"

"In candy canes."

"Obviously."

Once she's seated and has her seatbelt buckled, I turn the ignition and pull around the fountain.

I don't take the direct route to Long Sands Beach. If Layla wants thrills, then I know exactly where to go: my favorite biking hill as a teen. I got some serious air back in the day.

It isn't a steep incline, but as we near the top, I gun it and go over the crest at sixty miles an hour. The only thing that stops Layla from hitting her head on the roof is her seatbelt. Even in the front, I get the swoopy feeling in my gut. I slow down to the recommended thirty-five miles an hour as the road flattens out.

Layla laughs so hard tears run down her cheeks. "That was awesome. Much better than I expected from the town of York. Eight out of ten."

I glare at her in the rearview mirror. "That was perfect execution. How did I not earn a perfect score?"

"I need to give you something to work toward."

Time for another detour, this time to the park. I pull into the loop that surrounds the grassy stretches and the playground.

"This isn't the beach," Layla says, looking around at the houses on all sides.

I don't bother answering, but go over the first speed bump at eighteen miles an hour. Layla once again catches air before her seatbelt brings her down.

The next speed bump is a hundred yards away. We go over ten in the next two minutes as I drive around the park. Layla's in the air more than the seat, and she can hardly breathe from laughing. It's worth wrecking the van's suspension. I'll happily pay the rental company whatever it costs to replace.

By the time we exit the park, her head is on the back of the seat and she's huffing in air.

"Okay, okay," she gasps. "Ten out of ten. I definitely recommend your chauffeur services."

"We can go around again if you're not sure."

"I'm sure. In fact, twelve out of ten. I'll tell all my friends."

"I expect to be well paid."

"Noted."

When we get to Long Sands Beach, I pull up to the curb to park. From the sidewalk, it's two steps to the sand. The beach is a mile and a half long, but it's only one hundred feet wide. This early on a winter morning, there aren't any people out.

I open the passenger sliding door for Layla. She hops out and pats her stomach.

"I feel like I've already had my workout. I don't think I've laughed that hard in a long time."

"If you're not up for a run, I can always take you back to the cabin."

"Not if you can't catch me." She runs into the sand, her arms stretched out from her sides. She doesn't make it far before she stops to take off her shoes and socks.

I come up beside her. "Do I need to remind you it's winter? You're going to catch a cold."

It's much chillier and windier on the beach than I expected. I'm regretting not taking her running through the tree lined neighborhood where houses act as wind barriers. I prefer cold weather to hot, but this is downright frigid.

"It's worth it," Layla responds. "I love running barefoot on the beach. And this way I won't get sand in my socks. Come on. Take your shoes off."

"It's winter," I reiterate.

She shrugs, her lips pursed in a way that makes me think she's trying not to laugh. "I didn't take you for a wimp."

That's a taunt I can't ignore. I toe off my shoes and socks and Layla gives a cheer and jazz hands.

The tide is coming in so we run close to the surf where the sand is hard from waves. I'm a gentleman and run between her and the water. She is not a lady and keeps nudging me closer to the surf. At times the water comes up the shore farther than I expect and gets the side of my feet. It's freezing and I can't help but yelp.

Layla laughs.

"That's not funny," I say. "It's cold."

"It can be cold and funny." She raises her arms and waves at the sky. "Besides, who says I'm laughing at you? The sun is up, and it's a beautiful morning. It's the eve of my favorite day of the year."

I could get addicted to her enthusiasm for life. It reminds me of when she plays for the residents at Brock Pine. Her love of singing and the piano is contagious, just like her joy at being alive this morning. A few icy waves will not sweep away the grin that takes up residence on my face.

When we reach the end of the beach where the sand gives way to rock, we turn and head back the way we came. I move once again closer to the water, as if it's a road and I'm a barrier between her and oncoming traffic. She speeds up to pass me and swaps me places.

Fine by me. Brady said that a gentleman listens to a lady. My toes are frozen anyway.

At the last half-mile, she runs purposefully through the surf until the hem of her running pants are wet. She doesn't care about the cold which makes me feel like a pansy for complaining earlier.

As we near our starting point, Layla reaches over and tickles my side. She gets me at my most ticklish spot and it's enough of a shock to knock me off balance as I try to escape. I stumble forward, catch myself for a second, only to land wrong and fall to my side just a wave comes, getting me wet up to my waist. I squeal. Yes, squeal. Not a good moment for me.

Layla runs backward as she moves farther down the beach, laughing. This time, her laughter is definitely directed at me.

It doesn't take me long to catch up, and when Layla understands my intent, she faces forward and picks up speed. My legs are longer, and I pass her. I sweep my leg into the coming wave and splash her with ocean water.

She shrieks, but apparently she isn't one to back down from a fight. She kicks water at me, but stumbles. I catch her with a hand before she tumbles into the ocean. Instead of thanking me for the save, she leverages against me to jump with both feet, splashing water up to my chest.

"You did not just do that." It comes out weak because I'm shivering.

The only response I get is more laughter. I've been holding back, but no longer. I hoist her over my shoulder in a fireman's carry and step deeper into the ocean. It takes only a second for her to figure out my plan.

"I'm sorry!" she screams. "I'm sorry! I'll stop. Don't drop me!"

I gasp as the next wave hits above my knees. "You'll stop what?"

"Laughing at you." She's still laughing, so I know that isn't a realistic promise.

"Nope."

I take another step. She pounds my back with her fists and kicks her legs, but not hard enough to mean business.

"I won't splash you with water anymore!" she squawks.

"Promise?"

"Yes!"

I lean over the smallest bit, and her body slips an inch. Her hands grab onto the back of my jacket. She screams while still laughing. I think I've scared her enough and walk out of the water. I don't put her down until we reach our shoes and the water is too far away for her to splash me.

I place her feet on the ground. When I stand straight, we're less than a foot apart. Her laughter quiets as her eyes meet mine. She doesn't move back. In fact, she steps an inch closer and lays a hand flat against my chest. Heat suffuses through my body at her touch. Her hand rises and falls with each breath I drag through my lungs.

The connection I feel with Layla snaps taut, like it did last night in the hallway. I like her–no, "like" is a weak word. I absolutely, completely adore her. Not kissing her is torture. I don't know how it's possible, but not touching her today is even harder than it was yesterday. I want to wrap my arms around her waist. Kiss her temples, his cheeks, her neck. Her lips.

What I can't resist doing is lifting my hand and running my thumb along her cheekbone. Her skin is soft. She closes her eyes and leans into my touch, her breathing just as ragged as mine, and that isn't because we ran three miles. It's our closeness. Mere inches separate our bodies.

We belong together. Spencer cannot be part of her story. He would never put up with her splashing him with salty, cold ocean water. Watching a musical is a waste of time in his book. He barely carved out twenty minutes last night to sing a few carols while she played.

Like a news ticker on the bottom of a TV screen, questions cycle through my brain.

Do you laugh with Spencer like you do with me? Does he crave your company like I do? Does he understand what a treasure you are? Will you break up with him so I can date you?

I manage not to voice the questions out loud. It might make her move away from me, and I like the feel of her hand on my chest and the way she stands close enough for me to catch her lavender scent. I remain as still as possible.

Maybe Layla sees the questions in my head reflected in my eyes, because she steps away, her hand falling from my chest.

She picks up her shoes and runs toward the van without a word.

I stay where I am to recover my equilibrium. Difficult after what happened. It's the closest we've ever stood, and I can't blame my shivering completely on the cold. I've never had this physical response from only touching a woman's cheek. But this is Layla; she isn't just any woman.

I look out over the ocean. I've always loved visiting this beach. Spencer and I rode our bikes here almost every day that first summer I stayed. I miss the friendship we once shared, but we're not teenagers anymore. I don't respect the choices he's made, and he definitely doesn't respect mine.

If Layla marries Spencer like he plans, they'll both be miserable. Spencer will come to resent Layla for the drain on his time. She'll lose the spark of joy that is innately part of who she is.

I won't let that happen. I can't.

I'm going to romance her away from my cousin.

The moment I decide to pursue Layla is the moment I declare war on Spencer. Maybe it's the wrong decision and I should let things stay as they are, but if the right thing to do is to watch Layla lose her joy, then I'd rather not do the right thing.

Operation-Persuade-Layla-She's-Making-a-Huge-Mistake has begun.

That's a long title.

Title in progress, but the mission starts now.

Chapter Fourteen

OWEN

After breakfast, I go up to my room to grab my wallet. Hanging from the doorknob is a small paper Neiman Marcus bag. Inside? A dozen candy canes. My payment for entertaining Layla on our van ride this morning.

I'm still grinning fifteen minutes later as Brady and I grab our coats from the coat closet for our trip to the tree farm.

Sadie runs down the stairs and launches herself into my arms. I just manage to catch her. Her arms clamp around my neck, and she gives my ear a slobbery kiss.

I find myself missing Greta.

"Cousin O, Mommy says I get to pick my own Christmas tree for my room!"

"That's exciting." I glance over her shoulder and watch Tori descend the stairs. Her eyes are puffy and red rimmed. It's probably something to do with her divorce. Most days, I want to throttle her ex.

"Will you help me pick my tree?" Sadie asks. "It has to be this big!" She stretches her arms as far above her head as they'll go.

"I think we'll find you the perfect one." I tickle her belly, and she squirms as she laughs.

I reach out and tug Brady closer, then with one hand shut the book he holds. He scowls, but I ignore his annoyance.

"Sadie, do you remember meeting my brother Brady at breakfast?"

She nods like a bobblehead. "Our names rhyme!"

"Exactly," I say. "He's going to be your buddy today at the Christmas tree farm. Did you know his superpower is picking the perfect tree? That's why he's coming with us; otherwise, we'd leave him home."

Brady isn't happy when I foist Sadie into his arms, but he doesn't drop her, so that's encouraging. I'm sure this is the first four-year-old he's ever met.

"Cousin BB, I want a superpower like you," she tells him. "What can it be?"

Brady scrunches his face and looks over for help. I shrug and move toward Tori. He sticks his tongue out at me.

"Um, you're cute?" he says to Sadie.

"That's not a superpower, silly! I'm a girl! All girls are cute!"

When I reach Tori, I ask softly, "What happened?"

She flips her sunglasses over her eyes even though we're still inside. "My ex started dating a good friend of mine. I can believe he'd do this, but why is she?"

"Tell me where to bury the bodies."

That gets a small twitch of her lips. "I'd like to stay in bed and pretend the world doesn't exist."

I pull her into a tight embrace. "I'm proud of you for coming today."

"Sadie wouldn't miss this trip, though it crossed my mind to stay and send Sadie to the farm with you." An enormous sigh. "But I'm an excellent mother—no matter what Matthew implies in custody court."

"You're the best mother."

She pulls back and wipes under her eyes. "You're dang right."

Years ago, she would not have said "dang." She hasn't sworn since Sadie was born. Her ex never made similar concessions.

Grandmother comes up beside us.

"Owen, there are eight of us going to Trolley Farms today," she tells me. "Instead of taking two vehicles, would you drive your van?"

Even with sunglasses on, Tori's eyes visibly widen. "*You* brought the *van* parked out front? Are you married with eight kids and didn't tell me?"

I elbow her gently. "You should be flattered. I named the van after you. The Chevrolet Tori."

"You could have at least gotten a Mercedes-Benz if you were going to bestow my name on the thing. Ecclestons should refuse a Chevrolet on principle alone."

Which is why I don't consider myself an Eccleston. "I was more concerned at the time about not spending the night in the airport."

She smirks. "They have hotels nearby."

Ten minutes later, I'm behind the wheel with Grandmother in the passenger seat. Mom and Miles sit in the middle seat having a conversation that puts huge smiles on both of their faces. Brady's in the seat behind them with his book.

In the very back, Layla, Tori, and Sadie sit. Getting Sadie's booster seat back there wasn't easy, but it was worth it to hear her giggle as I go over bumps at a speed higher than the recommended limit. Even Tori is smiling as she bounces around.

Trolley farms is thirty minutes away. As we exit York, Grandmother asks, "Tell me about this landscaping you do. Are you enjoying it?"

Only now do I realize I've made a fatal error.

I'm trapped up front with Grandmother and no escape. No one is nearby to act as a buffer. She can ask me anything she wants, and I have to answer. Anything less than absolute truth feels dishonest, and I can't lie to my grandmother.

"Grandmother, landscaping is not all that exciting."

"Call me Granny. I've never liked how formal grandmother sounds."

"*Granny?*" I can't contain my shock. I have never thought of my grandmother as a granny. She's far too imposing. Or at least, she was when I was a teenager. The last few days I've seen a softer side. Still, *granny?* "I can't call you that."

"Why not?"

Because she does not look like a nice, comforting granny. She looks like the queen of England.

"Well, um, okay. *Granny.*" The shape of the word feels wrong in my mouth.

Granny laughs and that makes me smile. Yeah, the nickname will not work for either of us.

"Do you remember the first summer you stayed with us?" she asks. "You had a hard time falling asleep."

I think back, but it doesn't sound familiar. "No."

"You and I watched old episodes of *Murder She Wrote* together until you couldn't keep your eyes open."

Now that she mentions *Murder She Wrote*, I do remember. Over the years, the memories had faded until it felt like a dream, but now it comes back in a flash. That first year, I was homesick. If I stayed in bed I cried, so I began exploring the house while everyone else was asleep.

One night she caught me in the kitchen eating pie at midnight. I was sure I would be punished. She was imposing and ... old. Instead, she cut herself a slice and joined me. We talked about my family and school, then went up to her room where we watched Angela Lansbury solve mysteries. I was vocal about how stupid I found the show. Grandmother offered to watch something else, but I could tell she was enjoying herself, so I declined. I fell asleep in her room, but woke up in my own.

It became our tradition a few nights a week to eat dessert while watching *Murder She Wrote*. How could I have forgotten? It was one of my favorite things about that summer.

"I remember," I say.

"The second summer I went down to the kitchen every night for weeks, but you never met me there. You had better things to do with your time, which I completely understood. Charles was an exacting taskmaster, but you were up to the challenge. I know the boy Owen, but I would like to know the man you've become."

I have never felt so awful. That second summer, I thought about meeting up with Grandmother, but I knew if Grandfather found out I was wasting time watching murder mysteries he'd be disappointed. I didn't think she cared. At least, she said nothing. But even at such a young age, I understood Grandmother was different at night, just the two of us, than during the day. I should have sought her out.

As I look back on the time I spent in Maine as a teenager, I realize for the first time Grandmother was lonely. It makes me reevaluate my thoughts about her. I escaped Grandfather eight years ago, but she never did. I've been lumping her in with the rest of the family, but that hasn't been fair to either of us.

"I'm sorry I didn't find you that second summer."

She waves the apology away. "I didn't bring it up to make you feel bad. I wanted to remind you we were friends at one time. I'd like to be friends again."

Why not tell her about my life? What am I trying to hide? I've told none of the Ecclestons about the first company I co-founded because it's a lot easier to deal with their disappointment than their expectations. Remembering that first summer, I know Grandmother would accept whatever I tell her without judgment. Unfortunately, much like Grandfather overlooked her, so did I.

"I don't actually work as a landscaper," I admit. "I bought a landscaping business. Sometimes I help mow lawns or weed flower beds, but it's hard work and it's hot. During the winter, we shovel snow and put-up Christmas lights. That's more my jam."

She claps her hands together once. "How delightful. When did you decide running a business was what you wanted to do?"

While I drive, I talk about how my favorite courses in college were my business classes. For a group project, my friend and I mocked up a fake manufacturing business. When I quit Grandfather's firm, I called him and asked if he wanted to try it for real. I used the contacts I'd created through my brief stint as a lawyer and found investors. Our success was sudden, but well-earned. We worked hard to get our company where it is today.

I don't go into detail with Grandmother, but I explain that when I realized how our success was stealing all my time, I wanted out. I missed my mom and brother. I missed my friends. I missed living. So, I sold my half and got into landscaping instead.

"I have a lot more time since I mostly manage the crew's schedules. I'm able to visit Mom and Brady every other week in Elko."

Her expression glows with pride.

If I hadn't been wearing my anger at the family like a shield, could I have had this conversation with her years ago?

Grandmother surprises me by asking, "What do you know about Layla?"

I glance in the rearview mirror and see Layla and Tori talking. It's good to see my cousin smiling when thirty minutes ago she had tears in her eyes. And it's always good to see Layla.

"Why do you ask?"

"I think she's a marvelous influence on Spencer, but it's

obvious they don't love each other." She shakes her head, as if she's confused. "Do you think she's taking advantage of him for his money?"

A flash of irritation spikes through me. I speak calmly, but I am annoyed. "You're bribing your grandkids to get married. Did you expect any other outcome?"

Grandmother's mouth drops open. "I'm not bribing anyone. I'm giving a larger inheritance to those who have more familial obligations. You made it very clear that you're not interested in any inheritance, but not everyone in this family is as ... independent as you are."

I can't expect her to understand my point of view when she grew up with even more wealth than Grandfather. She's always lived in luxury. I'm grateful I did not, though my teenage self would be shocked to know it.

"I did a background check on Layla," Grandmother continues. "She has a large personal loan and outstanding credit card debt. She owes over one hundred thousand dollars and only makes fifty thousand a year. That's very irresponsible."

Layla owes that much? I glance at her in the rearview mirror again. She's smiling as she talks to Tori. My heart goes out to her. I'd guess she accrued most of the debt, if not all, for her grandma. I can't even imagine how much stress she feels in this situation. If only I was the one she would rely on for help. I would give her the money and not make her marry me to get it.

"In answer to your original question," I say, after taking a steadying breath, "Layla is not taking advantage of Spencer. Spencer is taking advantage of Layla's situation in order to get the bigger inheritance."

"What do you mean? What situation?"

"Her grandma has dementia. Layla has no family to help pay for her grandma's care. The debt isn't from buying things for herself. It's from making sure her grandma has a roof over her head."

"She told me about her grandmother." Grandmother looks out of the window thoughtfully. "Layla has very expensive clothing. And the Boudron. Are you sure?"

Even Grandmother knows about Boudron bags? They're more well-known than I thought.

"I'm sure," I say with conviction.

It's why Operation-Persuade-Layla-Spencer-Will-Not-Make-Her-Happy is so important. She's trading financial security now for misery later on.

"That is helpful information to have. Thank you for telling me."

After parking at Trolley Farms, Grandmother leans across the gap between the seats and pats my arm. "It seems you've made yourself a beautiful life. I'm proud of you."

Miles opens the passenger door and helps her down. He already has the wheelchair waiting. I stay where I am and allow her approval to wash over me. It's something I didn't know I needed. Subconsciously, I've been waiting for someone in my mom's family to trust me to make wise decisions and accept me for who I am, not who they wish I could be. The knot of anger in my chest loosens further.

When I look up, the van is empty but for Brady. "Are you coming or are you staying here to sulk?"

"I'm not sulking."

Brady shakes his head then jumps to the ground. I exit the vehicle and lock the doors.

Not far from the parking lot is a hay wagon that will take us to the barn further on. There are pre-cut trees available, but for a little higher cost, there's an option of hiking through their tree farm to cut down your own. I know this because I did research on the place before breakfast. All part of Operation-Romance-Layla-Away-From-the-Idiot.

Sadie takes Brady's hand and leads him toward the waiting hay wagon. Brady glances at me as if to ask for help, but Sadie will be a good influence on him. He needs experience with people outside of books and Dungeons and Dragons.

I turn to ask Layla how she enjoyed the ride in the back of the van and if I'll get paid in candy canes again, but after our charged moment on the beach, she has been intent on not looking in my general direction.

She and Tori talk as they follow Brady and Sadie. I follow behind and listen in on their conversation.

"I've never been to a Christmas tree farm before," Layla says. "My grandparents bought trees from the guys who sell on city corners."

Tori sighs. "I have never been to any kind of farm. It's not my aesthetic."

Layla laughs. "No, definitely not. But that doesn't mean it can't be fun."

Though I can't see it, I know Tori rolls her eyes. "Fun? We're heading toward a horse-drawn carriage filled with hay that I'm supposed to sit on to get to a barn. I can smell the horse poop from here. All I can say is I better not step in any of it. These boots are Jimmy Choo."

"It's called a wagon," Layla whispers. "Not a carriage."

Her correction is met with another eyeroll, this time

accompanied by a laugh. "See? Proof that this is not where I belong."

A friendship forming between them is not what I expected, but I think they both need a friend right now and I'm glad.

It's not as cold today as it has been, and I unbutton my coat and remove my gloves. It's perfect weather for what I have planned for Layla. I check my watch. We have forty minutes until it begins.

"I love this smell." Layla holds her arms out as if hugging the world. "Tori, don't you just love the scent of pine? I want a candle that smells exactly like this."

"I prefer to keep the smells of nature outside, where they belong."

Layla laughs. Tori glances over her shoulder at me and cracks a smile.

I love the scent of pine, too. It reminds me of tree hunting with Dad. He loved finding the perfect tree. After he died, Mom stopped buying real trees and stuck with a fake. I haven't been on a tree lot since. Nostalgia is a powerful, heady feeling. This visit is bittersweet.

Brady slows until the three of us catch up to him. "When our dad was alive, we cut down trees ourself. Do you remember, Owen?"

"Yeah, I do. I'm surprised you do. You were young."

"Not that young."

Sadie, who has been staring at the horses as we approached the wagon, tugs on her mom's arm. "Mommy, I want a horse! Can I have a horse for Christmas?"

"Absolutely not."

The quick response does not deflate Sadie's enthusiasm in the least. "I'll name him BB after my favorite cousin!"

Cousin BB blushes. I don't even mind my demotion.

Layla takes her buzzing phone out of her coat pocket. "I'll catch up. I need to take this call." She looks at me for the first time since this morning. "It's Brock Pine Home."

My thoughts instantly go to her grandma escaping yesterday. Did it happen again? Layla looks braced for bad news as she answers.

She walks to the left of the path as everyone else continues to the wagon. I wait for her, not trying to overhear her conversation, but I don't try not to either.

As she listens, her whole body droops.

"I sent the payment on Saturday night. ... Oh. Denied. How much do I still owe? ... That much. Okay. Can I get it to you on Monday? ... Yeah, I'll have money on Saturday, but with the banks being closed, the soonest I can get it to you is next Monday. ... Thank you. I appreciate your understanding."

Money for her grandmother. Can't she talk to Spencer today? Why does she have to wait until Saturday?

I want to hand her my credit card. I want to take care of this for her. What stops me is knowing that she won't accept and a fear that I'll embarrass her by calling attention to her financial situation again. If I manage a successful mission to romance Layla away from Spencer, she might let me help her. That's the hope.

Layla puts her phone back in her pocket and meets me on the path. We catch up to the others who are already in the wagon. Sadie's complaining about the scratchy hay, and Brady pulls her onto his lap.

At the back of the wagon are removable steps up into the bed. I hold my hand out to Layla. She won't look at me, but she takes my offered help. Even with her gloves on, her touch is like a branding iron, and I wouldn't be surprised if her fingers leave a permanent mark.

Unfortunately, she sits between Tori and the end of the wagon bed where there's not enough space for me to squeeze in beside her. I'm forced to sit next to Brady on the opposite side.

Grandmother doesn't take the wagon. It's probably too bumpy for her. She's on a golf cart up ahead, with Miles on the back holding on to her folded wheelchair. Mom sits next to him, both of them in deep conversation.

Brady leans closer and asks, "Do you think Mom likes Miles?"

I shrug. "They're probably just friends catching up. They knew each other when they were teenagers."

We watch as the golf cart jerks forward and Mom grabs onto Miles' arm with both hands for balance. Even after the cart moves smoothly, she doesn't let go.

"Or," I say slowly, not sure how I feel about their closeness. "Maybe it's more than friends."

Brady shrugs. "We'll be home in a few days. It can't go anywhere."

My attention veers to Layla. I disagree. A few days can change a lot.

Brady's thoughts follow my own, because he points his chin in Layla's direction. "What about you and her?"

Layla thankfully doesn't notice Brady's attention or hear his question. She's too busy talking to Tori.

"Nothing," I whisper.

"You stare at her all the time. She has a boyfriend, you know."

Hopefully not for long. "We're friends."

Brady snorts. "Sure. Friends."

"I like Lady," Sadie pipes up, reminding me she's listening to every word we say.

"Who's Lady?" I ask. "The horse?"

Sadie points to Layla. "Lady. She's nice."

Oh no. I wonder what tales Sadie will be spreading. I glare at Brady for bringing up the topic.

He smirks. "You're just friends. What are you worried about?"

When the wagon is full, the driver cracks the reins, and we lurch forward. The ruts in the road jostle us around like apples in a bag. It's a relief when we finally arrive and my feet are on solid ground again.

Children run around on the playground equipment to the side of the building, bundled up like Jet Puff marshmallow men in their snowsuits. Sadie pulls Brady toward the other kids, and he goes willingly, his book under his arm.

Layla turns in a circle, taking it all in. "I know this place."

"You've been here before?" Tori asks, one eyebrow raised as she looks around. She is not impressed. "Voluntarily?"

"No, but I definitely recognize that barn. They've filmed a few Christmas movies here." She laughs and points to the corner of the barn. "Right there is where Yolanda and Nathan kissed in *A Holly Jolly Christmas Tree Jamboree.*"

Besides the movie title being ridiculous, I love how she recognizes the movies being filmed here. I planned the perfect adventure to take her on today.

"Oh, wow." Layla points at the cut trees to the right. "I'm positive out that direction is where Harrison proposed to Caroline in *Christmas Carol Hoedown*." She claps and jumps a few times. "Meg is going to flip! It was one of her favorite movies a few years ago."

"I am not familiar with any of those movies," Tori tells her. "They sound fake."

My thoughts exactly.

"They're not fake," Layla says, pretending like she's insulted. "They're made-for-TV Christmas movies."

Tori rolls her eyes. "That explains everything. Who is Meg? Has she been admitted for observation to a psych ward?"

Layla laughs as she backhands Tori's arm playfully. "She's my best friend and a Hallmark Christmas movie junkie who will be green with envy when I tell her where I am."

Just as she did yesterday with the Christmas trees, Layla pulls out her phone and takes dozens of pictures, including a few selfies with her eyes wide and mouth open in shock as she points to different spots. She pulls Tori into a few, and Tori gives her signature fishy lips look, with a slight profile since she insists her left side is more photogenic.

"Will you send those to me?" she asks Layla. "My Insta followers will never believe I'm at a barn with actual horses."

After sending Tori the photos and taking a few more of the scenery, Layla types into her phone, but then abruptly stops. Her smile fades as she puts her phone back into her coat pocket.

"What's wrong?" I ask. "Did Meg not like the pictures?"

She shakes her head. "I didn't send them. She's with her family this week. I'll wait until I get home and tell her in person."

Is Meg's family what stole her joy?

When she moves into the barn, Tori and I follow. Tori doesn't notice Layla's somber mood. She nudges me with her elbow.

"I already have fifty likes. Someone thinks the photos are fake. Ha ha!"

Inside the barn is a country store and a small cafe that sells cocoa, coffee, and donuts. One full wall is filled with homemade wreaths and garlands. Grandmother directs Miles to take her in that direction, and waves for Layla and Tori to follow.

"I need your advice," she says to them. "We have the whole of the main floor to decorate. We need enough garlands to go up the stair banister. A wreath on every door. What else should we purchase?"

Layla's expression lifts as she talks with Grandmother about what to buy and how much. Tori raves about the wreaths and picks out her favorites. Mom and Miles grab coffee. Sadie runs in with Brady following, both of them breathless.

I watch them, surprised at what I come to realize: We're a happy family. There have been hints of it earlier this week, but now it's a fact. I've always felt torn between my mom's family and my family. There was conflict between the two, with me in the middle. When I quit the law firm, I thought they were out of my life forever, except for Tori. Now I see I can have both. Grandmother showed me it was possible in the van earlier; this is more proof.

There must be something in the barn I'm allergic to because my eyes water. Time to find my tour guide and grab Layla for our adventure. I'm even more committed to Operation-Show-Layla-How-Much-I-Care because the only thing I'm missing right now is my own family. As I watch her fawn over pink tree ornaments, I have no doubt she's the one I want to start one with.

Chapter Fifteen

LAYLA

The sales people love Rheta. She's almost bought out the entire store of decorations and greenery. The total cost will be staggering, and I leave before her purchases are rung up. After receiving the call from Brock Pine Home about one of my credit cards being denied, I can't handle how this family throws around money like it's inconsequential.

The colorful glass balls hand blown by local artisans draw my eye, but with the smaller ones costing twenty dollars apiece, I don't let myself linger for long.

I make my way toward the coffee counter before I remember that's a bad idea. I don't have money for coffee, and the smell tempts me to make a poor choice.

Owen comes up beside me. "Did you find some fun things to decorate the cabin?"

"Yes."

I glance up into his brown cocoa eyes, and for one

second, I wish things could be different. That invasive desire gets squashed immediately. Things aren't different, and it's a waste of energy imagining that they could be.

"I did a little research on this place before we came." He looks around, giving me a break from his penetrating gaze. "They've had eight Christmas movies filmed here over the past five years."

This is a nice, neutral conversation topic. "Wow, eight. Do they have a list on their website?" I pull out my phone, wondering if I've seen any of the other six. "Meg will be beyond jealous."

"They actually have a tour around the property where they show the different filming locations. Do you want to go?" He points to a man near the entrance with a clipboard. The man glances at his wristwatch, then looks back at us. "If so, it starts now."

A tour of filming sights? Meg would never forgive me if I turned down the opportunity. Except no one else has gathered. Will it just be me and Owen? Definitely not a good idea. We may be friends, but being alone with him will make it that much more difficult for my head to remember friendly boundaries.

"Let me ask Tori if she's interested."

Safety in numbers and all that.

"Actually—"

I don't wait to hear how he'll continue that sentence. I speed walk to Tori. She's negotiating with Sadie over what ornaments to purchase for the tree going in their bedroom.

It's strange how our conversation about fashion on the drive over smoothed out any issues she had with me when we first met. Fashion as art is one thing we can agree on.

How much fashion should cost is not. She comes across as a rich snob on first acquaintance, but she's actually quite fun to talk to.

"Tori, do you and Sadie want to go on a tour of the farm with me and Owen?"

She points to her boots. "Jimmy Choo."

That's all the answer I need. Everyone else in our group is otherwise occupied ... except for Brady, who has found a quiet corner to read. I head over and stop in front of his chair.

"Brady, do you want to come on a tour of the farm with me and Owen?"

He shrugs. "Sure." But after he stands, something over my shoulder catches his attention.

I follow his gaze to Owen. Owen quickly stuffs his hands in his coat pockets, turns his head away from us, and whistles.

"Actually," Brady says. "I'm at an exciting part in my book. Sorry." He sits down and goes back to reading.

I meet Owen in the middle of the barn. "What did you signal to Brady?"

"Nothing." He looks too innocent for me to believe him. For whatever reason, he doesn't want his brother to come with us. "Ready for the tour?"

I want to go. Owen keeps inviting me to fun activities, and I can't ever say no. It's a problem. One I'll worry about later.

"Yes, I'm ready," I say.

We meet the tour guide at the barn exit. As I feared, it's just me and Owen.

"Hi," our guide says to us. "Welcome to Trolley Farms!

I'm Max, and I'll be taking you around the farm today. I took some notes, but since you're the first two who have ever asked for a tour, I'm going to wing it. Let me know how I do."

I glance over at Owen. His cheeks have the lightest blush.

"You don't do tours regularly?" I ask Max.

"No. We've honestly never thought of it until he," Max points to Owen, "called and asked for one. If you enjoy it, maybe I'll schedule a few for next year."

Owen's cheeks turn a brighter red.

I give him the side eye. "Interesting."

I may appear annoyed, but in fact, I'm flattered that Owen asked for a tour for me. I can't think of the last time any man has gone to this much trouble for a date. Er ... since this isn't a date and just two friends hanging out, I've never had a *guy friend* put in any effort. My chest grows warm at his thoughtfulness.

"If you'll follow me," Max says. "We'll start at the spot where *Christmas Seasonings* filmed the scene where they went mushroom hunting. There aren't real mushrooms, but I hid a fake one and whoever finds it wins any one ornament from our shop."

A fake mushroom hunt! With a Christmas ornament as a prize. When I win, I will pick the largest glass ornament in their shop. I'll knit a special cozy so it doesn't break on the flight home.

We walk along a path toward a forest of pine trees.

"You better not let me win," I tell Owen. "I want real competition."

"I would never."

I don't believe him, and I glare to show him how much I mean what I said.

He holds up his hand in surrender. "Okay. Real competition." He steps closer, narrows his eyes, and hardens his lips "There is no way you're finding that mushroom. My eyesight is twenty-twenty with contacts. I am winning the prize, so don't think I won't."

Owen talking smack is a beautiful thing. I giggle.

"Thank you." I have to ask, "How did you know I like Christmas movies?"

"Something you said when we were getting fries last week about how you only watch Christmas movies with your roommates during the month of December. When I saw on their website how many movies they filmed here, I thought a tour would be fun."

"So much fun." I reach out and squeeze his upper arm. Mistake. There is some serious muscle in that biceps, even with his coat. My fingers linger longer than is appropriate before I drop my hand and hide it in my pocket. "I love this. Thank you."

His blush deepens. It's charming, just like him.

"You're welcome."

OUR LAST STOP ON THE TOUR IS A DIRT-PACKED CLEARING. THE second I enter, I know where we are. "This is the scene of the party in *Christmas Carol Hoedown*."

Max's grin expands. He doesn't seem to mind that I stole his line. I've been doing that a lot over the past hour, and each time he gets more enthusiastic.

"Right! I was a town member extra in that scene, so I learned the folk dance. I'm going to teach it to you now."

"No way! How fun." I glance at Owen. "I can teach it to my roommates next time we have a movie night."

"No way." His response is much less enthusiastic. "I think I'll sit this one out. I have two left feet."

I nudge him with my elbow. "You must have a hard time finding shoes that fit."

"Ha ha."

I clasped my hands together under my chin. "Please dance with me?"

His expression turns serious. "For you, anything."

My stomach flutters at the way he looks at me so earnestly. As if he would do anything I asked him to do.

He takes a step back and gets in what I can only assume is his dancing pose: legs apart, his arms akimbo. "I'm warning you, this will not be a pretty sight."

It's already a little frightening, though definitely entertaining. The fluttering in my stomach settles as I laugh.

After watching our interlude, Max turns his back to us. "I'll do it for you once, and then we'll take it slow together a few steps at a time."

From his phone Max starts the same song they had the band play in the movie. It's one written specifically for the show and has a simple, catchy rhythm. The lyrics, however, could use some work.

Max calls out each step as he goes. "To the left, hop, step, close step to the left. Now to the right. Hop, step, close step. Take mincing steps in a circle. Step, hop, step hop, step, hop."

It's easy enough, and I join in after watching for a minute.

"Show off," Owen mutters, but he's smiling.

Max stops the music. "Then it repeats from there. Ready to begin?"

He is a very patient teacher, which comes in handy because Owen can't dance. I wouldn't say he has two left feet, more that he has no rhythm and no memory of what order the steps go in.

Instead of getting annoyed or embarrassed, Owen keeps trying. He laughs each time he goes in the wrong direction. He applauds when I get the steps in the correct order. I love how he can have fun at something he does terribly.

"Go right. Your other right, Owen," Max says. "Owen, mincing steps means to step with your toes, not your heels. *Toes.* Do you know what your toes are? It's a hop, not a jump."

It's hard for me to keep up with Max when I can't breathe because I'm laughing so hard at my dance partner. My stomach aches.

Max studies Owen for a moment. "I think that's the best we can hope for. Ready to add the music?"

"Absolutely!" Owen says with enthusiasm.

Max starts the music from the beginning but doesn't join in. Instead, he records us on his phone. Owen is all over the place with his moves, a few steps behind because he's following me. Or at least trying to. Soon I'm off rhythm from laughing. When Max realizes we're a lost cause, he stops recording and throws up his hands, but he's smiling.

"That was dreadful," Max tells us. "But entertaining to watch."

"Will you send me that video?" I ask him. I give him my number.

"Please don't," Owen says. "Can you delete it instead?"

"Layla?"

I turn at the sound of my name.

Spencer stands ten feet away on the edge of the clearing. His long wool coat is open, showing his blue suit underneath. He wears his distinctive Berluti Oxford shoes. Everything about him looks out of place in the middle of a wooded area, but none more so than his expression: one of frustration mixed with anger.

The music stops behind me, and the only sound comes from the birds in the trees.

I wipe sweaty palms along the sides of my coat. "Spencer. You're here."

"What are you doing with Owen?"

Standing here like an idiot. I take a few steps and throw myself in his arms, mostly because that seems like what a girlfriend should do when her boyfriend shows up as a surprise and catches her having fun with another man.

I pull back and loop my arm through his. "We were learning a dance from a Christmas movie. This is Max."

Max shoots Owen a look, then me a look, as if he assumed we were a couple. An honest mistake, but one Spencer picks up on. He stiffens beside me.

"Do you want to learn the *Christmas Carol Hoedown* hoedown?" Max asks him. "It's easy unless your name starts with an O and ends with -wen." His whole body shakes with suppressed laughter. "Layla, however, is a natural."

"No, thank you." Spencer's tone is dismissive and my chest burns with embarrassment. He speaks to me only as he continues. "I'm waiting for information to get sent from the Salt Lake office and thought I'd spend a few hours with my *girlfriend*."

If this clearing wasn't saturated with awkwardness before, it is now. Worse than Spencer marking his "territory" is the way he's treating Max.

"That's so nice of you to come, Spencer." He will not cow me and I take a steadying breath before I continue. "You'll love it here. Max took me and Owen on a tour of the farm. He was telling us how every year the farm donates fifty trees to Sub For Santa. Isn't that amazing? We can get involved next year by buying trees and then donating them. It sounds fun, don't you agree? We should talk to Max about it before we leave today."

Spencer looks from me, to Owen, to Max, then back at me. He studies my face, and I hope he catches that I'm irritated with his behavior.

He must, because he holds out his free hand to Max. "It's nice to meet you, Max. We'll be in contact next year to see if we can work something out."

"That would be great," Max responds.

Spencer and I turn to head back to the barn. I stop and look over my shoulder.

"Thanks for the tour, Max," I say. "If you do set tours up next year, I will write a stellar review. You're an amazing guide."

"Thanks, Layla."

As we walk away, disappointment settles in my chest. I don't want to leave Max and Owen behind. I'm a horrible girlfriend. I can be better, and I'll start by asking Spencer about work.

"How is the trial prep going?"

He nods and a tentative smile breaks through his dark mood. "Gerald found a loophole in the investigation of our client. We're back on top. We still have a lot of work to do, but I'm not so frantic."

"I'm glad." Not for his client because he probably did whatever he's been accused of, but for Spencer because he works so hard to win.

Owen and Max's footsteps sound behind us. To fill the silence, I tell Spencer about the different filming locations on our tour. Besides finding the mushroom, my favorite stop was for *Stupid Cupid Christmas*. Since there isn't any snow, we "sled" down the hill on ice blocks. No matter how many times Owen and I raced, he always reached the bottom first. Even when I had a head start, his quarterback physique always passed me up.

I ramble on until we reconnect with the rest of our group in the lot of pre-cut trees. They've picked four, but still haven't decided on the last two and Sadie's small tree for her room. Sadie goes from tree to tree, trying to hug them all and getting a face full of pine needles for her troubles. It doesn't stop her from loving every single one.

Celebrating Christmas with a child is a different experience than celebrating with only adults. Everything is magical to Sadie, as if she's never encountered anything so wondrous. With this being only her fourth Christmas, maybe she hasn't.

After Brady convinces her to choose a tree, Tori shows me the bag of ornaments Sadie picked. Twenty painted animal figurines carved from local wood.

"I tried to talk her into something sparkly, but she is one stubborn girl. If she didn't resemble me, I would swear someone swapped her at birth."

When the last tree is purchased, they're all taken to a

machine where each tree is shaken before being wrapped in plastic for easy transportation.

"What are you doing to my tree?" Sadie asks the man when the machine stops. Her hands are on her hips and her expression is fierce.

"I'm unhoming the spiders who took up residence," the guy says.

Sadie scrunches up her face. "Huh?"

The employee smiles and bends down closer. "Sometimes when trees sit on our lot, spiders move in. Shaking the tree forces them to leave."

She bursts into tears.

Tori gets down on her level, one knee on the dirt packed ground. She doesn't seem to notice the dust accumulating on her Burberry jeans. "What's wrong, baby?"

"I want to take the spiders home with me!"

Tori picks up her daughter and lets her cry on her shoulder. She whispers to me, "She wants *spiders* as pets. Where did this child come from?"

Rheta schedules a delivery for the trees and greenery later that night, but has everything else packed onto two bench seats in the van, including Sadie's mini tree, so she can decorate it when she gets home.

I go to climb in, but Spencer grabs my hand. "I thought you would drive back with me."

He points to his rental car parked close by. I look back at the van and everyone laughing and talking as they get inside. I don't want to give up the camaraderie I've felt today with the rest of his family, and it would probably do him good to socialize with them.

"It's fun in the family van," I say. "Come with me? We can get someone to come pick up your car later today."

What's the purpose of having so much money if we can't be selfish once in a while?

He studies my hopeful face for only a few seconds before he nods. "Alright. Let's ride in a van."

It's a tight squeeze on the back row with four of us, which means I snuggle close to Spencer. In order to make room for our shoulders, he lays his arm along the back of the seat. I catch Owen's glance in the rearview mirror. His eyes look sad.

There's a tug-a-war inside my heart. I don't want Owen to see me snuggling with my boyfriend, and I don't want my boyfriend to doubt my commitment to our secret engagement. This is a mess and one I'm not sure how to clean-up.

As we pull out of the parking lot, Sadie sings, "The wheels on the bus go round and round, round and round, round and round."

It's enough of a distraction for me to cast off the concerns I have about these two men. I've made my decision. Owen knows that I'm with Spencer. Owen is the one who asked if we could be friends. He's the one who invites me to do friendly things with him. If he doesn't like seeing me and Spencer together, then he can stop hanging out with me.

I lean into Spencer's side and join Sadie in singing. Brady does as well. Tori rolls her eyes but smiles like she's about to cry.

"It's a van, not a bus," Owen calls from the front. He's so far away we can barely hear him.

"And its name is Tori, apparently," Tori mutters under her breath. "It's a little insulting."

Then she, too, joins in to sing about windshield wipers swishing.

Spencer does not sing, but he laughs. He laughs so rarely; it feels like a gift. Driving home in the van together was the right decision.

Owen sprays the windows and the wipers swish against the windshield. Sadie cheers.

This is turning out to be a fun Christmas full of new experiences. It was only days ago I felt melancholy about this year differing from past Christmases, but the differences have made this one so much more enjoyable.

It's surprising because I'm away from Nana. She escaped for the second time yesterday and was only found because she shoplifted a bag of chocolate chips and a bottle of window cleaner.

I miss my roommates. I yearn to tell them all about the tour today, but I can't reach out or they'll insist on knowing everything. There will be no communication between us for the rest of the week, no matter how hard it is for me.

I'm embarrassed that one of my credit cards didn't go through as part of the payment for January, and now I'm a delinquent because of one hundred thirty-three dollars.

But, I'm in beautiful Maine. I had a movie tour at a Christmas tree farm. I ran on a beach on the coast of the Atlantic Ocean. I made friends with my soon-to-be in-laws. My secret fiancé made the effort to surprise me with his presence at a *barn,* and now he's sitting next to me in a *van.*

Different is good.

Chapter Sixteen

LAYLA

I WAKE UP CHRISTMAS EVE MORNING WISHING FOR ANOTHER few hours of sleep. I stayed up late knitting gifts. Spencer may have insisted I not make gifts for his family, that they wouldn't enjoy something homemade, but after getting to know some of them, I disagree.

I spent hours' last night watching the 1995 *Pride and Prejudice* while knitting a horse for Sadie and mittens for Tori. It's a Norwegian style pattern that I love and they rival anything she could find at Saks Fifth Avenue. I still need to make three scarves, one each for Owen, Brady, and Miles. I brought the last of the shawls Nana made a few years ago and that I couldn't bear to sell. I'll give one to Rheta and the other to Marianne. As for the rest of the family, I would have to agree with Spencer: they won't appreciate anything handmade from me.

I blearily look at the time on my phone as I stretch. Nine o'clock. Breakfast time. I've been awake most of the last twelve hours since dinner, and my stomach is empty and unhappy about it. I better go before there's a full-on revolt.

I told Owen I wouldn't go running with him this morning. A wise decision since we've spent too much time alone together, but now I feel sluggish and a bit out of sorts. Seeing Owen before breakfast is like having a morning cup of coffee; it puts me in a good mood. Bad, bad, bad, bad, bad. I don't need an Owen addiction in my life.

Since Rheta expects everyone who isn't a lawyer to help decorate today, I pull on my favorite pair of jeans and a red University of Utah t-shirt I've spent years breaking in until it's soft. It's an outfit I didn't send back with the rest of my clothes, knowing I'd want to wear them if I ended up spending all day knitting in my room. I braid my hair and wear minimal makeup. Today isn't about looking sophisticated; it's about decorating for Christmas. I can't wait to transform every room for the holidays.

I'm the last one down to breakfast. Everyone is involved in a heated discussion about Boxing Day and they don't notice my entrance, except for Spencer and Owen. The two cousins both smile at me from different sides of the table, then when they notice the other's attention, they glare at each other. I turn to the sideboard, fill my plate, and I pretend that didn't just happen.

Tori and Sadie sit at the end of the table opposite Rheta this morning. It gives them more room to spread out. Theoretically, I could take Tori's seat on the other side of Spencer and not have to sit across from Owen, but I don't want to draw attention and have anyone ask me why I changed my assigned seat.

The moment I sit, Spencer takes my hand and kisses the back of it. For Owen's benefit more than mine, I'd guess.

"Good morning," he says quietly so only I can hear. "How did you sleep?"

"I stayed up knitting." I cover my mouth as I yawn. "When I finally turned out the light, I slept well. How late did you stay up?"

He does a shrug-nod combo. "Only midnight. The documents Salt Lake sent were helpful."

"I'm glad. Does that mean you'll help decorate today?"

"I have a few things to do on the case, but yes, I will. Prepare yourself; I've never decorated before. I may be horrible at it."

It's sweet how the tips of his ears turn red from the confession.

"It's something you can't really mess up."

He looks me up and down. His nose wrinkles. "Where did you get the clothes? I've never seen you in a t-shirt before."

Dorian calls out Spencer's name "Spencer, don't you agree?"

Spencer gets pulled into their conversation, and I get distracted by Sadie as she pushes her almost full plate away with a clatter and takes two of her animal ornaments out of her pocket. A pig and a cow.

"We put them on the tree last night before she went to bed," Tori tells me. "When I woke her this morning, she had all fifteen in bed with her. She's started naming them. The pig is BB because he's her favorite animal." She tilts her head and frowns. "I see many farm and zoo visits in my future."

I grin. "I'm sorry, but it's very cute."

Tori rolls her eyes and leans close. "Just don't tell her where bacon comes from. That's one thing I'm not willing to give up for my daughter."

Sadie stops playing and looks at her mom. "Where does bacon come from?"

"The store," Tori quickly answers before taking the cow ornament and prancing it around while neighing.

"That's a horse sound!" Sadie says around her laughter. "A cow says, 'moo!' Only horses say 'neigh!'"

"Are you sure?"

"Yes!"

"My bad."

I laugh at how expertly Tori changed the subject.

The conversation on the other side of the table grows louder.

"It will be too noisy and distracting having the house full of people," Gerald says.

"No one will go into your office," Rheta answers. "That hallway will be off limits."

"Noise travels," Dorian huffs.

"Wear earplugs," is Rheta's unsympathetic reply.

"Mother," Dorian booms, his voice filling the room. I flinch. He speaks extra slowly, as if it's Rheta's hearing that makes her not understand his opinion. "It's a bad idea inviting strangers into your home. They'll ... rob you."

That's a far-fetched accusation, and honestly insulting to the town of York. It makes me think he's grasping at straws since his earlier arguments against holding Boxing Day at the cabin have failed.

Rheta doesn't respond to his words or his tone. She sits placidly, her hands on her lap.

"Son, I respect your choice to work through the holiday. I'm not stopping you from doing what you choose, but now you need to respect my choice. I decide how to fill my time and who I invite into my home. These are my neighbors. If you don't like it, fly back to Salt Lake City."

Everyone at the table stills. I'm filled with dread. If Spencer leaves with Dorian, then I have to go with him. It would be weird if I stayed on my own, and I'm looking forward to spending Christmas with Tori, Sadie, Owen and his family. As well as the Boxing Day gift-exchange-and-eat-leftovers party.

"No, Mother," Dorian says, this time quietly. "We want to stay, of course we do."

Gerald, Ellory, and Spencer nod in agreement.

"Then stop trying to convince me I'm wrong," Rheta tells her children. "If you can't work in the house during the party, then go to the public library. I'm sure it will be empty since everyone will be here."

I stifle my laugh over Dorian's shocked expression. As if he's never walked through the doors of any public building, especially not a library.

"I only want what is best for you," he says meekly. "I'm your son. Can't I be concerned about your welfare? Preparing for a party at such short notice can be stressful."

"Oh, for goodness' sakes, Dorian. I'm old, I'm not dying."

MILES' PARENTS SUSAN AND MALCOLM ARRIVE AT TEN o'clock to lead the decorating committee. Twelve people from town arrive soon after, and they bring along a few children to play with Sadie.

Susan posts a printed schedule on the back of the front door. When I look for my name, I see it listed next to two women from town. We're going to work decorating the dining room. But first, we need to unpack all the decorations and lay them out on tables set up in the foyer, so they're easier to organize.

Susan and Malcolm are in their seventies, but that doesn't slow them down. They're unpacking with the rest of us, and when they come across mistletoe, they don't let the opportunity to kiss pass them by.

Sadie becomes the ringleader of the children. They maraud around the house with empty wrapping paper rolls and ribbons tied around their heads to cover one eye, pretending they're pirates. Sadie tapes the chicken ornament onto her shoulder like it's a parrot.

When I have most of the decorations for the dining room gathered, I take an armload in to get started. Owen is at the dining table untangling a string of brand-new lights. How they got tangled isn't the most important question.

"Why are you here?" I ask.

He glances up, then back down at the lights. "There's been a change in decorating partners. Do you think you can help with this? The kids got to it before I did."

I notice how he changed the subject, but for reasons I'd rather not think about, I don't dig into the why behind the change. With a smile, I pull up Christmas music on my phone and help him untangle the string of lights.

The theme for this room is silver and gold. We have ribbons and ornaments in all shapes and sizes. Even the tree skirt is gold with silver stars. I'm not sure how Miles and Rheta found all of this in two days, but it will be a beautiful room.

I climb the ladder to weave the ribbon through the branches, starting at the top and working toward the bottom. As we work, Owen whistles along with the music. I sing the words. It's companionable and kind of perfect.

"I have contraband." Owen pulls out a candy cane from his shirt pocket. "I thought we could hide it in the tree and see if anyone notices. It'll be like your pickle game, but since the candy cane is red and white striped, more of a Christmas-themed 'Where's Waldo.'"

I clap my hands and laugh. "I love it. Even better, we can hide one on every tree. After Boxing Day, we'll see if any of them are still there.

"Perfect. You hide this one. I'll hide the next."

As he hands it to me, my fingers brush his. My body shivers at the contact. I pull away, but my eyes stay glued to his. I didn't think decorating a Christmas tree could get better, but having Owen here has improved the process. We get stuck staring at each other.

"What's this?"

Spencer's voice comes from behind us and we both turn. I expected Spencer to show up to help, but not so soon. It's only noon.

"You're done earlier than I thought." I walk over on stiff legs and kiss him on the cheek. For a second day in a row, Spencer has caught me alone with Owen.

Spencer's nostrils flare and his lips flatten. He takes my

hand in a tight grip and stares at his cousin, even as he speaks to me. "I didn't want to disappoint you. I have the rest of the day off. Father and Gerald are taking care of everything that needs to be done until after Christmas."

He took time off for me. If he were only concerned for himself, he'd work over Christmas. He's trying to make me happy, which makes my guilt over enjoying my time with Owen heavier. As we decorated, I didn't think about Spencer once.

"That's wonderful." My voice sounds fake. I try again. "Thank you, Spencer."

"I did it for you." He plants a big kiss on my lips with no warning.

It's a territorial and possessive kiss. I know why; it's our audience. His arm wraps behind my back and pulls me closer like a vise. When he ends the kiss, I'm able to take a step back. My heart beat pounds in my head.

Owen stands next to the tree with his hands fisted at his sides. With a deep breath, his fingers loosen and he walks toward the door.

"Well, if you're here now, Spencer, I guess I'll go see if anyone else needs help."

I watch his back until he disappears through the door. I try to push him from my mind and enjoy Spencer being here with me, but after that kiss, it's hard. Harder still when Spencer turns off my music and looks at the tree like it's a piece of abstract art he can't understand.

"I didn't like the way you kissed me," I say. "I'm not your possession. Don't do that again."

The muscle in Spencer's jaw ticks. "I'm sorry if I made you feel that way. I don't think of you as a possession.

However, you are my fiancée. I don't want you to spend any more time with Owen, ever, but especially not alone."

His demand does not land well. I do as Owen did earlier and take a deep breath to calm myself.

"Again, I am not your possession. I can spend time with whomever I choose."

He paces along the table and runs his hands through his hair. "Owen's puppy-dog crush isn't so little anymore. It's the way he looks at you. Even Father has noticed, and it's humiliating. Ellory had the gall to insinuate that you return his infatuation. I won't have my family gossiping about us like this. It's unacceptable."

It's good that this conversation is happening now instead of later. Like after we're married.

"Spencer, if you think that our marriage is the type where you tell me what to do and I follow your direction without complaint, then you are wrong."

His head snaps back like I've slapped him, and his feet stop moving. Maybe the shock will help him listen, and we won't have this conversation again.

"Our marriage will be a democracy, not a monarchy," I continue, keeping my voice even. "We discuss things and make decisions together. Yes, I understand your concern about me and Owen. We're friends. I like him. I liked him before you proposed to me. But you have to trust me, just like I have to trust you. You'll be spending a lot of late nights at the office, but I won't be questioning your fidelity, so don't question mine."

His lip curls. "I would never have an affair. Especially not with someone at the firm."

"I trust you that you won't. Do you trust me the same way?"

"I trust you. I don't trust him. And what about the gossip? My father and aunt have noticed your *friendship* with Owen, and they only see you together at meals. They haven't had the misfortune of catching you staring into each other's eyes."

I'm suddenly exhausted and collapse into one of the dining chairs. It sounds terrible when he puts it like that and my anger drains away. "I can't control gossip, Spencer, and it's unfair of you to put that responsibility on my shoulders."

After a moment, he nods, the movement sharp. "That's fair. But I still don't like you spending time alone with Owen."

Understandable. I may not like how Spencer treated me when he came into the room, but I understand why he did what he did. He isn't blind. He can see how much I enjoy my time with Owen. I would be upset if Spencer was behaving similarly with another woman. This is horrible. I'm horrible.

I've chosen Spencer for practical reasons, survival even, and my heart needs to get with the program. My growing feelings for Owen are dangerous. I can't sabotage my future and Nana's because Spencer doesn't make me feel the way Owen does.

"Spencer, I can promise you that once we're back in Salt Lake City, I won't see Owen, at least not on purpose. We might run into each other at Brock Pine Home occasionally, but it's not like we're going to spend time together like we have this week."

"Really?" He sounds hopeful. "We all live in Salt Lake City. While I'm at the office, you won't invite him over to watch a horrendous Christmas movie or learn a dance or something?"

That sounds fun, and I have to swallow down my disappointment that it will never happen. I wish I'd never met Owen. It would make this decision so much easier if my heart wasn't pulling me in the opposite direction of my head.

"Unless we get together with your extended family, I won't make plans to see him."

He snorts. "Getting together with the Clarks won't happen again unless Grandmother stipulates it." He pulls out the chair next to mine and sits and takes my hands in his. "I'll be patient this week with Owen because I know I get to keep you forever."

My breath catches at the idea. Forever. Yep. Exactly. "See, it's not so hard to have a discussion instead of making demands."

"I'll remember that for next time."

"We're almost finished with the tree," I say as I stand. "But if we grab the last few decorations from the table in the foyer, we can begin decorating the rest of the room."

I take a step toward the door, but he doesn't let go of my hand and I stop.

He looks up at me with regret in his eyes. "I'm sorry for the way I behaved earlier, Layla. I never want to make you feel uncomfortable."

He kisses the back of my hand.

I wish I felt something, anything, at his touch.

My wish remains unanswered.

AFTER A QUICK DINNER, EVERYONE IS EXHAUSTED, AND WE ALL go up to bed early. Every muscle in my body aches from all the lifting and climbing ladders I did today. It was worth the effort. The cabin looks amazing. I feel as if I've walked into a Hallmark movie set.

As much as I enjoyed today, there's a twinge in my chest from missing Nana. Decorating the house was our thing. I thought about calling her on the phone, but it might confuse her, so I resisted. In three days, I'll be home with fifty-thousand dollars. The sacrifice now will pay off later.

I want to burrow into bed and sleep, but I have another night of marathon knitting. I pull up *While You Were Sleeping* on the TV and start a green scarf for Owen. I've always been a fast knitter, but my speed increased once Nana's livelihood depended on how much money I brought in each month. It only takes me a few hours to finish.

My phone buzzes with a text.

OWEN: *I have something for you. Will you meet me in the breakfast room?*

It was easy to avoid Owen this afternoon, since Rheta had him running errands. It's best if I don't spend time with him for the rest of the week. It isn't fair to Spencer, and the gossip among the older generation bothers me, too, even if I didn't admit it earlier.

I type out a message telling Owen I'm already in bed and can't come down, but my thumb won't move to the send button. After Saturday, I won't see him again unless it's at Brock Pine Home by accident. This might be my last time I ever have time with him.

My thumb suddenly receives the strength to delete my original message and write a new one.

LAYLA: *Be there in a minute.*

I grab the teal sweater Nana knit because it's within reach, not because Owen complimented my eyes when I wore it last. Just before I leave my room, I grab the scarf I knit for him. He said he had something for me and I can't show up empty-handed.

Besides, Christmas Eve is the appropriate time to exchange gifts.

When I open my bedroom door, I gasp. On the floor is a bouquet of white carnations, red roses, pinecones, sprigs of pine and fir, and candy canes in a beautiful glass vase.

Spencer didn't do this.

I can't encourage whatever it is Owen thinks he's doing, but my heart and not my head leads my feet as I pick up the vase and carry it down the hallway with me. The house is quiet as I creep downstairs. Even dark, the shadows of our efforts earlier today are visible.

It was easy to convince Rheta to hang some of Sadie's artwork in the foyer: crayon pictures of a tree, a family portrait, and BB the pig. Not that anyone would know what they are without the small plaques Miles made to put by each one. I don't think any of us would dream of turning down Sadie's requests.

When I get to the breakfast room, I expect the overhead lights to be on, but the only light comes from a string of lights along the middle of the table and the Christmas tree in the corner, giving the room a holiday glow.

The sewn ornaments from the Nubble Lighthouse and red glass balls adorn the tree. Under its boughs are four badly wrapped gifts. They must be another of Sadie's contributions to the decorations.

The space feels bigger than it is because the curtains over the windows and glass door are open, with the moon perfectly framed in the space.

On the table are two place settings across from each other. I drop the scarf and flowers on the end of the table and draw closer. Fine silverware. Glass goblets. Placemats with embroidered holly and berries around the edges.

I take in everything and ask myself, *what is going on?*

Chapter Seventeen

LAYLA

The serving door opens and Owen walks in holding two plates. The smell of curry gravy hits me first, but even then, I still can't believe what I'm seeing. Blutwurst, sauerkraut, and mashed potatoes with gravy smothered over everything.

"I hope you're hungry," he says.

"I ..."

I don't know what to say. Yes, I'm hungry. We decorated all day and never had a sit-down meal; just finger foods laid out in the dining room. I'd probably eat anything right now, but to find my family's traditional Christmas Eve feast in Maine leaves me speechless. Owen remembers everything about our conversation in his car on fry night.

Owen sets the fine China plates on the table, then disappears into the anteroom to come back a moment later with a basket of rolls.

I clear my throat. "What is this for?"

"It's Christmas Eve dinner."

He pulls out my chair and I sit, my legs weak.

"Yes, but why?"

"Because I want you to have the best Christmas, and that means celebrating Christmas Eve like it's meant to be celebrated."

I run my finger along the edge of the placemat, unable to look at him. "This is the sweetest thing anyone has ever done for me."

He sits across the table. "You should always have many sweet things done for you." It's a fact for him, as if I should expect nothing less. He points to my plate. "Tell me what you think."

That's all the encouragement I need to cut into the blutwurst and take a bite. An explosion of flavor hits my tongue. It's an earthy, almost coppery taste, so familiar I close my eyes to savor it.

Owen's silverware clinks against his plate, and I open my eyes. He's starting with the sauerkraut, brave man. He grimaces, one eye closing as he swallows it down.

"That's ... sour."

I laugh. "The hint is in the name." I take a bite of the warm, gravy-smothered sauerkraut. The tangy sourness is one of my favorites. It brings a smile to my face.

Owen chews a bite of blutwurst thoughtfully, as if deciding if he likes it or not. The flavor isn't for everyone. If I didn't grow up with it, I'm not sure it's a taste I would have acquired as an adult.

"Where did you get all of this?" I ask.

"Miles knows a German family who lives nearby. I talked

to them yesterday, and they were happy enough to make you a Christmas Eve dinner."

"Thank you, Owen," I say with utmost sincerity. "I wasn't lying when I said this was the sweetest thing anyone has ever done for me."

"You're welcome, Layla."

I tear a roll in half. The outside is hard, the inside perfectly soft. I dip it in the gravy. It's smoky and slightly sweet.

"Not a fan of the sauerkraut," Owen says. "But the sausage is good."

"It was Opa's favorite. Nana made it every year. As a word of caution, never look at the recipe. The year I found out what the ingredients were, it ruined Christmas Eve dinner."

He pauses with another bite of sausage smothered in mashed potatoes and gravy halfway to his mouth. "What's in it?"

"I told you; you don't want to know. Just enjoy the flavor and forget I mentioned it."

He places his bite in his mouth and chews. "That's good advice."

Every bite is delicious, and I am determined to meet this German family who shared their meal and thank them before I leave.

I eat every bite, even after I'm near bursting. I don't know when I'll have an authentic German meal again.

I lay my fork and knife across my plate. "Thank you."

"You already thanked me."

"And I will keep thanking you because twice is not nearly enough."

"You'll have plenty of opportunities because the

celebration is just beginning." He stands and waves to the tree in the corner. "Up next, the fake German tradition of finding a pickle hidden in the Christmas tree."

I'm in awe. "I can't believe you found a pickle ornament on such short notice."

"I didn't, so I had to make my own."

I move to stand in front of the tree. I can't spot the pickle with a cursory glance. "What did you make it out of?"

"A pickle."

I turn to look at him, wondering if I understood correctly. "You hid a *real* pickle in the tree?"

With a shrug and a lop-sided grin, he says, "I had an ornament hook, and I had a pickle. It wasn't hard."

I laugh. My chest warms, my thoughts turn to mush. Owen is a good, good man. The best of them all and I'm lucky to have him as a friend. Going against my better judgement, I reach out and pull him into a hug. It's only meant to last a few seconds, but I'm enveloped in the spicy scent of his cologne and a second later, the tight embrace of his arms. Any desire to end this moment flees. I feel secure and safe in his arms. He gives the best hugs.

The only thing that gets me to draw back is the thought of Spencer. I should not have instigated this, and I unlock my arms from around his neck and take three large steps back. It's best if I pretend that didn't happen and forget how nice it felt to be held in his arms.

I clear my throat and look at the tree. "Will you time how long I take to find the pickle? I have this down to a science."

He grabs his phone from his back pocket with jerky movements, and I wonder if he's as affected by the hug as I am. I still feel the warm press of his arms around my back. The tickle of his beard against my cheek.

I appreciate how he doesn't comment on the last thirty seconds and instead opens the stopwatch app on his phone. "On your mark, get set, go!"

After mentally separating the tree into blocks of space, I give each square all my attention, one at a time. My other trick is to always look at an angle and not straight on.

Nana hid the pickle at around her eye level. I'm not sure if it was to make it easy for me or easy for her, but I look at Owen's eye level.

Owen has done the same as Nana. I make out the green blob hidden behind another ornament. Tricky, but not tricky enough.

I unhook it from the branch and once it's free of the pine scent, I'm hit with a pickle smell. Ironically, I hate pickles, and I wrinkle my nose and hold it out.

He whistles. "Impressive. One minute, fifteen seconds."

"It's your turn to search."

That grin of his has my heart racing.

"Really? I didn't know I'd get a turn."

I ignore how his eyes dance. "Turn around so I can hide it."

Once he's facing away, I try to find the perfect spot. If I wanted to make it hard, I'd hide it in the bottom branches and near the trunk, but I decide to be nice and put it on the end of a branch at waist height.

"It's hidden. See if you can beat my time."

He doesn't look convinced it's possible. "Wish me luck."

I start the timer and he moves branches out of the way to peer deeper into the tree. Growing up, I wasn't allowed to use my hands, only my eyes, but he's a beginner and Nana isn't watching. I let it slide.

The seconds turn into minutes. I love his long fingers and large hands. I watch the way his muscles move under his button-up shirt. How he scratches his bearded cheek absently as he focuses on his task. The way his thighs tighten when he squats to look low. He hasn't worn shorts once since we arrived in Maine, and I miss seeing his legs.

As the minutes accumulate, he doesn't get frustrated or give up. He's focused, even if his search method is erratic; he's in one spot, then the next. He looks past the pickle at least three times before he finally pauses.

"Found it!" he crows and unhooks it from the branch. He turns, his face alight with his triumph. "That was harder than I thought it would be. How long did it take?"

His happiness at finding the silly pickle is sweet and sincere. It distracted me, and I forgot to stop the timer. I shave off a minute as a personal punishment for staring. "Six minutes, twenty-one seconds."

He blows out a breath and wipes at his brow with the back of his hand as if he's just run a seven-minute mile. "It seems I need practice."

"Give it twenty years, and you'll be a pro just like I am."

His eyes turn serious and his smile melts away as he studies my face. "I'd like to."

Time stops. A tangible current runs between us. He's so close I can reach out and touch his chest, just like I did on the beach. My hand lifts a few inches before I remind myself that this is my *friend*. The hug was pushing the friend boundary enough. Feeling up his chest is way too far.

Spencer had a right to his anger this afternoon. I'm angry

at myself for letting my feelings run this deep. I need space, so I walk to the other side of the room, putting the table between us, but I don't leave. There isn't anywhere I'd rather be.

"What's my prize for the quickest time?" My voice is wobbly, as are my legs. I steady myself by grabbing onto the back of a chair.

He glances at my lips for a split second before turning away. "I'll go grab it."

He exits through the serving door and this time when he comes back he has a tray with a stollen loaf cake covered in powdered sugar.

"Weihnachtsstollen," I whisper. The faint scent is enough to transport me back to my childhood.

"Um, what?"

Why does Owen have to remember everything I tell him? Why is he so wonderful?

"Weihnachts is Christmas in German. Weihnachtsstollen."

"Do you speak German?"

"Not enough to have a conversation, but a little."

Owen places the tray on the table and cuts a thick slice off the end. Inside the loaf cake are the bright colors of dried fruit, candied citrus peel, and almonds. Baked through the center is a rope of marzipan.

He hands me the first piece. I break off a corner and drop it on my tongue. I close my eyes as the memory of Christmases past envelopes me.

"This is just like Nana makes it," I whisper, my feelings of missing Nana so close to the surface that I have to sit down before I fall down. "I've tried to make it like this, but it's never had the right texture or mixture of spices."

"It looks like fruitcake."

If he were closer, I would smack his arm for the insult. "I am offended on behalf of Germany. It is not a fruit cake; it's *stollen*."

He uses a fork instead of his fingers, but his eyes widen as he chews. "This is delicious."

"I told you."

I savor each bite and appreciate Owen's silence as I do so. I need the mental space to collect my thoughts and feelings and package them away, never to think on again.

When I've eaten my last bite, he asks, "Are you ready for your gifts?"

Gifts plural? This is all too much. He's blurring the lines between friendship and more, almost as if on purpose.

"This entire night has been a gift, Owen. Please, nothing else. Thank you for making Christmas Eve special, but I need to get to bed. I'm exhausted."

I stand and walk toward the door, but he comes up behind me and catches my hand. His touch is light, a grip I can break easily, but I stand where I am, frozen as feelings course through me. Feelings of longing, regret, and guilt.

"Please, wait."

I stay where I am as he grabs the poorly wrapped gifts from under the tree.

"Merry Christmas!" He holds them out to me in both hands, a shoe box sized gift on the bottom, with three small, oddly shaped gifts stacked on top.

It's such a ridiculous sight. I laugh even as my heart breaks. "I thought Sadie wrapped those!"

A fake frown steals his smile. "Seriously? I spent a lot of time and tape to make these *presentable.*"

By the twinkle in his eye, he meant the pun. Honestly, the wrapping is perfect. Spencer would never go to the trouble to wrap gifts for anyone, and I both love and hate that Owen went to the effort to wrap these for me.

I grab the scarf from the end of the table, glad I brought it with me so I have something to give in return. "This is for you."

He doesn't have a free hand since he's still holding out my gifts. I lean forward and drape it over his shoulders as if it's some sort of award. Our faces are inches apart. I want to burrow into his warmth again and forget about money and responsibilities and Nana. All that matters in this second is Owen.

No! I will never forget about Nana. She sacrificed so much for me and Mom. I will sacrifice for her.

I step away until my back hits against a chair.

Owen gives me space when he looks down at the scarf lying against his chest. "You made this for me?"

"Yeah. It's just a scarf."

He looks up, his eyes soft and sweet. "Nothing you make is *just* anything. Do you know how jealous I've been of all the Brock Pine residents who have received something you've knit? You should hear them brag. Now I get to join in. Norman will be green with envy that I got a scarf from you, and he didn't."

My chest burns with pleasure. I had no idea anyone cared they had something made by me. It's like Owen knows exactly what to say to make me feel extra special.

"Thank you, Layla." His voice is soft, fervent. My skin

pebbles in goosebumps. "It's beautiful, and I will treasure it always."

He puts the gifts on the table and picks up the largest one. "Open this first."

There's an uneven weight inside that makes a clunking noise when I give it a little shake. I tear off the paper and open the box. I'm unprepared to find a thirty-two-ounce bottle of ketchup.

I laugh, dispelling most of my yearning for Owen over the past few minutes. This is a friendly gift, even if it is amazing how much thought he put into it. Into everything tonight.

"Thank you. I can't tell you how much this means to me."

He smirks. "It's a bottle of ketchup. I can get you more. They were on sale at the store, so it won't set me back much."

I slap his stomach with the back of my hand. Mistake. It's firm and warm. Touching of any kind is off limits where this man is concerned.

"I mean everything, smarty pants. The food. The pickle." A real pickle. A point to him for innovation. "The ketchup."

"I can't wait for you to open the rest of your presents if I'm met with so much appreciation for ketchup."

The second gift is the angel pendant on a silver chain from the shop at the lighthouse. The one I stopped and stared at for a few extra seconds. Of course, Owen noticed. He seems to notice everything about me.

The third is a bar of peppermint scented hand soap. Now I can smell like a candy cane every time I wash my hands.

Nothing is extravagant, but it's the thought he put into them. He knows me. He pays attention. He cares.

I realize for Owen, tonight is not about us being friends.

He is treating me like a girlfriend. I love spending time with him, but it's time for me to stop ignoring what's going on between us. We have to stop pretending.

I lay the items out on the table next to the last wrapped gift. "Owen, I can't accept these. I'm dating Spencer."

He leans his hip against the table and waits until I look at him before responding. "Spencer doesn't love you. His career will always come first. Are you happy dating a man who cares about his job more than he cares about you?"

Of course not, but I love Nana more than anything else in the world and she's worth it.

Instead of responding to his prying question, I turn away and head to the door, leaving everything, including the beautiful bouquet from earlier. "Spencer is a good man and a good friend. He might not take me on a tour of a tree farm or wrap his own gifts, but he gives me what I need; security and peace. Good night, Owen."

"Layla, let me help you." He sounds like I'm ripping out his heart, which pains mine.

I pause with my hand on the door and glance over my shoulder. I give him a carefree smile. "How? By accepting your inheritance and marrying me instead?"

I meant it as a joke to lighten the conversation, but the question comes out as if I'm serious. His hesitation in answering is a punch to my chest. In his eyes, I just jumped from friendship to marriage and he didn't follow. My cheeks heat from humiliation.

"I will marry for love," Owen says softly. "I won't marry someone who wants me for my money."

His voice is kind, but I hear an accusation hidden in his words because I will marry for money.

I study the tile beneath my feet. "I speak from experience when I say there is no nobility in being poor."

"I know that you're struggling to pay for your grandma's care," he says. "I can help you. There is no reason for you to date Spencer if all you need from him is money. I will give you what you need, and I expect nothing in return. I just want you to be happy."

He wants me to be happy. He's not throwing his hat into the competition for my heart. Of course not, there isn't any competition except in my head. What a fool I am. Tonight wasn't about Owen wanting out of the friend zone, it was about being a friend. *Get it together, Layla.*

"I want to help you," he says again. "Let's get your financial situation settled, then let me take you on a date. We can see where we go from there."

Maybe I'm not a complete fool. He still wants to date me, just not marry me. It's an appealing offer. I'd rather not marry for money, but Owen doesn't know what he's offering. He's a landscaper. He might own the business, but without his inheritance, he doesn't have the capital to help me financially. It isn't a thousand dollars here or there, it's seventy-five grand a year for as long as Nana lives. It's a hundred-thousand dollars of debt. If I tell him how much his help will cost, I'm sure he'd find a way, but then we'd both be financially ruined.

Maybe even more important of all, I can't use him for financial security like I can Spencer. Owen is too good and honest, and I have nothing I can give him in return. With Spencer, I have no such qualms because we're using each other. I get someone to pay for Nana's care, and he gets forty-million dollars and a wife to show off at work parties.

I will marry Spencer. I don't need thoughtful gifts and laughter and pickles on trees to be happy. What will make me happiest is for Nana to receive everything she needs for as long as she needs it.

Owen will find a lovely woman and be unencumbered by debt and live a happy life without me. It hurts to think of him with another woman, but I have no claim on him.

"Good night, Owen."

I head upstairs, expecting Owen to follow and argue, but all is silent. When I reach my room, I notice the light under Spencer's bedroom door across the hall. If he's awake, I would like to see him and get myself back into a realistic headspace.

Spencer answers my knock in seconds. I'm familiar with seeing Spencer in suits, and it's a surprise to see him in plaid pajamas. His pompadour flops to the side. A sleepy smile stretches across his cheeks. He is always handsome, but when rumpled like this, there is little that compares.

In his hand is a file folder that he hides behind his back. After he told me earlier today that his dad and aunt were taking care of everything until the day after Christmas, he might feel like a liar. Well, after the last hour with Owen, that makes two of us.

"Layla," he says in a scratchy voice. "Is something wrong?"

"Can I come in for a minute?"

He steps back, and I walk inside.

Besides his rumpled bed sheets, none of his belongings are visible. It looks as if no one is staying in this room. I sit on the end of the bed.

"Is something wrong?" Spencer asks.

The two of us have only ever been honest with each other, and I see no reason to stop now. My situation with these two cousins has my head spinning and my heart hurting.

"Tonight, Owen made me a traditional German dinner to celebrate Christmas Eve. We hid a pickle in a tree. Then he gave me ketchup as a Christmas present. As well as a bouquet and a necklace."

A flash of multiple emotions cascade across Spencer's face. Surprise, anger, confusion, and finally resignation. After our conversation this afternoon, he might be unsure on how to respond. I'm not sure how I want him to respond.

What he finally lands on is, "Why a German meal?"

The corner of my lips tip up the smallest bit. He's trying to make me happy in so many small ways, like taking time off from work today and tomorrow. Driving home from the tree farm in the van. Not lecturing me about spending time with Owen when, in this case, he has every right to.

"My opa was from Germany. I'm a quarter German."

Spencer sits next to me. "I didn't realize. I also didn't know Owen knew how to cook."

I chuckle, then sigh. "He doesn't, or at least I don't know if he does. He got the food from a local German family."

"Is this what you want from me? German dinners and a tour of a tree farm?" He takes my hand. "If so, you'll have to tell me because I'd rather not guess, then have you disappointed when I fail."

I give his hand a squeeze. "No, I do not expect any surprises from you." As much as I enjoy them, they aren't in Spencer's wheelhouse. There are other traits he excels in. "What I want from you is your time, your trust, and your honesty. I will give the same to you. Which is why I'm telling you about tonight."

Spencer taps his fingers against his leg. "I'm going to guess Owen tried to talk you out of marrying me. I know he wants you for himself."

"Essentially, yes," I say.

"Did he convince you?"

Unbidden, a wish that Spencer would break off our agreement flairs up. It's so strong it takes me by surprise and steals my sanity. I need Spencer. I don't want him to break up with me. What will I do for Nana? How will I un-bury myself from this debt? I can't do it on my own.

"No, he did not convince me."

"Good." Spencer kisses my temple. "I'm not the kind of person who changes his mind once it's made, and I'm glad you aren't either."

Instead of his loyalty bringing me peace, my chest tightens, much like it does every time I visit Nana. I don't allow myself to think about why.

"Are you ready for the proposal tomorrow?" he asks. "I'll do it in front of the family after we exchange gifts, if that sounds agreeable to you."

Oh gosh, the proposal tomorrow on Christmas. The tightness in my chest increases. "That will work. Good night, Spencer."

I'm off the bed and out of the room in seconds. I breathe a little easier in the hallway. At least for a few seconds, until I notice on the floor outside my bedroom the flower bouquet, the remaining stollen wrapped in plastic wrap, and the other gifts from Owen, including the one I didn't open.

Gifts in the hallway remind me of another German

Christmas tradition from growing up: St. Nicholas Day. Every December fifth I left a shoe outside my door and in the morning, it was filled with gifts and candy. One year, I stole Opa's winter boot because it was bigger than my tennis shoe. Nicholas, aka Opa, did not disappoint and filled the boot all the way to the top. I got a lot of fruit snacks and Hostess cupcakes from the pantry, but I loved it.

If seen, these gifts will add fuel to the gossip about me and Owen, something I want to avoid. I grab them, enter my room, and dump them on my dresser.

An ache for my Nana and Opa forms so deep and wide I collapse on my bed. If they were both alive and healthy, I could talk to them about this, and they would listen and help me figure out what to do. Except if they were alive and healthy, I wouldn't be in this situation. I feel so alone. Fear of the future, not just for my marriage but for Nana, nips at my thoughts.

I'm glad I have two more scarves to knit. The distraction will keep me sane. As I cast on, my eyes drift to the wrapped gift on my dresser. It taunts me.

"Fine," I mutter. "I'll open you."

I get off my bed and grab it. Whatever it is jingles as I tear the paper off. A bracelet falls to the floor. It's not until I pick it up that I see it's a charm bracelet with five charms. A candy cane, a lighthouse, a Christmas tree, a cup of hot cocoa, and a pickle. The last one has me laughing out loud even as tears stream down my cheeks. Who sells pickle charms? This year it's Owen who gets the good luck because hunting down a pickle charm is impressive detective work.

I love the bracelet. The problem is, I can never wear it because every charm reminds me of him.

How dare Owen be the kind, attentive, gorgeous, thoughtful man that I always dreamed would come into my life. He does something no boyfriend has ever done: he puts me first.

"Curse you, Owen."

Banishing every thought and desire that works against my resolve, I go back to my bed and grab my knitting. My alarm will sound in a few short hours, and I still have two scarves to make.

Chapter Eighteen

LAYLA

CHRISTMAS MORNING BEGINS IN THE BREAKFAST ROOM WITH everyone dressed in their finest outfits. In this family, that means designer.

The men wear suit jackets and ties, but for Owen who wears slacks and a polo. Brady looks handsome in a red sweater, with his hair combed back in a man bun. Tori wasn't wrong; give it a few years, and all the girls will be after him.

We women have dolled ourselves up as if we're headed out to a night at the Oscars. Ginger, who I've only seen occasionally at meals, drips with diamonds. Rheta is in a burgundy silk cinched at her waist. Ellory's midnight blue dress has a tulle skirt and embroidered bust. I'm so used to seeing her in business suits, it's a shock to see her in anything else.

It's good Spencer warned me about the dress code, or I'd have come down to breakfast in slacks and a blouse. I'm wearing my fanciest dress: black, sleeveless, and with silver beading along the top. I love a reason to dress up, but for nine o'clock on a Christmas morning spent at home, it feels excessive.

The exception to the dress code is Sadie, who comes to breakfast walking on her tip-toes and wearing a leotard, pink tights, and a tutu. When I give Tori a questioning glance, she raises her eyes to heaven. It seems to be a common thing where her daughter is concerned.

"Some things are not worth the argument," she says under her breath.

Breakfast has always been delicious at the cabin, but today it's warm crepes with a dozen different toppings and hazelnut coffee. Where has this coffee been hiding all week? It's the pick-me-up I need after two nights of little sleep. It's truly amazing.

Dorian, Marianne, and Ellory are chatty and linger over breakfast, which means we all do. Rheta sits at the head of the table with a huge grin, but when Sadie's impatience to open presents reaches a crescendo, we move to the family room. The decorations in here are very pink. It seems pink is the trend this year. At least, that's what we were told yesterday at the farm, but maybe the pink ornaments were all that remained so close to Christmas. Still, the pink is beautiful against the white of the room. Sadie loves it, and she dances around in circles.

Since yesterday, everyone has brought their gifts and placed them under the tree. There are at least fifty, and they're all wrapped in gorgeous paper and big, colorful bows.

The items I knit are in my Boudron slung over my

shoulder. I wrapped nothing, and am suddenly self-conscious to gift knitted items with everyone watching.

I don't need to worry, because my expectation for a Christmas morning where we gather on the sofas and open gifts one at a time isn't met.

Instead, everyone stands around in small groups talking and exchanges gifts one at a time. After Rheta gives gifts to Marianne and her sons, Spencer leads me to the tree so he can grab a large box wrapped in silver paper. He carries it in two hands as we walk to where Rheta sits in an armchair.

"Merry Christmas, Grandmother." He places it on the end table next to her and kisses her cheek.

"Thank you, Spencer. Layla."

She's careful with the ribbon and paper so that it doesn't tear. Spencer taps his fingers against his thigh with impatience. She is taking excessive care, but I don't want Rheta to feel rushed, so I take his hand in mine.

When the paper is off and the lid removed, the sides of the box open outward, revealing an elegant crystal vase with a fluted top. I gasp at its beauty and size.

"It's gorgeous," Rheta says. "Thank you."

Spencer preens. "It's Baccarat."

Rheta smiles like she's bestowing an award for giving an excellent gift. "It will look perfect in the dining room with roses or delphiniums." She takes a small wrapped box from beside her. "Spencer, this is something your grandfather and I wanted you to have."

"Thank you, Grandmother." After accepting the gift, he turns to leave, but I stay where I am.

"I have something for you as well," I say. From my

Boudron I take out the folded shawl and place it in her waiting hands.

Rheta gasps as she unfolds it. "It's like gossamer. Where did you purchase this?"

"My Nana made it."

She runs her fingers over the soft, web-like stitches. "How lovely. My mother had something similar that she purchased in Europe." She looks up at me, a genuine smile on her lips. "Thank you."

"Merry Christmas, Rheta."

She sandwiches my hand between hers. "I have something for you that you'll receive on Friday morning."

I don't need anything in return, but it seems rude to say so. "Thank you."

We take a few steps away so Dorian and Ginger can give their gift to Rheta. When she opens the box with diamond earrings, her face does not show the excitement that it did when she received my gift. Her fingers run absently over the shawl still in her lap as she speaks to them.

"It's a nice shawl." Spencer's voice holds confusion. "But it cost next to nothing. That vase is one of a kind and cost me six thousand dollars. You have to agree that's much more than what you spent."

It bothers me how he acts as if gift giving is a competition. "The shawl is quality workmanship. It's not about money. It's about the thought that goes into it."

Spencer snorts. "I put a lot of thought into that vase." With a sigh, his shoulders relax. There's disappointment in his eyes, but also respect. "I told you my family wouldn't want anything handmade from you. It seems I was wrong."

He is wrong, and I appreciate how he acknowledges it.

"Thank you, Spencer."

Ellory and her husband advance with a gift for us and our conversation ends. For the next hour, I follow in Spencer's wake, giving and accepting gifts from his family.

When Marianne approaches with Brady and Owen, my heart rate picks up. I've done my best not to allow my attention to land on Owen this morning, but now that he's beside me, it's hard to look away.

Owen holds out his hand to his cousin. "Merry Christmas, Spencer."

Spencer frowns as he takes his cousin's hand in a tight handshake. He doesn't hold any anger toward me for last night, but it seems he has yet to forgive Owen. "Merry Christmas," he mutters.

Brady hands Spencer a beautifully wrapped box. Spencer gives it to me to unwrap. It's heavy and I place it on an end table so I can tear off the paper. Inside is a wooden chess board with hand carved pieces made of what looks like amber.

This is a thoughtful gift. Not only is it well made, and I imagine expensive, but also, Spencer loves chess. He collects chess sets. The only member of the Clark family who would know such a thing would be Owen. I can't imagine he purchased this for Spencer himself when they haven't spoken in years, but he must have told Marianne what Spencer would enjoy.

"Thank you," I say. "It's beautiful."

Spencer remains silent. He has nothing to say to them, and it seems he has no gift to give either.

It's a good thing I came prepared. I pull from my bag the scarf for Brady and the shawl for Marianne.

She gasps as she takes it reverently. "This is gorgeous. I noticed the one you gave my mother, and I am thrilled to have one of my own."

She hugs it to her chest, and then she hugs me. It feels like a hug my mother would give me if she were alive, and I hold on to her for an extra second.

"Thanks for the scarf." Brady already has it wrapped around his neck, although with the fire blazing, it's hot in here.

"I haven't forgotten about your cloak," I tell him. "I'll get it started as soon as I get home."

He grins, then glances over at his brother. "You don't have anything for Owen?"

Spencer stiffens beside me, and Marianne glances between us. I can't read her expression. Disapproval maybe? Either she's heard the gossip about us from her siblings or she's come to her own conclusion.

Thanks for making this awkward, Brady.

"I made a scarf for Owen, and I gave it to him yesterday."

Now it's Brady's turn to glance between me and Owen. "Oh."

It's time for us to part company.

"Thank you again," I say, then Spencer and I head across the room to the two people we haven't exchanged gifts with yet, Tori and Sadie.

After Spencer gives Tori a Boudron diaper bag, he gets a phone call and walks away to answer. Doesn't anyone at the firm take time off for Christmas? It's honestly depressing to look into my future and see holidays spent with Spencer talking on his phone. I thought meals were bad enough.

Tori watches him leave before turning her attention to

the bag. "Does he think Sadie is a baby? She's practically potty trained." She runs a hand over the baby pink leather with the distinctive buttons.

"Either that or he doesn't know it's a diaper bag?" I say. "I don't think most people do unless they follow the company. It just looks like a shoulder bag."

"True."

Sadie jumps up from the floor where there are mounds of art supplies, clothes, toys, and stuffed animals. She tugs on the diaper bag strap.

"Can I put my animals in here?"

Tori lets her take it but not before she warns, "Do not put your art kit in here. Animals only."

I hand Sadie my gift to her, a knitted horse, stuffed with fluff I borrowed from my pillow. She gasps.

"He's beautiful!" She gives me a hug around my hips. "I'll name him BB."

"You have a pig named BB," Tori reminds her.

"My favorites are all named BB."

She runs away, galloping him around the room.

"Thank you," Tori says. "That was kind of you to remember Sadie."

I hand her the mittens. "I made these for you."

Tori's eyes soften as she takes them from my hands. For a moment she doesn't speak as she runs her fingers over the Scandinavian star design. "You made these?"

"I stayed up late the other night to get them finished by today."

"You made these for *me*." Her voice rises in pitch as she speaks. "I've never had anyone make me something that I didn't pay for." She swallows thickly as she looks back up. "I know I'm not the easiest person to get along with, but thanks for giving me a chance."

She pulls me into a tight hug and doesn't let me go until Sadie plows into our legs.

"Can I get a pig?" she asks as she looks up at me. "In pink."

"Sure, but it won't be today."

She frowns for a second, but nothing keeps her down for long. She runs off to show Brady her horse.

Spencer finishes his call and comes to stand beside me. We continue to mingle with his family, but I'm distracted. Any second now, he's going to propose. My palms sweat. I catch myself chewing on my thumbnail.

Spencer meets my eyes. This is the moment. I pull up as much enthusiasm as possible ... but he doesn't kneel on one knee. He tugs me from the room and down the hall to the office. Once the door shuts behind us, he turns to face me, a regretful expression on his face.

"Layla, I had a speech prepared to give in front of everyone, but I know I can't pull it off. I would rather give you the ring here and announce our engagement to the family."

My shoulders relax. I wasn't ready to give the performance of the year. "That is a great idea."

From his inside jacket pocket, he pulls out the now familiar ring box and pops it open. The diamonds are larger and more sparkly than I remember. My hand is only moderately shaking when I hold it out, and Spencer slips the ring on for the second time in less than a week. I feel a heaviness that comes from more than the weight of the diamonds.

He holds my hand in his and studies the ring. The fingers of his free hand tap against his leg. Why is he nervous? This is his idea.

"Are we ready to do this?" he asks.

"Are you having any doubts?"

He lets go of my hand and loosens his tie. "No doubt. Some nerves, maybe. Getting married isn't something to take lightly, and I'm trying to wrap my head around how our lives are about to change."

I've been so focused on getting the money for Grandmother, I have thought little about what happens after we're engaged, but he's right. Things will change. Wedding planning will take up my time. We'll move in together. I'll leave my roommates, and that's a hard thing to contemplate. Meg, Livy, and I have been together for four years, and I'll be replacing them with a workaholic who doesn't have the same taste in movies that I do.

This feels real in a way it didn't before. I feel queasy, but there is absolutely no turning back.

"Ready?" he asks.

"Yes."

We head back into the family room, hands clasped together tightly as we draw support from each other.

Owen is talking with Tori and is the first to notice our return. The smile on his face slips away the second he notices the huge rock on my finger.

I turn and face Spencer, so Owen is behind me. I don't want to see him right now. It's too late for doubts and second-guessing. It has been since the moment I said yes at *L'oie Bleue*.

"Attention please," Spencer says, and the room quiets as

everyone turns in our direction. "We have an announcement to make. I have asked for Layla's hand in marriage, and she has accepted."

I must have heightened awareness because I take in everyone's response at once. Dorian claps, a gleeful smile on his face. Ginger raises an eyebrow and yawns. Ellory and Gerald give half-hearted applause. Rheta smiles, but it doesn't reach her eyes. Where is her happiness in me joining her family like I expected after speaking with her a few nights ago?

Marianne and Brady clap, but their attention is behind me. On Owen. I can't resist peeking at him. Owen's shoulders fold inward. Devastation hollows out his eyes.

I feel his disappointment in my chest. A defense rises inside my head. *I'm Spencer's girlfriend; you knew that the moment you showed up at the cabin. Just because we have fun together doesn't mean we're meant to end up together. It isn't my fault you set yourself up for heartache.*

It's a weak defense that would never stand up in court. Our time together meant more to me than a way to wile away the week while in Maine. It was special. He made it special. He isn't the only one who's disappointed.

Tori is the first to offer us congratulations. At least one person in this room is thrilled about our engagement. If it can't be me, then I'm glad it's Tori.

Everyone else follows her lead and comes forward until we're surrounded by Ecclestons and Clarks.

Except for one.

Chapter Nineteen

OWEN

I knew Spencer planned to marry Layla, but I didn't realize he meant to propose on Christmas. Spencer isn't the kind of person who makes decisions quickly. I assumed Layla coming to Maine this week was planting a seed for a future engagement.

Layla is marrying Spencer. Operation-Show-Layla-She's-Worth-More-Than-a-Few-Million has failed. Why can't she see Spencer is completely wrong for her? They will make each other miserable sooner rather than later. At least she has her money. The thought carries a tinge of bitterness.

Brady elbows me. "Are you okay?"

"Of course. Why wouldn't I be?"

He glares like I'm stupid. "Because the girl you love just got engaged to someone else."

Love. It's a strong word, but with the way my heart feels torn to bits, he might be right.

"She was never mine to love." That didn't stop me from falling for her.

As everyone approaches the couple, I leave the room and go through the house to the back deck. It's cold outside, but the sky is clear and the sun is warm on my face. For once, there's no wind blowing off the ocean.

Layla is *engaged* to Spencer. I was so sure I'd be able to convince her not to marry him. It doesn't feel real. I don't know how long I stand outside, but I'm shivering when Miles finds me and wraps a blanket around my shoulders. I pull it tight across my chest.

"Don't you ever get a day off?" I ask. "Why aren't you home with your family?"

He leans his elbows on the railing and looks out at the ocean. "My daughters are with their in-laws this year. I'll see them on Sunday."

I remember his daughters, twins a few years younger than me. I didn't realize they were married. In my head, they're still fifteen.

"It's been fun being a part of your family Christmas this year," he continues. "Without my wife, taking care of everyone has kept me busy and my thoughts occupied."

"I wish I'd stayed home," I say. Now more than ever. At least then I wouldn't have spent the week with Layla, only to have her marry my cousin.

"It meant a lot to Ms. Rheta that you and your family are here," Miles says.

I raise an eyebrow. "Just Ms. Rheta? I've noticed you and my mom together often this week. What are your intentions?" I speak in a jovial tone to let him know I'm not upset, but I am curious.

He laughs. "We've been reconnecting. Though, I won't lie. If Marianne is interested in more than friendship, I'd like that."

It's what I suspected, and though I don't like thinking of Mom with anyone but Dad, life goes on. Mom hasn't been this happy in eight years, and it isn't only because she has her family back.

"You have my support," I say.

"Thanks. That means a lot to me." He looks back at the ocean with a wide grin, but then sobers. "I'm glad I caught you alone. There's something I want to tell you about your grandfather."

My mood instantly sours. "I'd rather you not."

Miles ignores my request. "He wasn't a horrible person. He wasn't perfect, but he loved you."

I snort.

"He missed you," Miles continues. "He never stopped hoping you would answer his calls."

I shake my head. "He only called to try to convince me to come back to the firm so he could control me, not because he cared."

"Mr. Eccleston might not have liked your father, but he wasn't a malicious man. Never did he want something horrible to happen to him. He regretted how he treated you and how he spoke about your father after his stroke."

I don't believe Miles. For Grandfather, it was his way or you no longer existed. He didn't care about me or Mom and definitely not Dad because we were outside of his control.

"He never said that," I argue.

Miles nods. "He did, on multiple occasions, and I thought you should know. You were a brilliant lawyer and I hate thinking you gave that up because of how he treated you and your father. He wanted to ask for your forgiveness."

I don't want to accept this as the truth. I take a few minutes to sort through my thoughts and emotions about why, and it becomes clear. It means Grandfather died with an apology he never got to give. I took that away from him, and that doesn't sit well.

Until I remember, there is more than one way to reach out. He could have sent me a postcard or hired a skywriter if he was desperate enough. Mom would have answered his call. If he made peace with her, then I would have spoken to him again. Maybe he regretted how he handled the situation, but he didn't try hard enough to tell me himself.

Still, I can't disregard all of of Miles' words. I loved Grandfather for half of my life. The summers I spent with him were my favorite months of the year. I think back to my time at the law firm. I might not have enjoyed practicing law, but I enjoyed working with him. Not only did I lose my father eight years ago, I lost my grandfather.

I hope what Miles said is true and Grandfather came to understand how his actions hurt my family. If so, then I accept the apology he never gave me. The last of the anger I've held on to disintegrates. If Mom can forgive and move on, then so can I. I breathe deeply, maybe for the first time since Dad's funeral.

"Thank you, Miles."

He nods. "I'm glad you came this Christmas. Your Grandmother has missed you. I've missed you." He slaps me on the back and walks toward the door. "Lunch is being served in the dining room."

Spencer will know the moment I walk in that I've been

sulking. Layla will see my devastation. Mom and Brady will offer silent sympathy. I can't handle everyone right now.

"I'm not hungry."

He stops with his hand on the knob and studies me. "I'll bring lunch up to your room and tell Ms. Rheta you're not feeling well."

I head upstairs to my purple oasis and eat the lunch Miles brings me. I flip through the channels on TV until I fall asleep. When I wake, it's dark. I lie in bed and think about Layla. About how much I admire her. How I love her. How there is nothing I can do about it.

Spencer won. I have to respect Layla's choice and let her go. My acceptance of the situation isn't easy; it's downright depressing, but unavoidable.

I've missed one meal, and that's enough wallowing. It would be a crime to miss Christmas dinner. I change out of my wrinkled shirt and head downstairs. As luck would have it, I run into Layla as she exits the family room.

"Owen!" She sounds shocked to see me and takes a step back, then makes sure the door shuts behind her as if us meeting in the hallway is something illicit. "Can I talk to you for a minute?"

"Yes." Seeing her with Spencer's ring on her finger is an ice pick to my chest, but I will listen to anything she wants to tell me.

The family room door opens. Her eyes widen. She takes my hand and pulls me to the first door she comes to, which is a walk-in closet full of towels, bedding, and cleaning supplies. It smells like lemon polish.

The door shuts, leaving us in pitch dark.

She feels along the wall, and a second later the overhead light flips on.

"Can I help you with something?" My eyebrows raise as I glance around at our intimate location.

She blushes. "I need you to understand me."

The humor I find in our surroundings flees. I rub my eyes. "Layla, it's honestly none of my business what choices you make. You don't owe me any explanation."

"I do. Even if you don't need to hear it, I need to say it. I don't take my decision to marry Spencer lightly." Her shoulders slump. "I'm tired of being alone."

There's more to her decision than loneliness because I'm standing right here. "Then why Spencer? Once married, you'll be more alone than ever because he's a workaholic."

She won't meet my eyes. They're focused on my chest. "When I was ten years old, my mom lost her job. She slept a lot and Nana assumed she was depressed, but it turned out she had colon cancer. No insurance. Four years of treatment. Opa and Nana worked past retirement to pay off the medical debt. We lived on a strict budget until they paid the last bill and they could finally retire. Opa died two years later."

I want to reach out and touch her, offer her comfort, but I remain still, my hands at my side. "I'm sorry, Layla. That's awful."

She glances up and meets my eyes for a second before she looks away. The sheets on the shelf have her complete attention.

"It was stressful. You don't know how that much debt feels, especially as a teenager. I worked hard for scholarships and grants because I knew we had no money to pay for college. When I started teaching, it was the first time in my life I didn't have to account for every penny." She hangs her head and rubs at her temple as if ashamed for her past actions. "I bought a nice car and went on vacations. I went clothes shopping every weekend. I lived it up and spent money like I would always have more. So stupid. I knew better."

"That's not living it up," I say. "That's living. You have nothing to feel guilty about."

"I should have saved for a rainy day. If there is anything I've learned in life, it's that a financial disaster is just around the corner."

"Layla, no."

I want to say more, but how can I argue? I've never been in Layla's situation. When I was growing up, we didn't have much, but we always had enough. We took a road trip every year and went out to eat at least once a week. I never felt poor until I compared my situation to my cousins.

Layla shakes her head. "I should have saved money instead of vacationing in Hawaii so that when Nana was scammed out of everything, we would've had something to fall back on."

Scammed. I know about Layla's debt and her reason for marrying Spencer, but to find out some person stole from her grandma has me furious. How do people like that exist in this world? My jaw clenches so tight that I can't get a word out, but what can I say except that I want to find that scammer and pummel him into the ground? What's done is done.

She surprises me when she pokes me in the chest. Hard. "For a year-and-a-half I've done everything I can think of to pay for Nana's care. I'm exhausted. So don't judge me. You don't know what it's like to be financially depleted and emotionally spent. To be drowning in debt with no way to pay it off. My future is bleak. Spencer has offered to take care of everything. I want relief. I want to breathe again. I want to live. Be happy for me."

I can't, now even more so than yesterday. My resolve from twenty minutes ago to let her make her choice without my interference disintegrates. I have one last chance to convince her this reasoning is wrong, and I can't let it pass me by.

"I can help you with money for your grandma," I say. "I sold my manufacturing company at the beginning of the year, remember? I have more money than I know what to do with. I ask for nothing in return. You don't even have to see me again after this week, if that's what you want." Though I hope that option isn't on the table. "Just don't marry Spencer."

She breathes out a long breath. When she looks at me, conviction shines in her eyes. "Spencer needs me, just like I need him. Our agreement to marry is mutually beneficial. I can't accept your money because there's no benefit to you."

I want to shake sense into her. "Helping you would make me happy. If that's not beneficial, then what is?"

Layla leans forward and kisses my cheek. Her lips are soft. The scent of peppermint clings to her, and I wonder absently how many candy canes she's eaten today.

"I can't pull you into my financial mess when I have nothing to give you in return," she whispers. "Thank you for a lovely Christmas."

She opens the door and leaves, flipping off the light switch before shutting me in the dark.

A second later, she reaches back in to turn on the light. "Sorry. Habit."

It doesn't matter if the light is on or off, the devastation Layla's caused remains either way.

LAYLA

Stepping out of the closet may be one of the hardest things that I've asked of myself. I'm leaving Owen behind for good. He truly wants to help me, but I can't accept. If only–

No. I'm not wishing for something that can never be. Spencer and I will have a functional, mutually beneficial marriage. We will be happy together.

Just as soon as I forget all about Owen.

It won't be easy. When he didn't come to lunch or show up this afternoon for the poker game in the family room, I kept glancing at the door, anticipating his arrival. It will be hard to untangle my feelings for him when all I want is to *be* with him.

One moment at a time, beginning now.

I need a few minutes alone to decompress. I've never shared with anyone the details of my childhood like I did to Owen just now. The emotions the memories brought up, as well as saying goodbye to him, have worn me out.

When I saw Owen, I was on my way upstairs to grab my phone charger since my phone is almost dead after all the pictures I've taken today. I'll take a breather in my room before going back into the family room.

Tori comes down the stairs as I head up them.

"Have you seen Owen?" she asks.

Um, maybe. Tori is the only one who hasn't caught on to my feelings for the wrong cousin, and I'd like to keep it that way.

"Why?" I ask.

"I went up to his room to see if he was feeling better, but he isn't there. Sadie wants to show him the drawings she made with the markers and paper he gave her for Christmas."

"I'm sure he'll show up. Will Sadie show me her artwork as we wait? I'd love to see her drawings."

I loop my arm through hers and head back to the family room. It's better if she doesn't see Owen exit the closet. It would lead to more questions and this entire episode needs to be put behind us.

Chapter Twenty

OWEN

At exactly ten a.m. on the morning after Christmas, the whole town descends on Grandmother's cabin. I don't know who these people are, but they know her. She's moved a wingback chair from her bedroom into the foyer and greets every person who comes through the front door. It gives me the impression that she is on her throne and the townspeople are her subjects coming to pay her tribute. The tribute being leftover Christmas dinner and unwanted gifts.

I've never seen Grandmother so happy.

Miles stands beside her and directs people to drop off the items for the gift exchange in the dining room and food in the breakfast room. The family room is set aside for games. Music and laughter spill out into the foyer. Within an hour, it's a rocking party.

Spencer, Dorian, Ellory, and Gerald hole up in the office. They did not take Grandmother's suggestion to visit the library, though I'm sure they're regretting it now. This place is loud.

Ginger had the right idea and is spending another day at the spa. I should have joined her. A massage and time spent in a sauna might knock me out of my foul mood. Except both Mom and Brady reminded me last night that I promised to make this the best Christmas, which means I can't disappear for the day again.

Brady's around here somewhere, surrounded by a flock of kids. Under Sadie's influence, they've decided that he's the best thing here, maybe even better than all the desserts.

Mom stays close to Miles' side. Whatever he's feeling for her, she must feel the same. There will be conversations about their budding relationship in the future, but that's definitely not something for today.

I catch glimpses of Layla and Tori together. They might be avoiding me. Either because I'm not good company in my current mood, or because Layla has decided I'm a distraction. Or maybe Spencer told her she can't see me anymore. Yesterday, she did make me hide in a closet to avoid anyone seeing us together.

I wander aimlessly from room to room until I'm sick of myself. Miles' mom Susan is in the kitchen directing help and warming food. I head there. As soon as I enter, she pats my cheeks like she did when I was a teenager, then puts me to work.

I gather empty serving plates from the breakfast room and take out full ones. Then she has me clean the fridge of leftovers from the past few days to add to what everyone else brought.

"After the family leaves on Saturday morning," she says, "It'll just be Mrs. Eccleston, and she can't eat all of this."

I come across the last of the strawberry cheesecake and grab a spoon so I can eat it myself.

When the kitchen empties of the few women who have been helping wash dishes, Susan asks, "What has you so down? I've never known you to be morose."

"Woman troubles," is as far as I get before the door from the hallway opens and Brady runs in.

"Hide me," he whispers, as he frantically looks around.

Neither Susan nor I move, too surprised by his sudden appearance. He ducks behind the counter just as the door opens and Sadie walks through.

"Where is Brady?" she demands. Susan and I both shrug. She stomps her foot. "He's supposed to play with me."

Once she leaves, we're silent until we're sure she's not coming back.

Brady bounces up and sits on the counter. "Thanks. I was her pony, and she'd pull on my hair when she wanted me to turn." He rubs his scalp. "She's cute, but she's demanding."

Susan chuckles. "Steal some of that cheesecake from your brother and have a break. He's telling me about his romance troubles."

Brady grabs a plate and a fork and takes half of my cheesecake. "Normally, I don't care about his love life, but I like Layla."

"Yeah, me too," I say. My sadness leaks into my voice. "That's the trouble."

"Isn't Layla engaged to your cousin?" Susan asks.

Brady and I nod.

She grabs a spoon and scoops a bite of cheesecake for herself. "You better fill me in."

I don't like talking about my problems, but I must need to get this off my chest because, after swearing them both to secrecy, I tell them everything. About how I knew Layla before this week, all I've learned about her financial situation, and the marriage agreement she has with Spencer. I pause as people come in and out with dishes, but pick up again when we're alone.

"This is too easy," Brady says with an unsympathetic shrug. He drops his plate in the sink. "Tell her about the millions of dollars you have from selling your bag business. I bet you have more money than Spencer does. She'll marry you instead."

Susan looks from Brady to me. "Bag business?"

Brady doesn't give me a chance to answer. "Yeah, Owen started a company with a designer friend of his. Boudron. Have you ever heard of it? Because everyone else has. I saw Zendaya in a TikTok ad last week."

Susan's eyes widen. "You own Boudron? Ms. Rheta said you owned a landscaping business."

Even Susan has heard of Boudron. The new marketing manager knows what she's doing.

I give her a weak smile. "I sold my half of Boudron and bought a landscaping company to keep me busy."

She nods as she takes in the information. "And Layla doesn't know? I agree with Brady. Tell her what you can offer her, and she'll see she has another option."

"No." They don't understand. "I don't want her to choose me because of my money. I want to give her money to help her and then have her choose me because I'm who she wants."

By the way Brady is giving me the side-eye, he's not impressed with my reasoning. "Don't be a tool."

I tap him on the back of his head. "I'm still your older brother. Be nice."

He scoots further down the counter so he's out of my reach. "I'm not being mean; I'm being honest. I don't get you and money. You have so much of it, but you drive the same car you did when you started the bag business. You live in a fifty-year-old house with only one bathroom. You had the money to fly us out to Maine in first class, but we squished into economy. You couldn't even splurge on business class. Look at me! I'm six feet tall! But you're cheap. You act like it's a sin to spend money."

It's a new level of low when my fourteen-year-old brother lectures me on finances. "I'm frugal, not cheap. I spend money."

Brady levels a look at me. "No, you don't. It's like you're ashamed to be rich. Since we've been here, it's obvious everyone thinks you're poor. No one knows Boudron is yours. Layla hugs her bag like it's a pet. Spencer gave one to Tori for Christmas. It's really cool what you've done, but you let everyone look down on you, and I don't get why."

This is the most I've heard Brady speak about anything other than a book in a long time and it's unfortunate it's to rag on me.

"Because money doesn't matter," I say.

My brother is not impressed. "Only someone who has money can say something so stupid. It obviously matters to Layla."

"Money doesn't give my life value," I amend. "Not having money doesn't devalue Layla, but she seems to think it does. She's acting like she's a commodity to be bought. I promised her I would help her. Repeatedly. She doesn't want my help. She doesn't want me."

I'm pouting, but I can't seem to stop.

Susan pats my cheeks again. "Taking money from Spencer will not break him. Maybe she thinks you're a landscaper like I did and didn't accept your offer, because she believes taking money from you will harm you financially."

"I don't want to be chosen because of money," I say stubbornly. "I want her to choose me because she loves me."

Susan tisks and shakes her head. "It sounds like she doesn't have the space in her life to worry about love. She might not feel like she has a choice. Tell her the truth and give her that choice. If she still chooses Spencer, at least you'll know you tried everything and so will she."

It's not that I don't understand what Susan and Brady are saying, but I don't agree.

"I've always respected how Mom gave up everything to be with Dad," I say. "The absence of money didn't stop them from being together."

"Your dad didn't come with a bucket load of debt," Susan says. "You'll have to decide what you want to hold on to more: Layla or your hate for this family."

"I don't hate this family."

"Ha!" Brady says.

"*Anymore.* I don't hate this family anymore." This week has given me the chance to forgive and see the good in people I've villainized for years. "Susan, what do my feelings for this family have to do with Layla?"

"It seems to me you do everything you can to *not* be an Eccleston. Every attribute you associate with them, you do the opposite. You quit the firm to become a businessman. This family shouts to high heaven that they're the best corporate lawyers. You hide what you've accomplished. You don't buy flashy cars or a big house or vacation homes. If Spencer is wooing a girl because he has the financial means to do so, you refuse to do the same."

"If I told Layla I have millions of dollars and she picked me, I don't want to wonder if she did because of my money. How is that a bad thing?"

"It's not, but do you believe Layla only likes you for your money? From everything you've told us, it seems to me she shares your feelings. Do you doubt that?"

I think back on our week and how happy she was when we were together. The beach, the tree farm, dinner on Christmas Eve. We've shared charged moments where I knew she wanted to kiss me as much as I wanted to kiss her. The attraction is not all on my end. Her belief I don't have money hasn't influenced how she's acted around me. She's never tried to convince me to accept my inheritance.

It's clear she isn't obsessed with wealth. Her engagement ring is huge, but she didn't expect Spencer to get her diamond earrings to match. She gave everyone knitted gifts quietly. Money doesn't seem to be a big draw for her, unless it comes to caring for her grandma.

"No," I say. "If I told her how much I have in my bank account, it wouldn't change her feelings toward me."

"How much *do* you have in your bank account?" Brady asks.

Susan and I ignore him.

"Tell Layla everything," Susan says. "Don't let her continue to believe she'd weigh you down with her problems. Show her you can take them on."

"Yeah," Brady says. "Stop being a snob about money."

It is becoming clear that I *am* a snob about money. What I have sits in my investment portfolio making more money, but it doesn't do anyone any good. What it does is make me feel superior to the rest of my extended family because I don't flaunt it like they do.

Grandmother is doing good with her wealth; I want to do the same with mine. Specifically, in Layla's life. Not only to help with her grandma, but to save her from a loveless marriage. She's rejected my offer to help before, but when she knows about Boudron, it might be enough to change her mind.

I will also be one hundred percent transparent with my feelings. She should know it isn't just a date I want, but all her years from this day onward.

First, I have to find her.

Chapter Twenty-One

LAYLA

Tori's room is a mess. Clothes, toys, and toiletries cover every available surface, even the little trundle bed where she wants to lay sleeping Sadie.

I move the clothes and stuffed animals from the surface and pull back the covers. Hidden under the blankets are the wooden animal ornaments. I scoop them into my hands and lay them on the floor next to the pillow.

Tori lays her daughter on the bed and removes her designer party dress before tucking her beneath the comforter.

"Fingers crossed she stays asleep," Tori says under her breath.

Sadie groans as she stretches her arms over her head. Our eyes widen as we wait for what comes next. She rolls over with eyes still closed. We tip-toe from the room.

Once in the hallway, Tori sags against the door. Fatigue seems to weigh down every limb, but she laughs. "That girl drives me crazy, but sometimes I can't handle how much I love her. It's a physical ache. I want to give her everything, but I can't give her what she wants the most: a dad who sticks around."

Her melancholy descends as swiftly as the laughter did. I wonder how much sleep she's had since she arrived.

Music and voices carry up the stairs for those who have yet to leave, even though it's past seven. It's been a fun, exhausting day. My favorite part was meeting the Zimmermans, the family who made me the delicious Christmas Eve dinner. I found out Owen paid them three hundred dollars for the food, even though they offered to make the meal for just the cost of ingredients. *Three hundred dollars.* I'm still in shock.

"Come on," I say, taking Tori by the arm and leading her to my room. "Let's take a break. I'm partied out."

Once there, we collapse on my couch and put our feet up on the coffee table. Instead of talking, we close our eyes and are half asleep when Tori's phone rings.

She pulls it from the hidden pocket in her maxi skirt. "Ugh. It's the ex, probably wanting to rub it into my face that he's with his new girlfriend."

She throws her phone across the room, where it smacks against the wall. It doesn't seem to concern her she might have damaged it.

"I'm sorry he's making you miserable."

She scowls. "I miss him, but I hate him. I hate how small he wants me to feel and how little he cares about Sadie." She scrunches her face. "Looking back, my motivation for marrying was because I hated practicing law. I wanted out of my job, and the only escape I saw was marriage and having a baby."

I wanted out of my job and the only escape I saw was marriage. Her words hit like a hammer to my skull. I want out of my financial predicament, and the only escape I see is marriage. That hits close, and my heart hiccups in my chest.

"My plan failed." She waves her hands through the air. "Not only is my marriage over, but Mom wants me back at the firm. I've put her off, but once Sadie starts kindergarten, I won't have any excuse not to."

Tori lifts my hand from the couch and studies my engagement ring, unaware that I'm close to passing out.

"I wish the best for you and Spencer. He's a wonderful guy. When my ex told me he wanted a divorce, Spencer was one of the first people I told. He dropped everything to come to New York for the weekend to help me. Surprising, since he reminds me of my parents." She drops my hand and blows out a breath. "Everything is less important than the people paying for their time."

More truth hammers into my heart. How sad that Tori felt her parents cared more for their clients than for her. Will my children grow up feeling like their dad cares more about his clients than he does about them? Of course they will, because I feel that way now. Tori didn't mention how much work Spencer did in New York while he stayed with her, but she didn't have to. His clients are never out of reach, no matter where he travels.

My tongue is stuck to the top of my dry mouth, and it's

an effort to push words past my numb lips. "How did you cope with your parents being gone so much?"

"I filled my time with hobbies and school. It helped as long as I didn't put too much energy into hoping they would show up to my golf competitions or praise me for my perfect grades. What's funny is I married a man who treated me the same way they did: as an afterthought." She tilts her head back against the couch and closes her eyes. "More horrifying than funny when I think about it."

Every word Tori speaks brings my future into frightening clarity. Theoretically, I know exactly what my marriage to Spencer will look like, but listening to Tori and seeing her heartbreak is real. It makes my future feel real in a way it hasn't before.

This week, Spencer has made time for me. He sacrificed what he could, as long as it didn't compromise his case. What about next year? Or in five years? Will he still be making these little sacrifices? Or will I become indistinguishable from the furniture?

"I'm an afterthought to Spencer," I whisper.

Tori sits up, her eyes wide, and says with false cheer, "Of course not. Spencer isn't like my ex. He loves you. I'm not sure my ex ever loved me. I was more of a trophy wife." She gags. "He works for the family firm; did you know that? He won the prize of marrying the granddaughter of the owner. I stopped caring how much jewelry he bought me once I realized all I wanted was to be seen for who I am and not who my family is. You don't have to worry about that. Spencer sees you. He adores you. He will never take you for granted."

I'm not so sure about that last part because Spencer

doesn't adore me. He may not want to marry me for my family connections, but he does want to show me off to his clients and increase his inheritance.

Tori's past is my present. Her present is my probable future. And right now, she is hurting and alone because of her ex-husband. I might throw up.

She continues her pep-talk. "You and Spencer are a great couple. You'll have the cutest little children."

Of that I have no doubt, but the idea of having kids with him hits me differently after spending the week with Tori and Sadie. I don't want to be a single mother, and even married, that is what I will be as Spencer's wife.

When I say nothing in response to Tori, she hesitantly says, "Did I upset you?"

"No." I can only hope my lie is convincing. I don't want her to feel bad for confiding in me. "Not at all." I swallow thickly. "Do you want to watch a movie?"

"Okay, but only if you're sure I didn't say something wrong. I can be thoughtless sometimes."

"I'm okay. I promise."

My smile must be persuasive, because after a few seconds of Tori studying me, she nods. I turn on the TV and start flipping through channels, paying little attention to what comes up on the screen until I land on Hallmark. When Tori's breathing levels out, and she falls asleep, I mute the TV and grab a blanket from the end of the bed and place it over her.

I want to talk to Meg and Livy, and even grab my phone to call, but I can't. Especially not now when I've seen a glimpse into my future. It will take very little to convince me I'm making a mistake, yet what is my other option besides marrying Spencer? I need the money he promised by Monday to pay the rest of January's Brock Pine Home bill. I need it to pay my rent. It would be nice to have food this month besides ramen and rice. There is nothing left in any account. It's gone. Nana supported me, and it's my turn to support her. I can't do it without Spencer. Alone, I fail.

A text comes through from Owen. He wants to talk, but we've said everything there is to say to each other. He thinks he can help, but I haven't told him how much debt I have or how much more I'll accrue. I'm too ashamed to give him the complete picture of what a mess I'm in, and it'll humiliate both of us when he admits he's not in a financial position to help me.

A knock comes at the door. My heart stutters. It's probably Owen, so I stay where I am and hope he doesn't peek inside. Another knock, but then all is silent.

My phone buzzes again and I expect a text from Owen, but it's a Facebook memory notification. I open it to find the video I made in honor of Opa after he passed. I press play.

It begins with pictures of when Opa was a little boy in Germany and through his teenage years until he moved to the United States and met Nana. The rest of the pictures are of them together, their lives entwined completely. My vision blurs as mom grows up, and then I'm on the scene. Mom becomes frailer in each photo until she's gone. Nana and Opa persevere, raising their granddaughter in a house they fill with love. I never doubted their complete devotion to each other or to me.

Nana always wanted the best for her family. She would be devastated to know what I'm sacrificing for her. If she were aware of my situation, she would understand that I'm destitute and be okay if she became a ward of the state. She wouldn't want me to marry a man I don't love to help her. It's a hard truth to accept because I want to give her everything she gave me. Maybe that desire has weighed me down more than the financial burden.

For the first time in a week, I allow myself to think through my situation in a way that doesn't include Spencer. What options haven't I considered?

Busking. A weak smile plays on my lips as I wipe tears from my cheeks. I don't discount the idea completely, but it's not a solid plan.

My roommates. I've never talked to them about my need for money because I don't want them to worry, and Nana is my responsibility. But, if I explained, they would help me cover my rent, at the very least.

Spencer. When I originally met with him at *L'oie Bleue* I asked for a loan. If I broke off our engagement, he would still give it to me. Maybe. It will take my whole life to pay it back on a teacher's salary, but I will try.

Or, if he refused to give me the loan, then I'd have to let the state step in. It's an option that physically hurts, but Nana will still be cared for, and that's what matters.

My knee bounces, but I don't realize it until Tori groans in her sleep. Too agitated to stay still, I pace the room while I chew on my thumbnail, thinking through the two options: marry Spencer or don't marry Spencer.

The more difficult road is breaking off my engagement. I've never shied away from hard work, but taking back all my debts is bleak. For one week, I was free. Now the financial demands feel like manacles around my feet.

Unfortunately, as I wear a line through the carpet, I know

it's the path that will make me happier in the long run. Marrying Spencer would be like trading one type of prison for another. I choose the financial prison over being locked in a loveless marriage.

It takes a few hours for me to build up the courage to talk to Spencer. I made a promise. I don't want to go back on my word, but there is more at stake here than disappointing him.

I have to tell him my decision now. I can't wait until we return to Utah. It's not fair to either of us, especially because the family is meeting with Rheta's lawyer tomorrow, and she promised me a gift. I can't accept anything from her when I know I won't be part of the family in the future.

Tori's still asleep on my couch, so I shut the door behind me with a soft click. All is quiet downstairs. I'm not sure if Spencer is still working, so I check his bedroom first. There is no answer to my knock.

I head downstairs. The house is dark, the remnants of the party waiting until tomorrow to be cleaned up. The office door is open. Spencer is inside, as are Gerald and Ellory. Even though Spencer told me building the case is going well, it seems they still need to spend fourteen hours a day on the thing. Seeing their slouched shoulders and weary expressions makes me tired.

"Spencer?"

He looks up and suppresses a yawn. "Layla. I thought you went to bed hours ago."

"I need to talk to you."

He stretches his arms above his head and stands. "I was about to take a break outside. I need the cold air to wake me up. Want to join me?"

I follow him toward the door, but not before taking the blanket from the back of the couch.

The moment I walk out on the deck, I'm surrounded by white. It snowed over the last few hours. A day late for Christmas, but it still brings me joy. I twirl with my hands out to my sides, and watch big, soft flakes tumble from the gray sky. For a few moments, I forget my reason for being here, until Spencer speaks.

"What did you want to talk to me about? Is Owen bothering you again?"

My joyful snow twirl halts, and I move to stand next to him under the shelter of the eaves. I don't know how to say what I need to say in any way other than blunt. "I can't marry you."

It's always fascinated me how clouds reflect light back to earth, making it seem lighter than the hour would suggest. Spencer's narrowed eyes and pinched lips are visible, and I wish they weren't. I hate how I've failed him, but I'd hate to fail myself even more.

"We have an agreement."

"I wish I could marry you. It would definitely make my life easier, but what we have is a counterfeit engagement that will turn into a marriage where we are nothing more than roommates. I can't help but see that down the road we'll make each other miserable."

He looks off into the distance, his jaw set, his hands in his pants pockets. "Misery is a decision. We decide to be happy and we'll be happy."

I can't tell if he's being purposefully blind or if he truly believes it's that easy. Maybe for him, it would be. Work is his first love, and if he only saw me for a few hours at night, then maybe that's all he needs to be happy. Except, he deserves to be loved just as much as I do. Even if he doesn't want that for himself, I wish it for him.

"Spencer, there is someone out in the world waiting for a man like you. I don't want to rob you of the opportunity to love and be loved."

"How altruistic of you," he says with a touch of sarcasm. "Except I don't want to marry for love. I told you about my father."

"Your father mistakes infatuation for love and he's given you a false idea of what to expect from marriage. When two people marry for love, they make sacrifices and they don't give up on each other. Like my grandparents and yours."

"In my experience, that is the exception, not the rule."

What a bleak outlook on relationships. If I believed like he did, I would spend all my time at work, too.

When he speaks again, his voice is pleading. "Layla, friendship can endure longer than love if you'd give us a chance. Let me prove it to you."

I think of Tori sleeping upstairs. The probability of us ending up like her and her ex-husband is greater than married bliss. Especially when I feel like I do about Owen. That isn't fair to either of us. Spencer believes he wants this marriage, but for the good of both of us, I have to refuse.

"I can't," I whisper.

Suddenly agitated, he rakes both hands through his hair. "This is because of Owen, isn't it? He swayed you into believing he's a better man than I am. Don't fall for his lies. He's a layabout who can't keep a job."

"This decision is about me and what I want for my future. I thought I could sacrifice love for security, but I can't do it." I shouldn't bring Owen up, but I don't like what Spencer said about him. He should know the truth. "Owen isn't a layabout. He's not just a landscaper, he owns the business. You might know this if you gave him a chance."

He snorts. "No thanks. He's stolen my fiancée. I think that's all I need to know about him. So, we're done? No longer engaged? You're giving up a chance to care for your grandmother so you can find a fairytale *love*?"

The most depressing part about my future is I won't ever find love. I refuse to bring Owen into my financial problems, and I doubt that will change with anyone else I meet going forward. Spencer doesn't need to know I'm picking a life of loneliness over him.

It's time to ask the big question. I overlook Spencer's anger. He has a right to it. I've done him wrong. But I still need money.

"I'm sorry I've hurt you, Spencer. It wasn't my intention, and I know you're angry, but I have a favor to ask. Last Friday, before you proposed, I asked you for a loan. Is that something you'd reconsider?"

He takes a few steps away, his attention on his feet as they crunch through the snow. He turns back to face me. Fat snowflakes gather in his hair. The longer he takes, the more I believe he'll say no. I begin to make a plan for moving Nana to a different home; one the state will pay for.

Spencer finally says, "Alright."

I slump against the side of the house, lightheaded with relief. "Thank you."

"Don't sound so surprised. I'm not a monster. My assistant will send you a contract on Monday. As soon as you send it back, I'll wire transfer the funds to your account."

He's going to be okay. He's hurt and angry, but not furious or filled with the need to cause me pain. I wish I could love him. This past year, each time we dated, I wished the same thing.

He tugs at the bottom of his sweater. "Anything else?"

"I should return your ring." I slip it off my finger and hold it out.

He doesn't touch it. He can't even look at it. "If you put it on the dresser in my room, then I'll be sure not to lose it." He turns to go back inside, but then pauses. "It would be better if you left tomorrow instead of Saturday. I'll change your flight and text you the details. I'm sure Miles will drive you to the airport."

"Thank you, Spencer. For everything." I hope he hears my gratitude in my voice. The words feel paltry compared to what he's given me and Nana.

He shuts the door firmly behind him. I'd rather not walk through the office after that conversation, so there better be an unlocked door somewhere in this house. Once again, I'm caught outside without a phone.

"Layla?"

I jump at the unexpected voice coming from my left.

Rheta, wrapped in the shawl I gave her for Christmas, steps next to me.

"It's a lovely night, isn't it?"

"Um..."

Did she hear my conversation with Spencer? Please, no. I want her to continue to like me.

She pats my arm. "I'm sorry you won't be a part of the family, but you made the right decision. Marriage is hard and without love, it's nearly impossible to make a go of it."

Shame colors my cheeks crimson. My whole body feels overheated. How far below is the ground? Close enough for me to jump and survive? I'm sure the two inches of snow will help cushion my fall.

"Rheta, I'm sorry for lying to you. I was desperate, which made me foolish."

"You didn't lie. Never once did you tell me you loved my grandson, and you didn't need to because it was obvious to everyone you two don't share those feelings. I wondered what the motivation was behind your engagement, and now I know. No lasting harm done."

I glance at the closed office door. I think she's right. I hope so.

"Thank you for understanding," I say, "though I don't feel I deserve it."

"Nonsense. Life is about learning, and in the process, we all make mistakes. Sometimes those mistakes put us exactly where we're meant to be."

That's an optimistic view of life. "Do you think so?"

"Yes, I do. Now, you're ready to go inside. My bedroom is two doors down. You can go through there."

My shoulders sag in relief. "Thank you. And thank you for a wonderful Christmas. I loved being here."

"I loved having you. You are a gift to my family, even if it was only for a week."

That is one of the sweetest, most earnest compliments

I've received. I'm sad I'll never see her again. This is goodbye forever.

"Goodbye, Rheta."

"Goodbye, Layla."

As I walk through her room, into the hallway, and up to my room, the familiar weight of financial ruin settles on my shoulders, yet I feel lighter after breaking off my engagement than I have all week.

Chapter Twenty-Two

OWEN

I couldn't find Layla or Tori last night. I sent multiple texts to them both, but no answer. They are definitely avoiding me. The family has a meeting scheduled with Grandmother and her lawyer at ten to discuss the updated will, and I need to talk to Layla before that happens.

I send her another text after my shower. No response. I stop by her room, but there's no answer at my knock. I head downstairs for breakfast. She's usually the first to arrive. Hopefully, I can convince her to reconvene in the hall closet for a few minutes.

The breakfast room is empty. Servers come in and place food on the side table. While I wait for Layla to arrive, I notice the snow outside. White covers the trees. It's a scene from a Christmas card, and I can't wait until Layla arrives so I can share this beautiful view with her. If she'll even talk with me.

I get impatient waiting, so I stop one of the staff. She won't know where Layla is, but she will know where I can find Miles, and Miles knows everything.

"Can you tell me where Miles is right now?"

"He left for the airport a while ago," she says.

"The airport. Why?" I can't imagine anyone in my family leaving hours before Grandmother hands out twenty million dollar checks.

"Layla's flying back to Salt Lake City."

Layla left? Why? Something must have happened for her to leave a day early. The entire purpose of getting engaged to Spencer yesterday was to get the extra money. Maybe her grandma's health took a turn. Or something's wrong with one of her roommates.

Then I have to wonder if this person even knows who Layla is. Maybe she's mistaken, and I'm getting worked up for no reason.

"You know Layla?"

A nod. "She said goodbye before she left."

Of course, Layla would say goodbye to the staff. She sees people that others, myself included, don't. What hurts is she didn't say goodbye to me. If nothing else, we're still friends. Or maybe, by the way she's been ignoring my texts, we're not?

"Do you know why she left? Sorry, what is your name?"

"Hannah. She didn't say specifically, just that it was time for her to leave."

"Thanks, Hannah."

I shoot off another text, but if her flight has already taken off, then I might not get an answer for hours. If she answers at all.

I head to the office to find Spencer. It's empty, so I take the steps two at a time on my way to his bedroom. Mom and Brady come down the stairs on my way up.

"What's up with you?" Brady asks.

Mom's brow wrinkles with concern. "Did something happen?"

"I'll explain later."

I bang on Spencer's bedroom door. When he opens, he's shirtless, his hair disheveled like I woke him up. This might be the first time he's ever slept past seven o'clock.

"What?" His lip curls. "Come to rub it in?"

I'm taken aback by his disdain. "Rub what in?"

"Layla chose you and a life of poverty over me. Are you happy?"

Sweet relief floods through my body. I feel faint and prop myself up with an arm on the wall. She broke up with Spencer. But then why didn't she come to find me? Why did she leave?

"When did she break off your engagement?"

He crosses his arms and leans against the door frame. "You expect me to believe you don't know?"

"I don't know," I say. "The last time I spoke with her was on Christmas Day, and she was one hundred percent committed to you."

He eyes me distrustfully. "Well, something changed her mind. She broke it off last night."

Whatever the reason, I'm euphoric. I laugh. Spencer glares.

"Spencer, I'm sorry you're hurt, but I'm glad she broke up with you. She deserves a husband who loves and adores her. You deserve a wife who can expect more from you than a paycheck. Don't you want someone in your life more important than work? Someone to help you through difficulties and disappointment? A woman who will stick by your side if tomorrow you lost everything?"

My passionate speech does not impress Spencer. He glances down at his wrist to check the time. He's not wearing a watch. "Is the TED talk finished?"

I tried. "I'm sorry if this hurts you, but I'm going after her. I would give up everything I have if it means I get to spend the rest of my life with her. Can you say the same?"

An expression ripples across Spencer's face I've never seen there before: envy. "I have a lot more to give up than you do, don't I?"

I'm not sure if my next words are harder for me to say or for him to hear. "Spencer, I co-founded the Boudron bag company with a college friend. I sold my half of the business earlier this year for fifty-three million dollars. With my current investments, it will double in the next few years. I own and manage a landscaping company with twelve crews who upkeep the grounds of private companies and city parks. I'm not destitute. I'm not lazy. I'm just not a lawyer, nor do I have any interest in an inheritance from Grandfather's estate. I'm sorry for lying to you this week, but after so many years of not speaking to each other, it didn't seem important."

He shuts the door in my face.

I deserve that. His fiancée broke up with him last night, and I'm thrilled. I have more money than he does, and I earned every penny. We may not agree on most things, but he's still family. I want to build a relationship with him, but not right now.

I call Miles as I rush to my room and throw my clothes into a suitcase.

He answers after two rings. "Owen."

"Has Layla's flight left yet?"

A slight hesitation. "No, it doesn't leave until eleven-thirty. Why?"

"Because I love her, and I have to tell her. Is she there with you?"

"I dropped her off fifteen minutes ago."

I have less than two hours to make that flight, and that's if there's a seat available. I can make it if I leave now and speed. That won't be easy in a Chevrolet van, but I've never shied away from hard things.

"Can you send me her flight number?" I ask.

"Let me pull over, and I'll get the details for you."

"Thanks. I owe you."

A few minutes later, I have the information I need. There is one more seat available; in first class. The cost is exorbitant, but I remind myself that I can spend money, and it doesn't make me a hypocrite. Also, Layla's worth it. She's worth everything.

I zip up my suitcase and run down to breakfast. I have five minutes to say goodbye to the family, then I'm off to tell the woman I love I don't want to live without her.

Chapter Twenty-Three

LAYLA

I'VE SPENT THE TIME WAITING FOR MY FLIGHT TO BOARD, reading through texts my roommates sent to each other in our group chat over the past week.

Livy didn't stay in Salt Lake City with Meg and her family like I expected. Instead, she drove to Wyoming to spend the week with her sister. When a snowstorm hit, she ended up at an inn with a handsome stranger. He's not a stranger anymore.

Meg spent the week with her family and her twin brother's best friend, Noah, at Nordquest Ski Resort. It seems she and Noah aren't enemies any longer. They might actually be more than friends. That's a plot twist I never saw coming.

I missed out on so much, and I regret not being there for them. Probably as much as they'll wish they had been here for me when they find out the whole story of my week.

I try composing a text to let them know I'm coming home early, fresh from a broken engagement, but I have no enthusiasm for the task. They'll be rosy with newfound love, and I'm melancholy about missing Owen.

It was pride that kept me from telling him goodbye this morning. My reason for avoiding him for most of this year is my reason for not wanting to face him now: I'm a black hole of debt.

I have read none of his texts, though the little red number is telling me the count is up to seventeen. By now, he'll know I broke off my engagement to Spencer, and that I've left. I hope he'll get the message and not expect anything from me when we're both back in Salt Lake. Even friendship feels dangerous at this point.

Not being able to resist seeing his face, I pull up the video Max sent me of Owen trying to dance. When it ends, I play it again. And again. It's like pressing on a bruise just so I can feel the pain.

My pity fest is interrupted when my phone rings with an unfamiliar number. I would normally ignore it, but it's a Maine area code and my curiosity motivates me to answer. Maybe something happened at the cabin. Or maybe it's Owen, and I'll get to hear his voice for a few seconds before I hang up.

"Hello?"

"Is this Layla Adler I'm speaking to?" an unfamiliar female voice asks.

I hate how I'm disappointed it's not Owen. "Yes."

"This is Sofia Vega. I'm Mrs. Rheta Eccleston's attorney. She asked me to inform you that a certified check for one hundred thousand dollars will arrive tomorrow morning by courier at your address in Utah." She rattles off my address. "Is that the correct address?"

My heart stops. My lungs refuse to function. I can't speak.

One. Hundred. Thousand. Dollars.

Enough to cover Nana's care for the next year. Or to pay off my bank loan and most of the credit card debt. I cover my mouth with my hand so Sofia Vega doesn't hear my gasp as my body begins to function again. It sounds more like a sob.

"Ms. Adler? Is that your address?"

"Yes," I croak. But why is Rheta sending me money? I'm not engaged to her grandson anymore. She has no reason to give me anything.

Sofia Vega continues. "Mrs. Eccleston has also set up a fund that will disperse seven thousand dollars a month for the next ten years to go toward the care of Mrs. Ellen Adler. My contact information, as well as the parameters of the fund, will be included with the certified check. Do you have questions?"

I find my voice so I can inform her, "I can't accept this."

"Yes, she thought you might say something to that effect." She's grinning on the other end of the line. "Mrs. Eccleston wanted me to tell you that you can take her help. She only wishes the best for you. I suggest you graciously accept and send her a thank you card. Good day, Ms. Adler. Have a happy New Year."

She hangs up. I sit in shock. Did this really happen? Am I dreaming? The tears on my cheeks are real. As is the cold air blowing on me from a nearby vent. Now that I've determined the call happened, I need to decide if I should take what Rheta has offered.

It doesn't take me more than ten seconds to decide yes; I am accepting her generosity. She has no ulterior motive. She gives monetary gifts to people, businesses, and organizations she believes in. I don't feel like I owe her anything in return, like I did with Spencer, or that I'm indebted to her like I would with Owen. This is a gift offered in love, free and clear. A thank you card feels paltry compared to hundreds of thousands of dollars, but I have nothing else to give her except my undying gratitude.

Tears stream down my face, but I'm also laughing as I rock backward and forward in my seat. I have my life back. My future opens before me and it is bright.

"Are you okay?"

I wipe my eyes and turn to the young teenager sitting beside me. I'm glad she asked because I need to tell someone.

"My nana will have everything she needs."

Her nose scrunches in confusion. "Okay."

I rub at my cheeks as more tears fall. I woke up this morning dreading the years ahead of me, and now they're full of possibilities.

The crowd lining up to board the plane parts as someone pushes his way through. The man looks like Owen pre-Maine. He has the same long stride, trimmed beard, and cocoa-colored eyes. Instead of wearing slacks and a button-up shirt, he has on a t-shirt and shorts during winter. At least he has on a jacket with a green scarf hanging from his neck.

I recognize the scarf because I made it. That, more than anything else, convinces me that this isn't a man who looks like Owen. It *is* Owen. When he sees me, he jogs over and kneels on the ground at my feet. His grin melts away when he notices the tears on my cheeks.

"Layla? What's wrong?" He sounds concerned and runs a thumb under my eye, wiping away the tears.

My heart gallops in my chest. It takes forever for me to find my voice. "Nothing is wrong."

"You're crying."

"Tears of happiness." A full-bodied laugh accompanies my words.

His eyebrows lower, and he tilts his head to the side. "What happened?"

Not only am I financially free, my heart is free. I'm a single, twenty-nine-year-old woman who is face-to-face with a gorgeous, caring, funny, thoughtful man who followed her to the airport. He's what I want. I will never run away from him again. He doesn't know what he's in for because I never want to leave his side.

I scoot to the edge of my seat and throw my arms around his neck. My knees bracket his hips. His arms go around my waist. His beard rubs against my wet cheek and his breath is warm on my neck. I feel just as secure in his arms today as I did on Christmas Eve, but now I feel no shame or regret. He is mine. My chest is about to burst from all the happiness I hold inside.

"You're worrying me," he says.

"I'm happy. For so many reasons, but right now, I'm happy you're here."

"You're glad I came?" He sounds hopeful.

I laugh again. "Yes, I am definitely glad you came."

He pulls away far enough to look at me. "You broke up with Spencer."

I nod and laugh. "Yes."

"But you left without saying goodbye?"

"I didn't know how to tell you what a mess I am financially. It was not a little money I needed, it was over one-hundred-thousand dollars and on top of that, another seventy-five-thousand every year. I couldn't put that sort of financial stress on you. You deserve better. But now, everything is different."

He studies my face and tenderly moves a lock of hair behind my ear. "Different how?"

Manic, happy laughter burbles out of me again and I pull him close, burrowing my head in the crook of his neck. The scarf he wears is soft against my cheek.

"Rheta is providing everything for my nana's care. I just got the call. She's paying off all my debts and giving Nana a monthly stipend. She's given me my life back. Owen, I want that date you asked me for. I want to spend every day with you. If that isn't what you want, tell me now because I'm already building dreams for my future and you're in every single one."

My declaration is met with silence. I expected Owen to be as enthusiastic as I am now that the barrier keeping us apart is gone, but I must have misunderstood why he's here. I pull away, but he doesn't let me go. Our eyes meet. His lips lift in the grin I adore. He must see my confusion at his silence. I essentially told him I love him and he hasn't said a word in response.

"I want to be a part of those dreams, Layla. I'm thrilled that Rheta stepped in to help. But before I tell you how much I love you, I have to share with you something else and I'm nervous you'll be mad."

My heart soars, then sinks. What could be more important than his love for me? "What do you have to tell me?"

He unwraps his arms from around my waist and leans back on his heals. I shiver as the cold air blows against my back. Trepidation sinks into my soul. This is bad.

"That manufacturing company I started with my friend?"

"I remember."

"We manufactured bags."

Not what I expected after the introduction he gave to this confession. "Bags?"

He points to the Boudron at my feet. "Those bags."

My jaw drops. I need confirmation that I understand correctly. "Boudron is the company you sold?"

"Just my half. Believe me, our success surprised no one more than us. It was all about timing and getting the attention of the right fashion designers and celebrities. Without social media, we'd probably still be working out of his garage."

It's not computing the words he speaks. "Boudron? The hottest designer bag on the market for the past three years? That Boudron?"

He smiles as he nods. "I'm sorry I didn't tell you. I have a complicated relationship with money and I didn't want you to pick me because of what was in my bank account. I should have been honest. Are you mad?"

I'm shocked is what I am. I also feel a fool. I didn't think he had the money to help me pay for Nana, and he probably has enough in his bank account to purchase a hundred assisted living homes outright.

"Layla, what are you thinking?"

Good question. What am I thinking? I'm thinking about how much I want to kiss him.

"I'm not mad you didn't tell me. Honestly, it's better you didn't. Now that Nana is taken care of, I don't care about your bank account. All I care about is you."

He has me in his arms in seconds. His lips land on mine, but only for a second. I want them back where they belong, but he's speaking. "Layla, I love you. Thank you for not marrying my cousin. Family reunions would have been the worst."

I laugh and then get lost in his eyes. I run a finger through his beard. Over his lips. Under his eyebrows. Owen is mine. I can touch him whenever I want. Laugh with him. Hug him. Kiss him. All wonderful things that I don't have to feel guilty about. I savor his arms around my waist. The warmth of his skin. His soft brown eyes drinking me in. They skip down to my lips. Mine veer in the same direction.

"Are you going to kiss again?" someone says, shattering our moment.

We both turn toward the teenager sitting in the next seat over. Right. We are in an airport terminal, not alone. Something I should have remembered sooner.

"If so," the teen continues, "Hurry it up. They just called for section three. If you take too long, you'll miss the flight."

The line for boarding is half as long as when Owen showed up, but we still have quite an audience.

Owen turns to me. "Actually, I think I want to miss our flight. I'm not ready to go home. Will you stay in Boston with me? There's an Italian restaurant I would love to take you to. We can do whatever else you want. A museum or the freedom walking tour."

I'm reminded that Harvard University is in Boston. Owen lived here for three years going to law school. I want to see the city through his eyes.

Except ... Spencer was generous and gave me a first-class ticket. It feels wasteful not to use it, especially since I deserve the economy section.

"What about our tickets? I don't want to waste Spencer's money."

Owen turns to the teen who is listening to every word of our conversation. All she needs is popcorn to truly enjoy the show.

"Who are you traveling with?" Owen asks her.

The girl points to the woman sitting beside her. "My mom." From her wide eyes and interested smile, she's enjoyed my reunion with Owen just as much as her daughter.

Owen takes my hand and pulls me up to standing. "Let's see if we can get these lovely women in first class, shall we?"

"Really?" The girl's squeal is so high, I'm sure the service dog down the corridor heard it.

It doesn't take long to have our seats transferred and to rebook a flight for tomorrow night. The whole time, Owen is touching me or I'm touching him. Almost as if we can't believe this is happening; we're free to be together.

Our suitcases are on their way to Salt Lake City, but Owen contacts a friend to pick them up for us so they aren't sitting in the airport for a day.

We leave the airport hand in hand. Snow falls in fat flakes. The tops of our heads are quickly covered in white.

"Ready for an adventure?" Owen asks.

A hundred times, yes. A thousand. A million. But first ...

"In one second," I tell him.

Before I get too distracted by Owen and the city, I send my roommates a quick message.

LAYLA: *Sorry I haven't responded this week. Maine has been a surprise in more ways than one. I'll explain everything when I get back tomorrow. Sorry if I worried you!*

I zip my phone in my Boudron and ignore it as it buzzes. Right now, I want to be with Owen.

We head to the taxi stand, but before we reach the line, Owen pulls me into an alcove. My back is to the building, with Owen blocking everything behind us. He leans close, one hand on the wall next to my head, the other on my hip on the inside of my open coat. The warmth of his body so close to mine sends electricity coursing through me, from the tips of my toes to the top of my head. My skin pebbles with goose bumps.

"Is this okay?" he whispers.

All I can do is nod. People pass, but they may as well be miles away for how little I notice. My attention is one hundred percent dedicated to Owen. His jacket is open, and I lay my hands flat against his beautiful, firm chest. I feel the beat of his heart through my palms.

His hand moves from the wall to cup my cheek and he runs his thumb over my bottom lip. I lean into his touch. His attention veers to the hollow of my neck. I shiver as if it's his fingers touching me and not just his eyes.

"You're wearing the angel necklace."

I pull back the sleeve of my coat and shake my wrist. The charms on my bracelet jingle. "This too."

His grin grows. He leans forward and breathes in. "Is that peppermint soap I smell?"

I laugh until he drops a kiss just below my ear. It turns into a gasp.

His lips move against my neck as he says, "I promised I would tell you how much I loved you after I confessed my secret."

"You did?" I remember nothing beyond this moment. My eyes lids flutter as his lips skim over my jaw.

"Yes, and a promise is a promise." He kisses my chin, then stands straight and meets my eyes as his expression grows serious. "I love you more than I love strawberry cheesecake."

His declaration surprises a laugh out of me. It's going to be like that, is it? I fist his t-shirt in my hands and pull him closer.

I kiss the crease next to his eye and whisper, "I love you more than candy canes."

He grins against my cheek. "I love you more than I love opening Christmas gifts on Christmas morning."

I'm smiling as I kiss his jaw. "I love you more than my Boudron bag."

He kisses next to my ear and whispers, "I love you more than fifty-three million dollars."

I gasp at the amount, but before I can ask what that means, his lips are on mine. We give twin sighs. He's been wanting this kiss as much as I have. I wrap my arms around his waist. We're so close, he could zip me up inside his jacket. His hand moves to my neck, and his fingers weaving through the hair at the base of my scalp. The other cups my cheek and tilts my face to the perfect angle to deepen the kiss.

As we spend the next however long hiding in an alcove built specifically for us, trading secrets and toe-curling kisses, I'm amazed at how my counterfeit Christmas ended. If I hadn't come to Maine as Spencer's secret fiancée, I'd still be avoiding Owen, hiding around corners at Brock Pine Home, so he wouldn't find out my credit score. I never would have met Rheta. I'd still be stuck in debt with no escape and too prideful to ask for help.

Rheta was right. Sometimes our mistakes put us exactly where we need to be.

Epilogue

ONE YEAR LATER

LAYLA

Christmas Eve dinner is fantastic. Sausages, sauerkraut, mashed potatoes, and hard rolls from the German bakery, all of it smothered in curry gravy. It's filled with memories, and I can't help but smile at every bite. *Nana would love this* is the only thought that dims my joy.

As delicious as the food is, the company is better.

Owen and I are back in York, Maine, staying with Miles' parents in the house Rheta gifted them for their many years of service. It's the house Rheta received as a wedding present from her parents. She kept it even after her husband built the big house closer to town.

It's large, but homie, unlike the gargantuan castle where Rheta still lives. Rheta invited us to stay with her, but Marianne and Miles were married last month and they asked us to stay with them, Brady, and Miles' two daughters and their husbands here at the cottage.

Epilogue

They were all kind to allow for my German Christmas Eve traditions. It's honestly been the most fulfilling family Christmas I could ever wish for, and it isn't over yet. We still have the nativity and carol singing. Tomorrow we'll head up to Rheta's cabin for a Christmas party.

Rheta invited all of her family for Christmas, but we were the only ones to come. Tori is stuck in New York because she doesn't want to be far away from Sadie, who is spending the holiday with her ex and his new wife.

Spencer is in a new relationship with an oncologist who is on call this week. From what he's said in the few texts we've exchanged, things are going well with her. How well things can go when they both work sixty-hour weeks is hard to determine, but he's happy, and that's all I want for him.

Miles stands to clear the table from dishes, but both Owen and I insist he sit down. The man should have at least one day off from taking care of everybody else. Owen and I carry the dishes to the kitchen ourselves. He rinses and packs the dishwasher while I put away the food.

"Has Christmas Eve been everything you wished for?" he asks.

"It exceeded expectations." My smile falters for a second. "I miss Nana."

Her dementia has grown worse, but she's well taken care of. Under the circumstances, it's the best I can hope for.

Owen comes up behind me and wraps his arms around my waist. I lean back against him. No matter where we are, his arms feel like home. His beard rubs against my cheek as he kisses the corner of my lips.

"We'll visit Nana as soon as we get back and bring her sausage."

Epilogue

"It's called blutwurst."

"I know. I just like hearing you say the name. It's sexy."

"Only because you don't know the ingredients."

He nibbles at my ear. We might never leave this kitchen if he keeps carrying on like this. I push him away with my elbow. "Get back to work."

He plants a kiss on my lips before returning to the sink. "Did you notice how many applications were submitted yesterday?"

"I haven't looked since we arrived. How many?"

"Nine. Your foundation is doing good work."

"Our foundation," I remind him. The foundation we set up with his inheritance from Rheta and a chunk of money he made from selling Boudron. Its purpose is to help those who struggle to financially support family members living in residential care. Every month when we disburse payments, I'm giddy with joy. We are doing good things.

Owen is on the board, but he has also begun practicing law with a non-profit part time. It gives his life purpose to help others.

When the kitchen is clean, we meet back in the living room for carols. The family is talking and laughing. It's everything I imagined a family Christmas to be. And we are family. Owen's step-sisters have been welcoming to Marianne and her sons. Susan and Malcolm treat me like their granddaughter. Before dinner, we took a family picture with all of us in our matching pajama bottoms. I picked the pattern this year: cows wearing Santa hats. Sadie would love them, which is why I sent a pair to her and Tori in New York.

I'm about to sit at the piano when Owen takes my hand and stops me.

Epilogue

"Before we sing carols," he says loud enough for everyone to hear. They quiet in record time. "It's time for our annual pickle finding competition."

"Really?" This is news to me.

"It's not annual if we've never done it before," Brady points out.

"Our *first* annual pickle finding competition," Owen amends.

"What's the prize for finding it?" Brady asks.

Owen winks at me. "A kiss."

"Eww." Brady's face scrunches with disgust as only a fifteen-year-old's face can. "That's not motivating."

Owen shrugs. "Then you get the satisfaction of knowing you have the best eyesight of everyone here."

Brady frowns. "Also not motivating."

"Is it a real pickle or an ornament?" I ask.

"An ornament. No using your nose to sniff it out this year."

I slap his stomach with my hand. Mmm. He's warm and solid, and I keep my palm exactly where it is. "I didn't use my nose last year."

He smiles. "Prove it." Once everyone has gathered around the tree, he calls out, "Go!"

Regretfully, I drop my hand from his abs and begin my search. I'm one hundred percent focused on winning that pickle prize. No one will steal my kiss.

Something sparkles in the tree, reflecting the shine of the white Christmas lights, and draws my eye. And there, next to the sparkle, is the green pickle camouflaged by tree boughs.

"I found it!" I call out as I grab the ornament. The

Epilogue

something sparkly comes with the pickle. They seem to be tied together.

It takes a second for what I'm seeing to make sense. It's a ring. A white gold solitaire diamond engagement ring. Simple but beautiful. My mouth drops open. I turn to see everyone has disappeared into the kitchen, but for Owen. He's down on one knee.

"Layla, I love you. More than I ever imagined was possible. You bring a joy and purpose to my life I didn't know was missing until I found you. Will you go through this life with me by your side, be the mother of our children, the person who I wake up next to every morning and kiss every night? No matter what comes in our future, I promise I will never leave you. I will never take your love for granted. I will always see you, cherish you, love you."

I remember the wish I made last Christmas the night Spencer proposed his crazy plan.

I wish to be happy in my marriage.

I know I will be. Mom and Opa are looking down from heaven, so happy for us, as I take Owen's hand and pull him to his feet. I see our lives together stretching out before us, our good times out weighing the bad, because we have each other.

"Yes."

I kiss him with all the love and devotion I feel, and those feelings are reflected back as he kisses me. We don't pull away until family applause breaks through our happy haze.

I lay my head on his shoulder. "I love you."

"I love you. Merry Christmas."

Epilogue

If you are wondering if Tori has a happy-ever-after, then you are in luck! She has her own Christmas novella called *If Wishes Were Snowflakes*.

Thank you for reading *Her Counterfeit Christmas*! I hope you enjoyed Layla and Owen's love story! If you would like to be notified of future releases, sign up for my newsletter. You can do this through my website, gracejcroy.com. When you sign up, you'll receive the novella, *Kiss Me, Jane* for free.

If you enjoyed this book, please let other readers know! A great way to support authors is by leaving a review on Amazon, Goodreads, or BookBub. A few words is enough to make a difference!

Also by Grace J. Croy

It Must Be Love Series

It's Not Like It's a Secret

It's Not Like It's Fate

It's Not Like It's Real

It's Not Like It's Forever

It's Not Like It's Meant to Be

Christmas Wishes Series

Her Christmas Rescue

Her Christmas Movie Kiss

Her Counterfeit Christmas

Is Kisses Were Snowflakes (novella)

Magical Regency Series

Intuition

Bronwyn

Stand-Alone Titles

The Lonely Lips Club

Love Checks In

About the Author

Grace's favorite things include reading, writing, traveling, and her cats.

She lives in Utah, in a little house at the bottom of a little mountain, where the snow piles high in the winter.

When she isn't writing, she works as a librarian, planning awesome community events and advising readers on what book to try next.

Her favorite places to travel include New Zealand, California, and Paris. No matter how long she's away, she always loves coming home.

Made in the USA
Columbia, SC
11 September 2024